GOD OF THE DEAD

M.C. Norris

In celebration of my Volga German heritage, I'd like to dedicate this book to those stalwart settlers who sowed the seeds of my wonderful Kansas family. Arnholds, Norrises and Harrisons, by blood or marriage, I'm pleased and proud to always find myself in such fine company.

Love you guys.

Chapter One

The prospector bobbed on the stern of his balsa, at the heart of the city of rafts. Foam oozed through splits in the rubber air hose clenched between his golden teeth. Taped and spliced at random intervals, the tubing slithered haphazardly around the deck to its point of connection to a prattling compressor. Air streamed through the hollow of his mouth in a continuous howl, as the man with the gilded grin surveyed the fleet of ramshackle vessels. A curved *cutacha* jungle knife dangled from a cord lashed around his waist. Chipped from years of misuse, the rusted blade of his weapon was hilted to the cropped handle of what looked to have once been a child's baseball bat.

His was a hard form, lithe and blackened, as if by some inferno in which he'd been forged. Poised on the transom of his vessel, he seemed to exist as a living mockery to whatever kiln had failed to contain him, to smelt the precious metal from his mouth, to tarnish the pearl of his outgrown nails. If the man had eyes at all, they were hidden somewhere in the swath of shadow slung beneath the brim of a faded army hat. However, in all his apparent tranquility, his subtlety of motion, the profound calm that seemed to emanate from this watcher of people belied his natural placement in the chaotic *garimpo*. He was different from the rest, apart from them, like a dark image burnt upon the setting. A prospector of prospectors, he studied the behavioral patterns of the crewmen throughout the bobbing shantytown with the dark interest of a cat regarding some birds. The other miners were too preoccupied to pay him notice. Their eyes were trained downward, their arms sifting tons of dredged sediment conveyed through the sieves in their tireless search for a few flakes of gold. Unseen were the suppliers, fifty feet below. Working blindly in absolute blackness, the divers plunged their suction hoses into the muck, feeding the process that was the *garimpo*, as it crept over the Rio Iaco as a collective machine designed to transform pristine rivers and their bordering forests into smoldering paths of destruction.

The prospector slicked back his brimmed hat to reveal a wild tussock of hair. He flung the cap across the deck in the direction of a knot of deckhands hunkered miserably beneath the sagging plastic awning that afforded their only sanctuary from the heat. The nearest of the lot responded with an almost imperceptible nod. They moved as a pack of cooperative predators coordinating some plan through a slight discourse of body language and glances, wordlessly taking to their stations around the balsa. The prospector hefted a large sack of dripping stones, and he affixed this crude system of weights to the nylon cord around his waist.

Orienting himself toward some point on the horizon, he inhaled deep breaths of compressed air through the hose, eyes brightening, as he rose to his toes upon the transom. Beyond the entropy of the encampment, the growling generators, the great bonfires of felled trees that imparted plumes of ash over the verdant reefs of Brazilian rainforest loomed the jagged peaks of the Andes. To these elder gods of fallen empires, the prospector dealt a last glance before stepping off the stern of his balsa, and down into oblivion.

The yellowish color of the water quickly dimmed, as his limp body trailed the sack of stones down into the depths of the Rio Iaco. He plunged until his ears rang and popped, until the fading brilliance of the surface was evidenced only by a sickly effervescence that waned until all trace of the world he'd left behind was snuffed in the grip of absolute blackness. His ears welcomed the tinkling concert of migrating pebbles, the rhythmic chugging of the dredge suction lines. At last, his bare feet were received by a layer of frigid muck at the river bottom. Waiting, just breathing from the airline, he allowed his senses to become reacquainted with this hostile and lightless environment. Once stabilized, he turned in the direction of a familiar groaning resonance, and then traversed the abyss with great moonwalker's strides until he'd located his dredge's suction hose, the secondary tool of his trade. Hugging the great vacuum in the bend of his left arm, he released the razor-edged *cutacha* from his hip.

This was his world. Above, he amounted to nothing. Son of a murdered Maldonado whore, he'd squabbled daily amongst the destitute shat upon this world without a hope or a prayer, all blowing like motes of litter in the wind toward whatever opportunity for new failures arose. Up there, he was shit, but down here—he rotated his body in the direction of the other chugging dredges, and the divers who blindly manned them—he was a god.

Few in this mining camp were experienced. They just drifted in, lost souls with sad histories, piratical minds and criminal records, whose miserable existences floated them through every loathsome occupation as they drifted the natural course of depravity, until at last, they found themselves caught in the great filter of human dregs that was the *garimpo*. This would be their final stop. Just enough gold could be gleaned from the river bottom to support their indulgences, which were steadily supplied by the droves of peddlers and prostitutes who followed their customers ever deeper into the jungle. The *garimpo* was a prison without walls, crowded with violent inmates incarcerated on their own volition, a place where the only sentence could be death.

On the bottom of the Rio Iaco, no one ever saw him coming. Slashing airlines, he'd learned, was a novice's mistake. A loose hose waggling in the current promptly alerted crews to the struggle down below before their mining site could be plundered. Cutting throats was the best method. They died complacently this way, struggling like little lambs against a tether as he gripped their airlines until they bled out. The lightless conditions denied him the pleasure of watching his victims die, and that was a shame. Down here, he could only listen, feel and imagine the dramatic spectacles that he created.

Once he'd dragged his *cutacha* across their throats, they panicked, so shocked by what had just happened that they never thought to release their oxygen supply line, and swim for the surface. Even as that icy flood of water rushed into their lungs through the gaping holes in their necks, and the river warmed with the spillage of their blood, they never let go of their airlines. They just kept pulling on that hose, pulling until they died with bubbles streaming through their opened throats that the prospector liked to feel fluttering warmly through his fingers.

He advanced through the nightscape in slow-motion leaps. Each bound brought him closer to the sounds of his target, three balsas away. It was the poor bastard's own crewmen who'd betrayed him. Experienced crews knew better than to show excitement while anchored over a rich mining site. In these waters, it was a deadly mistake to grin like apes, cheering and slapping backs while crowded over a sieve. Ironic, their diver, the only crewman who'd no idea what his labors were producing, would always be the one to pay the ultimate price for his topside crew's naivety.

The chug and rush of vacuumed sediment was an alluring beacon. He could hear the pebbles rattling up the dredge, the torrent of bubbles spewing from the diver's airline, and something else—was it singing? The prospector smiled, as he vaulted through the blackness. Sometimes they sang. Fearful, inexperienced, they crooned their garbled hymns over their airlines to alleviate the alienation of the worst position on a mining crew. As the prospector neared the voice in the darkness, he recognized this particular song. It was the *Himno Nacional del Peru.*

Largo tiempo el peruano oprimido
la ominosa cadena arrastro
Condenado a cruel servidumbre
largo tiempo en silencio gimio

How wonderfully appropriate. The prospector hummed along with his victim, as he seized the fool from behind, wrenching his arm around the man's face and thrusting the *cutacha* blade beneath his chin. This was his favorite moment. As the diver struggled to escape his deadly headlock, he could feel himself starting to get an erection. For some funny reason, he felt like cutting this one's head completely off.

The prospector heard his own burbling scream, a sound he'd never produced before, as a bolt of agony shot up through his thigh. Steel squeaked against bone. His *cutacha* was clenched in the diver's viselike grip, while the bastard reamed a shank down into the joint of his hip just as deeply as the blade could be driven. The prospector abandoned his suction line to defend himself better against that twisting dagger. White strobes exploded throughout the blackness, as the bridge of his nose was suddenly pulverized by the back of the diver's skull. It was a moment before his senses cleared, and he realized that he'd lost his airline. The diver escaped with a flurry of kicking legs, leaving the prospector airless and anchored to the river bottom by his own sack of stones.

Pulsing blood throbbed inside his ears. He jerked the shank from his hip. Swarms of voracious fish began to attack the open wound. They rushed out of the blackness from every direction as he sawed at the nylon tether. He felt them slapping at his body with their fins, pummeling his thigh in a burning torrent that he knew would never subside, only increase in intensity, until their collective bloodlust had reduced him to a pile of bones.

He swatted at the living darkness, sawing at the cordage until at last, with a liberating snap, the prospector was rocketing skyward through the swarm, threshing the water in an effort to confuse the ravenous horde until he'd distanced himself from the worst of them. The piranhas pursued him, tearing away gobbets of flesh with every strike, but lack of air was his greatest agony. His eyes bulged, his throat swelled and collapsed, as burning lungs fought to pull a lungful of water through his clenched teeth. Thrusting higher with every kick, he could finally see an amber effervescence of light, just beginning to radiate down through the gulfs of blackness from somewhere high above.

He was going to surface right beside his victim's balsa. The danger was obvious, but at this point, it wasn't possible to deviate from the most direct course to the surface. Even if his lung capacity was sufficient to carry him back to the relative safety of his own vessel, there would be no sanctuary for him there. By now, his escaped diver had surely alerted the whole *garimpo* to the presence of pirates, a threat that no one took lightly. Every miner in the city of rafts was going to be up there waiting for him. Lost divers were a regular occurrence. So long as his victims never surfaced, no foul could ever be proven, but this time, he'd blown it. His herd of prey was keenly aware of the lion in their midst, and they were going to turn on their predator. He'd prowled the *garimpo* long enough to anticipate the brutal justice that would be in store. He and his crew would be blamed for every diver who'd ever gone missing. Odds were, his shipmates were already dead.

The shimmering aura of the surface brightened with every thrust. The temperature of the water warmed as he broke through some frigid barrier, yielding to whorls of golden light. At last, his shaggy head exploded from the surface, wide-eyed and sucking air like some awestruck troglodyte newly birthed of the primordial soup. When the hacking *cutachas* didn't flail upon his skull, when his ears failed to detect the cries of outrage, the pop of small arms fire that he expected as his welcome back to the surface world, he whipped his head around, confused. He was all alone. Alone and treading water in a floating ghost town of abandoned rafts.

He pinched the water from his nose, coughed, and spat. Most unsettling was the lack of background noise. Not once, since he'd joined the *garimpo* could he recall a single moment of stillness. Not a single compressor prattled. Not a dog barked. There were no shouting voices. Even the churning conveyers had been halted. Belts hung slackened, sieves dripping. There was not a solitary sound emitted by any living or mechanical thing, from the *garimpo* to the dense jungle beyond.

The prospector hovered on the surface, blinking in the sunlight, still expecting an angry mob to appear at any instant. There was a peculiar odor in the air, he noticed, as well as a strange haze that seemed to have fallen over the Iaco valley. It wasn't tenuous like a bank of fog, or even mist. It was more difficult to perceive, like some trick of weary eyes that imparted a slightly greenish tint to the color of things. The prospector squinted up at the sky, where the effect was most noticeable. It was not exactly blue. No less hot and bright, still spangled with clouds, normal in every way but in its hue, which had somehow fallen out of normal spectrum. Strange, how such a slight adjustment to ordinary tint could feel so bothersome to the eyes, bumping everything off-kilter, making the world feel so alien.

The prospector swam toward his balsa. The smell that hung so available in the air was equally perplexing. He peered cautiously at the other rafts as he neared his own vessel, still anticipating some form of reciprocal violence to erupt, some consequence to his actions, but no penalty was delivered. The odor was twofold. Its base was comprised of the mustiness of forest litter, the slimy stuff beneath rotten logs that reeked of mold and snails, a fungal wildness that emanated from the essence of decomposing wood that was somehow both pleasant and off-putting to the senses. It was the reek of bygone life, and of every creature that reveled in life's destruction. The sharper edge was something acrid, yet nutty, something more difficult to compare to any known scent but perhaps that of toasted almonds and crushed ants. He didn't know. The prospector hauled himself wetly onto the deck of his raft.

Facedown on the timbers, he was afraid to examine the throbbing agony at his hip. Eyes clenched shut, he breathed deeply for several seconds, focusing on the gentle lap of water against the transom. His fingertips slid over the lashed timbers, down his flank, to a raw and ragged mess that was his upper thigh. He winced, cupping his hand over the fist-sized divot that had been scalloped right out of the muscle by the fish. He'd known more than a few miners who'd died as a result of infections they'd contracted while working in these waters, and his wound felt worse than most he'd seen.

The prospector's eyes flicked open in response to a nearby splash. Raising his head from the timbers, he peered up over the low transom. Two meters astern, rings of water expanded from a gently fluttering form. Beating wings slowed, as a small bird pirouetted on the water's surface. Within seconds, it was still. Dead, but hardly alone in its lifeless state, it shared the river with brown and glistening backs that were suddenly evident, drifting between the anchored balsas in a grim migration. Miners, amidst countless fish, all floated together through the eerie silence of the *garimpo*.

Pushing himself up from the deck, eyes wild and searching, the prospector swiveled his head in the direction of his raft's makeshift cabin, and there they were. Beneath the plastic awning, his crew lay still. Upturned faces, bloated to caricatures by the effects of their strange deaths, they extruded their blackened tongues at the sky.

Snatching his *cutacha* from the timbers, he leapt to his feet, heart drumming inside his chest. He rotated in the center of the deck, poised to defend himself from the unseen threat that had to be lurking in the sky, the water, or in the dark jungle beyond. His logical mind demanded something, some hint of an explanation, but nothing was granted him. Nothing but the delicate forms of winged insects that fell from the air like bits of ash to settle soundlessly, lifelessly, upon the water. The distant slap and crash betrayed the occasional bird falling down through the forest canopy.

The prospector grimaced with every breath of tainted air that he sucked into his lungs. The greenish tint to this new reality, the acrid mustiness, these were the only clues as to what plague must have passed over the area while he was down on the river bottom. Cupping his hands to either side of his bearded mouth, he succumbed to the wild impulse to release an earsplitting bellow. Only the echo of his own anguished voice resounded through the desolate undergrowth. As minutes passed without response, the prospector was left with little choice but to accept the fact that for unknown reasons, he alone had managed to survive.

The outboard motor wouldn't start. After several attempts, he weighed anchor. Employing a paddle as a rudder, he rode the current, maneuvering his balsa through the floating necropolis of rafts, where whole crews were slumped into their conveyers, giving them the appearance of lazy hogs asleep at their feeding troughs. On almost every vessel, bodies were folded over the sieves, imparting themselves headfirst into the same muck over which they'd toiled. Dead divers trolled from the ends of taut lifelines. Their corpses rolled languidly in the current.

The encroaching forests on either side seemed to sag with collective despondence. Withered boughs of foliage hung dully from branches, divorced of that natural luster that was indicative of vegetative life. Beneath these sickly bowers, the banks of the Rio Iaco were strewn with the residents of what had so recently been a bustling sideshow to the *garimpo*. Campfires still smoldered amongst the collapsed forms, four-legged and two, all reduced to an ominous state of equality, as macabre markers on every spot where a peddler, prostitute, dog or a chicken had drawn a last breath. The prospector's gaze lingered on a blackened torso whose lower half extruded from the cooking fire that she'd been tending.

Downstream, the odor grew stronger. He clasped a hand over his mouth and nostrils, as if his fingers could filter it from entering his lungs. Not that this stench appeared to do him any harm. At least, not immediately. If the poison in the air was in any way connected with the extinction of so much life, then it was a guess that the lethal concentration of this mysterious gas must have dissipated as quickly as it had been unleashed. He was just lucky, damned lucky, to have been down on the river bottom, and separated from his air hose at the precise instant that a wave of death swept over the city of rafts.

It was getting late. The sun had just begun to slip beyond the peaks of the Andes. Darkness was falling. Throughout the jungle, he heard no sound but that of withered leaves, dropping from their stems to the forest floor with a gentle clatter. It was perhaps that utter absence of life and that empty vacuum all around him that made the new presence so terribly apparent. His eyes widened. Something else was out there, and it was watching him.

The prospector flung his paddle to the timbers. He snatched up his *cutacha*. Straining his eyes, he gaped through the snarls of dead vegetation. His heart hammered so hard against his chest that every beat snagged a breath in his throat. He hadn't seen anything specifically, nor had he been alerted by any sound. It was something else. His perception of a maleficent presence had simply manifested itself in his consciousness, just as distinctly as if his balsa had floated right into some field of sentience, but it was a two-way effect. He'd drifted into something's territory, and they both were aware of the other.

The prospector shouted at the forest. He stamped his foot against the deck, slashing at the darkening air, and smacked the flat blade of the *cutacha* against his bare chest. The stench was intoxicating. Whether it was the effects of his heightened emotions or something airborne, he began to feel lightheaded. The nutty pungency numbed his lips and tongue, while its more astringent edge seared the linings of his nostrils. Everything was changing. He rubbed at his eyes, smeared his hands over his slackening face. It began to feel as though he'd drifted completely out of his own world, and into another. His raft was floating through the whorls of a vast termite colony, where he inhaled redolent fumes of rotting wood and royal secretions, where some pulsating queen controlled her castes from the deepest grotto.

The prospector advanced to the edge of his balsa, reeling in the mind-bending vapors. No fight left in him, he surveyed the tangled vegetation with a dulled complacence. A silvery thread of drool swung from his lower lip. He found himself nodding at all the things that he now understood. Yes, he knew things, important things, things recently inferred, or perhaps things unearthed that had always been buried somewhere in his brain. He smiled, because his path in life seemed so clear to him now. The twists of his meandering past had always seemed so random, but every action he'd ever taken now appeared to have been calculated as critical directives in some greater plan. Every drone in the termite colony had a specific job to perform, and so far, he'd performed his duties well. He sensed that the queen was pleased with his work. Tonight, he was going to receive a promotion.

The prospector straightened up a little when he heard the trunks of trees begin to snap. Cracks resounded through the jungle like rifle reports. Dead canopies whispered, as trees toppled in a great wave of roiling foliage that shifted, parted, and finally afforded an unobstructed view of the Andes Mountains, as a wide path tore its way through the jungle to the river's edge. One of the queen's soldiers, bringing news of his promotion. He wiped some snot hastily from his nostrils, and smoothed back his wild hair. The last row of trees splintered and crashed into the Rio Iaco, teetering the prospector on the edge of his balsa.

There, it loomed, as immense as a drug lord's mansion. The jungle presence glowered down full upon him, its eyes a cluster of portals straight to Hell. The stench was ferocious. The prospector found himself trembling in its shadow, but not from fear. He trembled with excitement. At last, his hard work had been noticed.

The thing leaned down, bending along a seam at its midsection until it was close enough to set the prospector's balsa aglow in the hellish eminence of its eyes. The hair on his arms stood on end as currents of weird energy fished all through his body. He hooted when sparks spat from the outboard motor.

There was magic in the air. The air compressor prattled back to life, with a gaseous hiss and a glottal roar. The jangling system of conveyers lurched back into motion, carrying sieves around the auger in a jolly promenade. In the darkness, their shadows marched across an infernal backdrop cast upon the awning. He suppressed a powerful urge to begin dancing around the raft like a goblin. Instead, he remained at full attention.

It was beautiful. The prospector smiled up into the crimson spotlights, sparks flitting from his golden teeth. Orders from the queen had arrived. Every drone in her ranks had a special job to do, each within his unique capacity. Some had really big jobs that the prospector didn't fully understand, involving corporations, computers, and national defense networks. His job was simpler, but no less important to the future of the colony. His task was to find her, the deep dreamer, and put an end to her before any problems could arise.

The prospector fired up the outboard motor, and he brought his balsa about. Never before had he felt so empowered, so alive. He offered a parting wave to the looming thing in the jungle as he piloted the raft back upriver. It would be a long journey, out of one country and into another, taking him all the way to the ends of the earth, if that's what his mission required. Nevertheless, he was determined to succeed. He would find that little bitch, and when he did, he was going to cut her head off.

Chapter Two

The colonel snapped a rigid salute as the bunker doors swung wide. Backlit by sprays of fluorescent light, a twisted form was escorted into the central command room, flanked on either side by armed squads of Unit 777 commandos. The colonel swallowed down the knot already tightening in his throat, faltering in his effort to maintain some semblance of professionalism, as the rows of masked troops hustled into tactical positions on every side of the room. They were taking no chances with this one, not even here, in the most secure underground bunker in all of Egypt.

The colonel's heart rate increased as his eyes met those of the shadowy figure, stepping forth from his guardsmen once the bunker doors had slammed shut behind him. He crossed the room with a soundless cadence upon bare and calloused feet. Lancet light pierced the holes riddling his tattered tunic. His approach was aggressive, fearless, corroborating the accounts of the few who'd managed to survive their brutal engagements against this animal. Despite the ragged garb of a tribal warlord, he appeared quite comfortable in the sterile confines of a military facility, advancing with an air of entitlement toward what would soon be his new appointment as tactical commander over the largest army in the Middle East.

As the colonel stood face-to-face with the infamous warmonger, he suspected few officers could be endowed or even indoctrinated with the level of militant solidarity simply to stand by, unaffected, on the threshold of such a monumental blunder.

Here was a madman, a freak, who'd made quite a name for himself under some rather pretentious pseudonyms, but he was perhaps best known as "the Green Man." None knew him more intimately than those thousands of butchered innocents whose mutilated remains filled mass graves all over the Middle East. Only a handful outside of his mercenary network had ever managed to catch a fleeting glimpse of him, and no one, to the colonel's knowledge, had ever survived an opportunity to look full upon this living nightmare. The colonel tried not to stare into the gaping hole in the middle of the Green Man's face, but he failed. The sallow tone of his greenish skin was to be anticipated, of course, but no amount of wartime casualties could have prepared the colonel for the extent of the Green Man's malformations.

"Everything has been prepared in strict accordance to your instructions. Egypt stands by, awaiting your command. It will be an honor to serve you, Sir," the Colonel said, clearing his throat. He lowered his salute, and stared into the Green Man's vapid eyes.

As a detective strives to understand a killer by analyzing the wounds inflicted on his victims, so was the colonel left to ponder this tyrant's assignment to one of the world's most powerful positions. The order had come down from the top, and under the highest level of classification. In just twelve hours, all regular army personnel throughout Rashid Field Headquarters were reassigned in advance of the Green Man's arrival. By the zero hour, the facility had been entirely repopulated by Unit 777 commandos, supported by a regiment of the colonel's own Sa'ka Special Forces. The base was on lock-down. No one entered, no one left, until the Green Man had accomplished whatever objective Egypt had employed him to complete.

"With all due respect, Sir," the colonel said, "by what title would you prefer to be addressed?"

The Green Man cocked his misshapen head. Those vacuous eyes belied nothing. His was a visage divorced of any trace of humanity. It was no more possible to intuit what this man was thinking than what thoughts entertained the mind of a coiled viper. The colonel felt himself give an involuntary jump when one of the Green Man's hands struck suddenly upward, mashing a small device into the greenish folds of his throat. Vibrations from the instrument rattled through a wreckage of vocal cords, producing a robotic intonation. "I am the Voice," he replied, drawing a loaded revolver from the folds of his tunic, leveling the barrel to the colonel's forehead, "and I'm here to relieve you of command."

"Pyramids. Why the hell else would anyone want to visit Egypt?" The American dropped his hand to his wife's thigh with a fleshy smack. "Outside of the outstanding class of people, of course, and those miles of gorgeous wasteland. No, we naturally came to see those pyramids, along with everyone else in this restaurant, and now, having seen them, I have to say that I'm pretty relieved to have checked this one off my bucket list."

"Pyramids." The engineer nodded, gesturing with a slice of pizza toward the massive monuments that loomed beyond the plate glass windows, silhouetted by the sanguine light of a dying sun. "This trip was supposed to have been my professional retreat, but I brought along my son." He cast a glance toward the dark-haired teen seated next to him, who was toying with his phone. "His mother is Egyptian. Bringing him to Giza was always her dream, but she didn't care to join us, not under these circumstances, but I couldn't pass on the opportunity. My colleagues, they all went into Cairo for a nicer sort of dinner," the engineer tipped his head in the direction of his son, "but this guy wanted to stay for the laser light show, and of course, for the pizza."

"Hey, who doesn't love pizza?" The American grinned at the kid, whose eyebrows hitched, but he never looked up from his phone. "We all do. Every goddamned one of us. Personally, I think it's testimony to what's quite possibly the perfect cuisine. A man can travel halfway around the globe to admire one of the Seven Wonders of the World from right across the street, sitting in a weirdly familiar, air-conditioned fast-food joint, stuffing his face with pizza. It's just fantastic."

"You really think so?" His wife raised an eyebrow.

"Obviously, I was being sarcastic. When the builders of these eternal monuments were sliding those first huge blocks into place, what do you imagine they might've thought if they could've foreseen that one day, many thousands of years after their demise, the eyes of their Great Sphinx would be staring right into the front windows of a goddamned Pizza Hut? I don't think they'd be too happy about that." He clapped his hands and chuckled, glancing over at his wife. "Pyramids and pizza. Laser light shows. I just love it."

"Did you enjoy your tour?" The engineer's eyes fluttered closed for a moment, as he seemed to draw a breath of air in hopes of diluting the forced atmosphere of this company of perfect strangers. Seating was limited in the crowded restaurant. Tables had to be shared.

"Sure." The American man nodded, sticking out his lower lip. "It was very—archaic."

"Were you bothered at all by the merchants?" the engineer asked, directing his gaze to the American woman. "They can be aggressive, and rather lewd."

The American shrugged, looking to his wife.

"No," she replied. "I expected that I might attract some unwanted attention, being a western woman and all, but I don't feel as though we were targeted in any way."

The American pinched his nose, leaning back in his seat. "Those disclaimers are all over the Internet. Don't come to Egypt! Stay away! The pyramids are such a dangerous place! I mean, come on, those aren't their pyramids." He directed a thumb at the throngs of local merchants down on the plaza, then straightened up in his seat and leaned over the table. "They're our goddamned pyramids. Right? They're your pyramids. They're his pyramids to enjoy." The American tipped his chin toward the teen, whose eyes flicked up momentarily from his phone before settling back down into his technological bubble. "These people? The people who occupy Egypt right now? Their culture is just as alien to the builders of those monuments as we are. Don't let them fool you. They don't own the pyramids, even though they might try to convince you that they do. No-no. The pyramids are a gift to all of us." He tapped the pad of his index finger against the center of the table. "No matter where you travel abroad, they're always going to see you coming. You know what I mean? Different languages, same old set of tricks. They'll always see you as an easy target, a scared little tourist quivering in his flip-flops, and of course, carrying around a fat wad of cash in his wallet, right? Bullshit. You can't let them bully you. Otherwise, the terrorists win, right?" The American chuckled. "The two of you, I'm guessing Germans? Ya?"

The engineer and his son nodded, as their mouths were too full of pizza to reply.

"Well, then you know exactly what I'm talking about. They'll always see you coming if you're from a more developed country, but we don't let it bother us, do we?" He glanced toward his wife. "We love to travel, wherever and whenever possible, and I refuse to let anyone push us around."

"I don't travel too much outside of Europe," the engineer replied, swallowing his food. "It's become too dangerous. These countries, they don't care about protecting their tourists, or even developing any sort of a tourism industry. They have a much more fundamental attitude. My wife, she was born here, yet, she was very worried about me bringing him along. That says a lot."

The American narrowed his eyes and smiled. "We've travelled all over the world, the two of us. Africa, Australia, Asia, Peru ... and I honestly can't say that I've ever felt unsafe anywhere. Not for one minute have I ever felt like things were out of my contr—"

The American frowned through the front windows, as a tight formation of military helicopters ripped through the gap between the pyramids and Pizza Hut, billowing dust beneath their chopping rotors. The German teen looked up. He raised his phone with both hands, snapped a picture, and then lowered the device back into his lap, already texting. After completing a circle around the area, the squadron peeled off to the south, and drifted off into the twilight.

"As an engineer, I should be mostly interested in the design and construction aspects of the pyramids. That's why my firm chose this location for a retreat, but you know what I really find most fascinating about the pyramids?" the engineer said, dabbing his mouth with a paper napkin.

"What?"

"They are symbolic of a much bigger phenomenon. They are not really tombs for dead kings, as we've always been led to believe. That's a misconception. Tombs were never their purpose. No mummy of a king has ever been found inside of a pyramid. The bodies of the ancient rulers were always buried in Saqqara, and down in the Valley of the Kings. The purpose of the pyramids was something entirely different."

"I'm listening."

"When we think of pyramids, we always think of Egypt, right?"

"Yeah."

"Pyramids are not unique to Egypt. Their appearance was a global event. Five-thousand years ago, pyramids were popping up all over the world. It was as though all people, all around the world, were all being inspired to create the same type of structure at the same point in time. I'm a logical man, and that is illogical. I can't believe in some golden age of enlightenment. That is ridiculous. I believe that a far more physical transfer of knowledge took place, from one culture to another." He gestured toward the pyramids of Giza. "These were not the first."

"No?"

He shook his head, and took a sip of his lukewarm tea. "You mentioned travelling to Peru. That was actually where the Age of Pyramids began, down in the Brazilian rainforests at the three corners of Brazil, Bolivia, and Peru. Very little remains of those structures because they used earth and shells as construction materials rather than stone, but those were the first pyramids. In South America, there are estimated to be many hundreds, perhaps even thousands of them, and none of them were tombs."

The American looked to his wife, and winked. "You must have been on a better tour than we had. I mean, they offered us a camel ride, but ..."

"Well, if they aren't tombs, then what are they?" the American woman asked.

"That is more difficult to explain," the engineer replied, "and perhaps irrelevant. What is obvious is that in most every case, a pyramid's foundation is a separate structure than the pyramid itself, built from different and older material. All around this area, there are ruins of a far more ancient society, crystal altars, obelisks, and nameless temples. Much older civilizations once existed, but they were wiped from the historical record. Pyramids are often found atop the ruins of these older structures, as if a pyramid is more of a political statement than the fulfilment of a purpose. I like to think of a pyramid as an enduring symbol of the dominance of a new culture over the remains of an old one, an immovable capstone, a seal that cannot possibly be broken, planted over the gates to more ancient knowledge." The engineer pointed accusatively at the great pyramid of Giza. "The enslaved construction workers who built these structures were probably the last traces of those cultures that were erased."

The American screwed up his brow. "Erased by whom?"

"By the star worshipers."

"Star worshippers?" The eyes of the American woman widened.

"Yes, a worldwide astronomical cult of stargazers and calendar makers that appeared five-thousand years ago, in every corner of the world, leaving behind the pyramids and celestial calendars as their legacy."

"I've heard of the whole cocaine and nicotine thing, South American plant residues turning up in Egyptian mummies, suggesting some sort of a transatlantic trade route between the Old World and the New."

"Yes, but in the other direction. It was a route from the New world to the Old, by a movement that arose in the Brazilian rainforest, and spread like wildfire around the world. Europeans are so arrogant in their insistence that we were the first seafarers to circumnavigate the globe, when there is so much obvious evidence to the contrary. This feat was already accomplished many thousands of years ago by what seems to have been a rather aggressive religious movement."

"Well, now we can all enjoy a good laugh at their expense, because we've watched every one of those goddamned doomsday calendars run out, and the world keeps right on turning."

"Unless," the engineer said, raising a finger, "those calendars simply indicated the approximate end of an era, and the beginning of a new one."

"Dad! It's starting!" The teen lifted his phone to the plate glass window, and began to record a shaky video. Outside, the enigmatic face of the Sphinx was illuminated in an eerie spray of greenish light, haloed by shimmering holograms of scarab glyphs. The lighting inside the Pizza Hut dimmed. Overhead speakers crackled with the unmistakable static of an old record needle on dusty vinyl, followed by the tinny voice of a narrator whose canned recording had almost certainly been employed, in one form or fashion, since the 1950's.

"Civilizations are like islands in an ocean of barbarism," the narrator stated, in a curtly nasal voice. "Over this, I have watched, for five thousand years. Man is but an insect before me, yet it was man who built me. I am the Sphinx."

A discordant reed soundtrack reminiscent of some dated educational program wavered through the speakers. The flow of music was synchronized to a gradual change in color of the Sphinx's hooded countenance, from neon green to blue to purple, and finally, to a hellish red. Flickering symbols of ancient portents appeared in neon instants all across the horizon, as the pyramids blazed into view, one after another, bathed in fountains of crimson light.

The staccato of chopping rotor blades disrupted the mystical ambiance. All heads in the restaurant swiveled from the Sphinx to the squadron of gunships, tacking deliberately through the dusk in the direction of the Giza Plateau. They were back, but something was different. This time, there was a menacing aspect of purpose in their approach.

The clamor of conversation and clinking flatware throughout the restaurant was muted, as a thumping chopper came to hover directly over the Pizza Hut. The recorded symphony music was overwhelmed by the aircraft's deafening pulse. The remaining gunships fanned out over the plaza, where the crowds of tourists and merchants dispersed.

"What the hell is going on?" the American asked, gawping up at the restaurant ceiling, but his words were scarcely audible over the pounding cadence of the hovering machine. The casual dining ambiance devolved into the erratic behavior of a frightened mob. Customers left their tables and bolted for the side doors. As they made their escape, they were swallowed by plumes of windblown dust that roiled with oceanic turbidity. Thundering boots on the Pizza Hut roof ignited chaos throughout the restaurant. Women screamed, clutching their squalling children, as dark, villous forms descended through the brownish haze. One after another, they dropped like a hatch of spiders from their dangling ratlines.

The engineer leapt from his seat. "Get up. We've got to go. Now!" He seized the arm of his boy, who was still snapping photos with his phone even as he was hauled to his feet.

"Where are you going?" the American woman howled. "Richard!" Her husband had left the table. She cranked her head around, searching. He was gone, already lost amongst the mindless stampede for the nearest exit.

The engineer and his son rushed for the foremost flank of the crowd, where blows were being thrown. Bodies toppled over tables and chairs. Stepping through the enmeshed patrons and pizza, the teen tried to snap photos of writhing bodies, as his father shoved his way through the portal, dragging the distracted boy behind him.

"Richard?" The American woman rose from her seat, her gaze flicking from the dining room chaos to the squad of masked commandos that rushed past the opposite side of the glass. Enveloped in blinding dust, the first trooper reached the doorway, where he dealt a vicious strike with his rifle butt to her husband's teeth. The American woman screamed, raising her arms reflexively as the prattle of automatic weapon fire filled the dining room. A wave of toppling bodies cleared a path to the doorway. A face she recognized appeared suddenly on the other side of the glass. Blood-drenched, gawping like a clubbed fish, the engineer slapped his red palms against the windows. His crazed eyes met hers as his body collapsed, streaking a gory arch down the glass.

Distant bursts of gunfire across the plaza were marked by muzzle flashes, accompanied by the ongoing show of laser lights. Stilled bodies littered the ground. Others crawled, or hitched forward through the sand like half-crushed insects. From its altar of artificial light, the Sphinx glowered down upon the massacre with lofty indifference, as if scenes of slaughter were a common occurrence in the court over which it had long presided.

Overhead, the chopper's engines began to whine. The speed of the pulsing rotors increased. The aircraft lifted up and away, billowing filth around the dozens of masked commandos who were storming into the restaurant. Any possibility for escape was over. The crowds edged back from the phalanx of troopers, herding like sheep into the center of the dining area. A hush fell over the room as a final invader entered the restaurant, a hooded man who strode casually through the carnage.

Unlike his company, he wore no military uniform. Nor did he wear any aspect of subservience on the hideously deformed face that leered beneath his ragged cowl. He was a living incarnation of the Sphinx, with a gaping crater where a nose was once presumably situated, bearing every scar of abuse that a lifetime of war might inflict. Commandos moved into their positions by directives so subtle that they couldn't be discerned. They seemed to hear and obey his unspoken orders, as if their mind were somehow possessed by the rind-skinned monster who walked barefoot through the gore and shattered glass.

The entire restaurant trembled on its foundation as a titanic shockwave inspired a collective scream. Restaurant patrons crumpled to the floor. Some crawled under tables and covered their heads as a wave of blackness rolled over the Giza Plateau. Facedown in the gloom, the American woman's jagged breaths were amplified in the new and stifling silence. All power in the area had evidently been disrupted.

Another dull fusillade rattled the sheets of glass in their panes. This impact was succeeded by a tremor so deep that it seemed to emanate from the upset organs of the planet itself. The American woman scrunched her eyes shut, whimpering against the greasy tiles. Through her eyelids, she could perceive the room brightening and waning, as if the darkness was occasionally pierced by flickering bolts of energy. The resonating trundle of what sounded like toppling boulders seemed to originate from the far end of the plaza, in the vicinity of the Great Pyramid. The thunder rolled on for several terrifying minutes until absolute silence reclaimed the Giza Plateau.

No one spoke. No one dared to move. Only a single set of footsteps disturbed the absolute silence. The lone presence maneuvered casually through the wreckage, as though quite comfortable in chaos, at home in Hell. From beyond the proximity of her own jagged breaths, the American woman followed this dark attendant with her ears, as it drifted from the rear of the establishment to the front windows. Once there, the being stood silently beside her, as if admiring the view of whatever cataclysm had just transpired. She heard a muffled humming, not unlike the vibration of an electric shaver. This sound was soon accompanied by a robotic rendition of human speech.

"You are the lucky ones," said the voice.

A strange earthy odor permeated the dining room, like almonds and acid. She noticed that something was wrong with her throat. It was closing. The American woman's eyes bulged. She sucked for a breath that wouldn't come. She couldn't breathe. She rose to her knees, jaw oscillating, clawing at her sealed windpipe, retching on a swollen tongue that was already extruding from her mouth. What had so recently been a cheerful restaurant, had become a cave of death. She stood and reeled through her final moments, twirling amidst her fellow dancers in a ghastly performance that seemed to entertain the hooded silhouette who loitered at Armageddon's threshold.

"You are the harbingers of a blood dynasty." The words rattled from the throat of the man with no nose. Arms folded over his chest with an air of grim satisfaction, he maintained his sphinxlike stoicism, fearless, even as the lumbering horrors on the darkened plaza swiveled their massive heads, spotlighting the restaurant in the volcanic glow of their clustered eyes. "The first of seven-billion to die."

Chapter Three

"I've never been involved with this kind of an investigation before," the agent said. He placed the blunt remains of his right hand atop the evidence file that was situated on the conference table in front of him. He hung his head with an ingratiating air of admission. Shadows oscillated in the flickering glow of the gaslights. "Maybe it would be best if you told me how I'm supposed to begin, Ms. Raquet."

"You can begin by calling me Cecile."

She trusted the agent, despite his whiskers, mismatched clothing, and grime. A lot of folks distrusted the IDC, but this man didn't try to hide the pain behind his eyes. He'd lost a lot, probably his whole family, but he was carrying on. That was more than could be said for a lot of folks who'd just given up, crawled into their holes and died. He was still interested in working. That was good. She liked the flavor of his smoke.

"How do we begin, Cecile?"

She smiled at him. "Usually, we start with a personal object. Like an article of clothing, a piece of jewelry, something like that. Best if it's something they were wearing, or had with them at the time of their death."

The agent's gaze fell to the manila folder. He shook his head. "In this case, I'm afraid we don't have anything like that." He looked back up at Cecile. "I might as well tell you right now that the individual in question is not dead."

"Not dead?"

The agent slowly shook his head.

"Honey," Cecile said, raising a playful eyebrow, "you do know what a spiritual medium does, don't you?"

The agent stared across the table, but did not reply.

"I commune with the spirits of the dead." She clicked her chipped fingernails on the surface of the table, and her gaze returned to the abbreviated nub of the agent's right hand. Purple scars mapped the hems where someone had stitched him hastily back together. She looked back into the depths of his eyes, and she decided that he'd performed the surgery on himself. "Did you lose someone special, a year ago?"

The temperature of the agent's stare suddenly dropped by twenty degrees. "Didn't we all?"

"Would you like me to—"

"No."

Cecile pursed her lips and cleared her throat. She straightened up in her seat and drew a long breath of air. "Honey, what *do* you want me to do?"

"I have a photograph." The agent thumped his scarred appendage against the file. "We hoped that with your gift, you might be able to help us."

"I can't commune with the spirit of an individual who is still living."

The agent nodded. "I understand that, but I guess we figured that spirits of the deceased are not exactly in short supply these days. We hoped that in some roundabout way that you might be able to point us in a new direction, tell us something we don't already know. Anything would be a big help. We're at a dead end in this investigation."

"Can I see it?"

The agent opened the file with his left hand and removed a single print. He glanced at the image, and then placed it face down on the table. "This is the only known photograph of this individual in existence." With a quick thrust, he slid the picture across the surface of the table.

Cecile lifted her hand, and placed her palm on the back of the image. She cleared her throat, settled into her seat, and closed her eyes. "The person who took this photograph is no longer with us."

"That is correct," the agent replied.

"It was taken by a boy. A teenaged boy. One year ago." Cecile's eyelids fluttered. "He sent this picture to his mother, just before he died. His father was with him at the time. He died a violent death as well. They both did."

"All of that is correct."

Cecile opened her eyes, and gazed across the table at the agent. She'd turned him. It was always obvious when she'd made a believer out of a skeptic. They were always skeptical at first, until she softened them, and those walls came tumbling down. "I don't want to scare you, Honey, but before I go any deeper, I have to warn you, because you're new to this and what you may see and hear, might just be a little disturbing."

"I understand."

"Now, this is a little bit backwards from what I'm accustomed to doing. Normally, I try to connect with the spirit of victim of a violent crime. I earn their trust, and then, I try to coax them into revealing some clues about the circumstances of their death, but this is different. We ain't solving a murder mystery here. We aren't looking for clues about the death of a child photographer. You already know when, where, and how he died, and I'll bet you even know who did it. The boy's killer is on the photograph in front of me."

"That is all correct."

"So, what exactly do you want me to try to find out that you don't already know?"

"Just help." The agent's countenance hardened, flushing with hot patches of color. "Help us find this son of a bitch."

Cecile turned the photograph over. She frowned when her gaze fell upon the strange face staring back at her. "Can I ask you what you already know about this person?" The blurry image was that of a hooded man with no nose, enveloped in a cloud of what appeared to be windblown dust.

"We don't have a name. Only aliases. Last seen in Egypt, on Zero Day."

"On Z-Day? Then how can you be sure that this man is still alive?"

"We can't be absolutely sure. We aren't sure of anything. All we hear is chatter. That's why we brought you in." The agent stroked his whiskered cheeks with his good hand. "You made quite a name for yourself in New Orleans, with the LBI. Helped solve something in the neighborhood of a hundred-and-fifty cold cases? That's impressive, but I can assure you, in all the investigations you assisted, there has never been a killer more desperately in need of being apprehended than the man in front of you. We call him the 'Green Man,' on account of his skin discoloration. Maybe hypochromic anemia, chlorosis … again, we don't know." The agent's eyes hardened. "We do have good reason to believe that he's the ringleader of an underground terrorist network that crippled our world's national defenses at the moment we needed them most. If we can establish the right connections, we'd like to be able to hold the Green Man responsible for Z-Day," the agent said, placing his hand upon the twisted stump of the other, "as well as everything that came afterwards. We need this. The whole world needs it, moving forward."

Everyone lost something that day. Most lost everything. New Orleans was hit first, and hit hardest. Cecile was amongst the few folks in that city who were lucky enough to survive the first night, to crawl from dawn's devastation like a collection of insects that had somehow survived a passing crop duster's fumigation. Like every survivor, she'd learned to carry around a strange burden of guilt. The guilt was strange in the sense that while she could never understand why she was permitted to rise from amongst those billions who'd fallen, her so-called luck came bound to an obligation to witness civilization's collapse, the erasure of familiarity, and the gradual extermination of all her world's species. It was a strange new reality that fostered a burning resent toward the governments that had failed to warn them, toward the armies that had failed to protect them from the horrors that invaded and promptly desecrated their world. Most folks called them dragons, because wherever they flew, cities burned.

There were thousands of them. All emerging from below at once, like a great hatch of cicadas, the dragons wrought terror throughout their wakes of devastation, but they were not despised.

Not exactly. That was the strangest thing. On one hand, the dragons were beautiful to look upon, but Cecile supposed they were forgiven their sins because they weren't specifically killers of people. They attacked structure, and Dragons were just animals, after all. Much like a lion's prowess, or a great bear's majesty, their awesome destructive force was perceived as a natural dominance that was appreciable, even respectable, to human beings. There was no malice in an animal's actions. Only intelligent life forms can commit the act of murder, and same as it ever was, it was people murdering people. True hatred was reserved for the new race of traitors to the human race who breathed the toxic air and walked freely amongst the titans, performing their unthinkable duties.

"Most importantly, we have good reason to believe that the slaughter going on up there is not just some natural byproduct of a social meltdown. Immunity to the toxins isn't just some freakish biological accident. I'm afraid that the Hunters are all part of a plan."

Cecile furrowed her brow. "A plan?"

"Insurance." The agent nodded with grim conviction. "They were bioengineered to insure a total holocaust, and every lead that we follow brings us right back to him."

As if humankind hadn't suffered enough, Hunters were the most sickening insult. While the dragons were up there doing what came natural to their species, so was mankind—not humanity—*man*kind—all the way to the bitter end. Cecile refused to believe that we'd appeared on this world for no other purpose than to teach an unnecessary lesson in the futility of intelligent life, taught and learned by the same doomed experimental race. No, she had to believe that something, somewhere along the line, had gone terribly awry, and that we'd willfully departed from a better destiny that had always been so easily within reach, right up until the final moment, and we'd failed to grasp it, even after our erasure began. Our demise had never been a foregone conclusion. We'd had promise, but that promise was forsaken.

"They're using some system of communication, and the Green Man seems to be at the hub. Our path seems pretty clear. It's become the IDC's top priority to find the Green Man, and to kill him."

"Tunnel vision."

"Pardon me?"

Cecile cocked her head, narrowing her eyes in the flickering gaslight. "Linear thinking. It's a male trait. When it works, the male mind works well, but you realize it's also what got us into this mess."

She laid the photograph back on the table, and placed her palm over the Green Man's distorted face, lowering her eyelids. "Those things came from beneath the pyramids. They were all down there inside their eggs for five thousand years, hidden beneath pyramids that were scattered all over the earth, thousands of them. There were pyramids we didn't even know about. Pyramids buried in the deserts, lost in the jungles. Pyramids hidden under the goddamned sea." Cecile reopened her eyes, and scowled at the agent. "Did you know that the appearance of pyramids marked the beginning of our decline, under a new patriarchal culture that appeared at that exact same time, one that persisted right up until Z-Day? It's true, but for better or for worse, it's all over now, Honey. This big mess, it's all nothing but a reboot. Your time has passed."

"*Our* time?" The agent raised his eyebrows. "Meaning, men?"

"Mm-hm." Cecile tapped her fingernail against the surface of the table. "This world was all out of balance. It was being utterly disrespected. There wasn't no other direction but down. Our time as a people was running out, and you know it. If it hadn't been for Z-Day, our end would've come by war, starvation, disease, or just by poisoning from our own polluted lands and water. We had it coming, Honey. We sure enough did, and there ain't no *man* left on this ruined world who's ever going to tell me any different. You did this. You menfolk, with your brutal, linear-thinking minds. You brought our Mother Earth down to her knees in five-thousand years, when women had been ruling this world just fine for twenty-thousand years before that. That's right, we did, and you'd better believe that I know what I'm talking about." Cecile flared her eyes at the agent. "I got some very old friends on the other side who remember a balanced and peaceful world when we had it pretty good before y'all took over. Shame on you, Honey. Shame on all of you."

The agent leaned back in his seat, hands in his lap. "I'm not sure where all of this is coming from, or why you're directing it at me, but I'm open to suggestion, Ms. Raquet."

"Cecile," she said, with a wink, "and I'm not trying to give you a hard time."

"It kind of feels like it."

"I just want all menfolk to know that if humanity has a chance, if we can somehow overcome this situation that we find ourselves in, then it's only going to happen by starting things off on the right foot. Accept where we went wrong. Put the female back in her rightful place, and maybe, just maybe, we can put this poor ruined world back into some kind of balance that we once strived to keep. Maleness is an offshoot of femaleness. Remember that. All life is female, from the get-go. The earth is female. God is most definitely female. Respect the mother, respect the earth, and one day our sins just might be forgiven."

"With all due respect, Cecile," the agent said, rubbing his face, "in what direction, then, would you suggest we proceed?"

"There ain't no directions in the Land of Nod. There are only voices, and you need to shush now, so I can try to hear them."

Almost at once, Cecile could feel them pressing in. Not yet discernable, but palpable, like rows of caged animals in a darkened zoo. She could feel their desperation, their longing, but she wouldn't let them overwhelm her. That sort of behavior was not allowed. The dead would love to talk the ears right off anyone able to hear them, because all things that speak want to be heard. Get enough of them jabbering all at once, and you'd no doubt lose your mind. Her Nana Hess had taught her that.

Nana Hess used to say that the living mind wasn't made to visit Nod. The minds of most folks, anyway. Kind of like being underwater, way down at the bottom of a lake, where you can hear things, but you can't tell which way they're coming from, and you can see things, but it's hard to tell just what you're seeing. Some of them might once have been people, but most are other kinds of things, things that ain't got no name, and probably ain't up to no good. Maybe they were things once lived, maybe not, and God willing, never will.

"Ain't no Heaven or Hell," Nana had said, "just Nod, where you'll find your good and evil, beauty and danger, predator and prey, just as you see in any direction you turn your head. Anywhere in creation is the same as any other in that way. Don't you ever cross that stream thinking there's going to be a land of milk and honey just awaiting you on the other side. Mm-mm. You got to watch out for yourself, C.C., same as you got to watch out in the living world. If you don't, then you're just a little bug, kicking around atop the water. Soon enough, there's going to be something coming on up to get you."

Her Nana Hess taught her to turn them all away, every one of them. Taught her that hers was the only voice in Nod that she ever needed to hear. "You tell them to move on back, C.C.," Nana said, on the morning poor old Slim met with a terrible end, and the gates to Nod blew wide in Cecile's fragile, young mind. "You turn them back with this here *gris-gris*," Nana placed a leather pouch filled with gunpowder, metal shavings, and Lord knew what else, onto Cecile's sweaty forehead. "If they got something worth saying, then you make them find a way to show you instead of all that telling. Turn off your ears. Turn your back on them. Don't think for a minute they're special just because they're dead. You make them work for it. Love yourself, C.C. Don't ever let no one, living or dead, come and step all over you like a doormat. My Grandbaby is worth so much more than that."

Old Slim got bound forever to Nana Hess that day, whether he much liked it or not. Weren't too many indignities left that he might've thought were left to suffer, after those devilish nigger boys got through with him, but Cecile's favorite cat had one more indignity coming. Long as Slim's dried balls hung in that pouch around her Nana's neck, he couldn't ever wander too far, not in this world or the next. Just to be sure, Nana Hess made sure that poor cat's manhood went with her, right down into her grave.

"A day might come when you decide to come and find me," Nana had whispered to Cecile, a day before she passed, "and when you do, I may look something different than what you'd like to remember, but old Slim, he'll look just the same." She smiled, and patted the pouch of *gris-gris* upon her withered breast. "When you ready, you come on over to Nod, and when you do, you call for that cat just the way I taught you. He'll come a-running, just the same as he always done, and he'll lead you right to me." She winked. "That's how you'll know your Nana Hess, over there on the other side."

The vibrations flowed through Cecile's body, until it felt like she was about to fall to pieces. Time slowed and stood still as she slipped between moments, into a place where she could move while the agent sitting across the table stayed frozen. It was a powerful sensation, drifting between moments. That's why the Styx appealed so well to men, with all their dark designs. You could travel the world in an instant, pay some nasty little visits to folks too, if that's what suited you. That's why no goodness ever came from the Styx. Only devilishness. It could get ahold of a man's mind, take him away in its current, and drift him so far away there wasn't no chance of him ever getting back. Women didn't have a place there, at all. It took a man's sort of magic to fool around in that realm, where the worst sorts of witch men still wandered, but Cecile wasn't too worried about them. She was set on going deeper, across the stream of collective consciousness to a world where not even the worst witch man could follow.

The last veil was a jarring transition, where something thin and connective had to be pulled and stretched, darned near yanked loose from her body until she worried every time that whatever it was could snap and set her drifting for all eternity. A lost balloon between moments, with her empty husk of a body left behind, pampered for years by folks in white suits who didn't mind getting their hands dirty. She could feel that stretching clear down inside her womb, as she bucked loose of that fleshy anchor, wriggling like a tadpole toward the light, toward the misty realm that Nana Hess called the Land of Nod.

They rushed in from all directions, smothering her with their yearning. There were so many nowadays that she could hardly move. Nod was overrun with the restless souls of billions lost that hadn't yet found their places in the shades. Cecile held tight to that satchel of *gris-gris*, clenching it hard in the grip of her mind's eye. None could speak. She would not hear them. Only one was allowed near her bubble, the one she called to her side by buzzing her lips like jimson moth's wings.

Old Slim rubbed his sleek cheeks against her bubble. He knew who she was, straight away and every time. Cecile couldn't tell for all the earth what she must look like, but somehow that old cat always knew her for who she was. She longed to pet him, to stroke her fingers over his head and arched back in the same old way that she'd always liked to love on him, in life. Such was Nod, where nothing was quite the same. She floated around Slim, giving her cat a playful bump now and then, as she followed him through the shades to the place where Nana Hess rested.

Hers was a world within worlds, where clustered and colorful avenues wound in dreamlike whorls through what must've been Nana's memories, all twisted into convoluted niches sometimes inhabited by interpretations of the souls she's known and loved. Cecile even caught glimpses of herself here occasionally, portrayed as the shy ghost of a child who never remained in sight for long before darting from one shade into another.

She followed the black cat along its meandering path, where it paused to mark the threshold of every nook with a good rub from the side of its face. Nana Hess used to describe the effort to get all of her grandbabies off to church as, "herding cats." Cecile liked that expression, but it was tiresome enough to imagine herding any more cats than just one. She guessed it was peculiar that a voodoo queen like Nana Hess would even think to take her grandbabies into a church house, but she supposed that like most everything else Nana did, it was more for the effect of her actions on the ever-watchful people, rather than for any real purpose. Voodoo was complex. It was a lifestyle, a religion, an artistic expression, and of course, a great big show, all designed to transfer what was sometimes money, and sometimes some element of control, from the hands of the more powerful to those who were less so, in a manner so deft that the victims never felt a thing. That bamboozled element was not something that could be measured, or even defined, but any three-toed fool could see its effects. You could see it in the way that folks turned their heads to stare whenever Nana Hess walked through the door. You knew something was off-kilter by the way those white folks were always coming and going from her house. People admired her, and they needed her, inasmuch as they feared whatever it was that they perceived her to be. Not even the police would dare cross her. After so many years trying to discern exactly what her Nana Hess was, Cecile decided that it was easier simply to become it.

"Communing with the dead ain't voodoo," Nana said, "it's a gift, runs in the blood of our women, but ain't nobody but me and you ever needs to know that. You hear? We keep that a family secret. We let them think our gift is voodoo," she said, with a smile and a wink, "'cause that just gives voodoo some more power."

The voodoo died with Nana Hess. It was her life and her livelihood, just like her mam, and her mam's mam, before that. It had offered those women a chance for hope and respect, back when it seemed there was no other way of having those things. Times had changed. Cecile's mama went a very different path, one that took her straight to the grave, and delivered her baby into the care of Nana Hess. Never a day went by that Cecile wasn't grateful for those formative years with her Nana. Lord only knew what might've become of her had she been raised by her mama, spending her whole childhood in Storyville, a pit of madness and depravation that swallowed people whole.

"Your mama had the gift, same as the both of us, but she couldn't handle it. That girl could listen to all the dead in the world jabbering in her head at once, but she would never once listen to me."

"How'd you know I was thinking about my mama?" Cecile asked, floating toward the shifting heap of red yarn that was her Nana, in the Land of Nod. "Were you smoking me?"

"You know I was smoking you, C.C. I like the flavor of my Grandbaby's smoke."

Slim sauntered over to his master, sniffed the threads, and stepped delicately but purposefully into the pile. The cat turned three times, pressing its paws luxuriously into the soft bed of crimson fibers, before curling into the slight depression, purring and squinting his yellow eyes. Truly a cat in Heaven.

The collective light of a hundred candles, inset into every recess of Nana's collection of African artwork, cast flickering shadows of her innumerable keepsakes and dried articles that hung stiff and strange from the billowed upholstery of her ceiling. The place smelled of incense, cocoa butter, and the savory aroma from those pots of food forever simmering on her stove. Every piece of Nana's eclectic trappings was representative of something from her former life. Each item had a special place, and a deeper meaning. Some, she would explain. Others, she would not.

"That man you're looking for ain't got no place here. Not yet, anyhow."

Cecile floated toward the pile of red yarn as it rose, twisting itself into what was at first a column, before taking the form of a plush interpretation of Nana Hess's old face. She did this for Cecile's benefit. Nana preferred formlessness, but she knew that it brought her Grandbaby happiness to see something of the woman she'd known and loved in the living world.

"He's still alive, Nana?"

"Yes, he sure enough is."

"Can you tell me where to find him?"

"You know I can't do that, C.C. Not from here. I ain't got no connection to that side, anymore."

"How can I find him, Nana? Ain't there some way?"

The fibrous face stretched into a wide smile. The twin holes in the yarn that represented her eyes gave a slow, incredulous blink, just as they would have in life. Cecile floated around her Nana's form, which twisted at the base to maintain their eye contact.

"You going to wind your Nana up into a knot."

"I'm sorry." Cecile reversed directions until her Nana settled back down. "Didn't you ever try to use your gift to track down folks in the living world, back when you were still connected to it?"

"Hmm, won't say if I did and won't say if I didn't, but I'll say this much—there ain't usually no goodness coming from those kinds of tricks. We've been down this road before, you and me. What devilishness are you up to, child?" The fibers of Nana's brow folded into a frown. "Why are you trying to bother that poor man?"

"He's a bad man, Nana. Real bad."

"So you think he needs killing to fix what he done? That's what you're up to, ain't it?"

Cecile knew all too well that there was never any sense in trying to lie to her Nana Hess. The woman could smoke you right down to your last ember. "Yes'm."

"Child, that's a man's way of thinking. Ain't no problem so simple that it can be fixed by killing folks. Now, I know you know better after all we went through over that damned cat. Somebody put you up to this? You tell your Nana the truth."

"I'm working with someone."

"Some man."

"Yes, Nana. He's a man."

"Women in our family don't need no men. We make them to need us. Nana thought she taught you that. You're getting me riled, Cecile."

"You did teach me that, Nana, and that's just what I'm doing. He came to me, Nana, just like men would always come to you when they were helpless. The man I'm speaking with ain't got a prayer of catching this devil without me."

"You expect to be paid, don't you?" The column of yarn leaned close, until Cecile was staring down into those glowering poke-holes for eyes.

"Yes, Nana."

"You don't ever help no man for free."

"No, Nana." It was a bit of a half-truth. She and the agent had not yet discussed any terms of payment for her involvement in the Green Man's case, but collecting some form of payment for her assistance didn't seem too very outlandish.

"Well then," Nana said, relaxing back into her amorphous, crimson heap, "that maybe changes things."

"How do I find him, Nana?"

"Just like I taught you. With a personal object. You bring that with you, back to Nod, holding it tight in your mind's eye, like you hold them *gris-gris*, and you and I will just take it from there. Don't necessarily have to be something of his. Could be something belonging to someone close to him, someone who's already over on this side. See what I'm getting at?"

"Yes, Nana, but I don't have a personal object. I don't even have nobody close to him. We got nothing but a photograph."

"That might not be enough," Nana replied.

"No. It isn't. Not usually."

"Hmm. You think about the man in that photo, real hard, put him right there in your mind's eye. Let your Nana Hess just see what she can do."

While Cecile focused her mind on the man without a nose, the heap of red yarn churned and flowed with a serpentine sensuality. Slim perked up, eyes brightening, studying the movement all around him. He pounced on the trailing end of a red string, pinning it to the floor with his forepaws. He took it up between his teeth, cocked his head, and chewed contentedly on its frazzled tip.

"Let me introduce you to someone," Nana finally replied, "who might help you find that personal object you'll need to make a better connection. She's right behind you now."

Cecile turned around. She searched along the shelves and crannies for any sign of a lurking spirit. They could take any form, in the Land of Nod. Confident ghosts, like her Nana Hess, could adopt any form that pleased or suited them, but many ghosts lacked that confidence. Broken people, the lonely and tormented who may have taken questionable paths, or through no fault of their own, were born into terrible circumstances, the souls cheated and deprived of a fair chance at life, and were often manifested in Nod by a basic representation of their essence. There was certainly a presence in the room. Cecile could feel it, and it was not a pleasant one.

Cecile drifted along a wall of cowhide shields, past shelves peopled by the carved totems of lithe African women, inset amongst the ranks of books and candles. She could feel the glowering presence of the spirit getting stronger as she neared an ill-lit corner at the back of Nana's abode. There, on the floor, spread a reeking pool of black liquid.

"Hello, Honey. My name's Cecile. What's yours?"

The puddle shimmered dully, but did not reply.

"I could feel this one lurking, the more you started focusing on that man. I believe this one knows him pretty good. In fact, I believe she your man's own mama."

Cecile floated down to the floor, and came to rest at the edge of the dark puddle. It glistened, but cast no reflections. The swirling images upon its surface were being generated from within. "You his mama?" Cecile asked, softly. "You want to talk about your son?"

Black and tenuous tendrils of steam rose from the pool as it began to churn, ripple and simmer. A montage of images shimmered over its surface. Strange and disturbing, this woman's memories reflected the sort of abuse that Cecile might've suffered all her life, had she not fallen into the care of her Nana Hess. There was a school bus, overgrown with volunteer cedar trees, a ramshackle house, mostly hidden from view. She saw a fluttering clothesline, a battlefield of broken toys, beer bottles and aluminum cans. A mailbox on the shoulder of a dirt road. The school bus. Fields of wheat stubble racing to the horizon. The school bus kept reappearing with increasing regularity. The rusty mailbox bore the name "Cyrus" in plated letters, nailed vertically to its crooked post. A battered bicycle was propped against an elm tree. The school bus. A peering face, pacing behind the bus's cracked and tinted windows. Handcuffs. Pliers and a bloody box-cutter. Handcuffs. Burning skin. Something's not right with him, not right in the head. Handcuffs. A malformed boy, running naked down a moonlit road. Not right in the head. Idiot child. Mind is gone. Idiot child without a nose.

All at once, the show was over.

"I'm sorry, Honey," Cecile whispered to the puddle, which had thickened into bubbling tar. "I'm so sorry for all you had to go through, you and your boy. You were cheated out of a good life with him. That wasn't your fault. You couldn't get away from that monster, could you? There wasn't nowhere for you to run."

The puddle had coagulated to a dry and cracked burn on Nana's floor, where it continued to smolder. This one had said enough, all that it had the strength to say. It had burned itself out for a while.

"How'd she do, C.C.?"

Cecile rose from the colorless stain in the corner, and floated back over to the sentient pile of yarn. Through the sifting folds of crimson thread, she spotted something slithering, therein, something that wasn't yarn. A mass of threads toppled, spilling over the coil of scaled hide, and it was gone. Cecile intuited that this was one of those sorts of Nana's secrets that wasn't going to be worth asking about.

"I think I got a last name," Cecile replied, "and a pretty good feel for the place where he grew up, but I'm not sure where that place is. There were wheat fields, stubble, anyhow, and a broken-down school bus, parked behind a poor old house. It was pretty bad, what all she showed me. It was real bad."

"Indeed it was, child."

"You were watching, Nana?"

"I was watching you, and that was enough."

"Did you see anything else in my mind's eye? Anything I saw, but didn't see?"

"There was some writing on the side of that school bus," Nana replied.

"What did it say?"

"USD-269."

Chapter Four

Malcom raised his vials up to the amber glow of the sodium light to check the color of the six cartridges of potassium permanganate. He gave each one a little shake, turning it between his fingertips. The first two were no longer bright red, but they hadn't yet gone green. They were somewhere in the middle, brownish, around sixty-percent oxidized. The other four cartridges were still blood red. These, he snapped back into the compartments on either side of his mask. The two brownies would have to go.

He removed a flask from the hip of his web belt, and popped the stopper. Using his thumbnail, he unlocked the cap of each cartridge with a half-turn, and then dumped the contents into the galley sink. He turned on the faucet, rinsed out the gritty residue, shook the vials dry, and then filled each cartridge up to the white mark with an acidic solution from his flask. Setting the cartridges carefully to the side of the sink, he retrieved his canister of potassium permanganate from a weathered holster at the small of his back. He unscrewed the lid, and then removed the little, plastic spoon that was hiding inside. Tapping out the crust, he then dipped out a level scoop of the purplish-bronze needles, and tipped it into the first cartridge. As the KMno4 crystals settled, the solution inside the little glass cylinder flashed to a brilliant crimson. He capped the vial back off, locked it down with a turn of his thumbnail, shook it gently, and then snapped it back into the side of his mask. He repeated the same process with the remaining cartridge, and then snapped it into place. Once all six cartridges were reloaded, he snapped down the locking manifolds of plastic tubing.

Lately, he'd watched a lot of troops taking chances, letting all six of their cartridges burn down to ten percent before changing them out. That was stupid. The call for deployment could come at any time. There was no good reason to take unnecessary risks here in port, where KMnO4 was available in ample supply. Soon enough, there would be plenty of risk, and it wasn't going to come with an option.

He sat down on the edge of his cot and stared at the mask in his hands. The mask stared back. This was a soulless countenance of rubber and plastic. It seemed to possess a sentience all its own, perhaps imbued with the terror of its enemies whose last sight was this stark face, as they stared into its soulless black eyes and pretended to know what thoughts haunted its mind. They couldn't know the half of it.

As Malcolm held this headpiece to his exoskeleton layer, he was reminded of those pet hermit crabs that he'd kept as a child. Indomitable, in life, the little knots of chitin and claw marched fearlessly across their miniature battlefields, hefting that purple shield in the face of any perceived threat. What was most memorable about those creatures was that whenever the crabs sensed that they were dying, they always crawled out of their shells. Why did they always do that? Malcolm hated that. It was as though those little soldiers felt compelled, in their final moments, to admit the truth, to reveal that all along that they'd been nothing but a cowardly stinking worm hiding their whole lives inside a shell.

Malcolm was ready for the call. More than ready. Over the last few days, he'd found himself praying for it, rocking on the edge of his cot, pressing his face into his hands. Anything but this. He'd come to loathe the feel of his own grease on his fingers, the whispering sound of his unmasked breathing, the smell of his own human musk. He was sickened by the sight of his thin, hairy forearms, the map of veins beneath his wan skin, the hollow eyes in the mirror that peered out of that worried visage tilled into his brow. He hated that face filled with weakness. He looked down at the mask in his hands, and he longed to be back inside of it.

A lot of people thought that the world out there was a lost cause, a living Hell, an enduring testament to humanity's last and greatest failure. Maybe it was. Maybe it was our just punishment, our penance, but if that was Hell out there, then what exactly was this? Malcolm looked around the welded steel walls of the four-by-eight bunker, in which he'd paced for two weeks, feeling himself slowly dying under the sickly glow of a sodium light, just waiting for someone to give him permission to go out and do the things that the man in the mask was trained to do.

Malcolm rose from the cot and strode back over to his locker. He wanted to smash his knuckles into the metal and leave a dent behind, something for the next prisoner of this hole to ponder. More and more often, he found himself suppressing some senseless urge to lash out at an inanimate object. It was an urge that was becoming more insistent with every passing hour inside this bunker.

He sucked a deep breath through his nostrils, and exhaled through his teeth. He reopened his eyes, and instead of punching a senseless dent into the locker door, he gently opened it. Removing his satchel of vacuum tubes, he held each one up to the light, scrutinizing the state of their filaments. They were all good, of course. They were just as good as they'd been the last fifty times he'd checked them. He took down his cyanide poisoning antidote kit, and popped the plastic hasps. He checked for leaks in the bottles of sodium nitrite, sodium thiosulfate, and looked for any cracks in the glass ampules of amyl nitrite. Needles and hypodermics were all in place. His hand-crank ham radio mounted into his Kevlar helmet was at full charge, with a fresh vacuum tube snapped into place. The M-16 rifle was meticulously cleaned and oiled. The thirty-round magazines in his bandolier strap were all loaded. Five were black, containing standard antipersonnel rounds, and one was red, which contained incendiary rounds. His water filtration kit was readied. Emergency duffel was stocked with compressed cans of rations and water, first aid, and a couple packs of smokes. Most of the Americans chewed tobacco. Malcolm didn't have the stomach for that. Wasn't much of a smoker either, but in dire situations, tobacco was a good form of currency.

He pulled his mask up over his face. God, it felt so right. He closed his eyes and inhaled a big lungful of the sour, sulfuric air through the filter cartridges to perform a quick seal check. Maybe he just missed the taste of it. Holding the blade of his knife up to either side of his jaw like a thin mirror, he studied the flow of bubbles through the series of KMnO4 cartridges on either side of his black plastic snout. Beautiful.

Checking every piece of his gear was the first step of his morning routine. It wasn't just an obsessive compulsion. That's what he told himself, anyway. Things went missing. It was a world of thieves up there, where no one could be fully trusted. It was also paranoid world, and a shrinking one. Every day, human territory seemed to shrink a little smaller than the day before, while the range of the dragons kept expanding.

From the moon to the ocean depths, through the trenches of every war since time's beginning, the cruelly adaptable human animal had always been ready to gear up for deployment. Every challenge we'd ever faced had presented unique constraints to test the endurance of the human body, the cunningness of the human mind. We'd passed every test. Malcolm stared into the blade, drawing long bubbling breaths through the permanganate filters, relishing the taste of chemicals in his mouth. The challenge up above was no different. Humanity would overcome it. We would kill our enemies. We'd clean up the giant mess and rebuild our world, just like always. Life would go on. Malcolm had to believe that. He had to believe in some promise for validation, some justification for all of the shit he'd done. If the day ever came when he'd have to put his mask away in a box, the world's redemption would mean his own irrelevance. If and when that day arrived, he'd probably have to stick a gun in his mouth.

There came a sharp pounding on his bunker portal. Malcom sheathed his knife. He pulled his helmet over his head, and ascended the ladder. He slapped the latch aside, gave the airlock valve a few counter-clockwise spins, and yawned to pop his ears, as the chamber depressurized with a hiss of escaping air around the seal. Once the pressures had equalized, Malcolm rapped back against the portal three times. With a squeal of hinges, the steel cover was lifted from the outside, and thrown back against the deck of the barge with a massive thud. Masked faces peered down at him like a couple of weird bugs.

Malcolm scowled up at them. It was bright out there. So bright that it hurt. He raised his hand to wipe the sleep from his eyes, only to clonk his knuckles against the tinted visor of his mask, like this was his first day at Boot Camp. Churning bubbles in the soldiers' K-cartridges indicated their amusement. Malcolm flipped them off. He dragged himself up through the portal, and stepped out onto the gently rocking deck. A friendly hand slapped the center of his back.

Malcolm stretched the kinks out of his spine, groaning with a mixture of pain and pleasure through his mask. He stood there, blinking in the morning sunlight that gleamed upon the steel bow of the St. Louis Arch until the sleep had roamed to the corners of his eyes. Not much had changed. On all sides, he was still greeted by the ruins of the same city from which the Corps of Discovery had departed, two centuries ago, under the command of Captain Lewis and William Clark. The Americans had once called this place "The Gateway to the West."

"What's the good news?" he asked.

"Today's your big day, Sir." The nearest soldier pointed westward. "You're headed upriver with a rifle squad on the Tom Sawyer. Kansas City is going to bring power back up at 15:00-hours, put out some dragon bait."

"With what?"

"Klystron generator."

"Where the fuck did they get that?"

"Fort Leavenworth. Brought it down by rail."

"They've got a train?"

"Yes, Sir. The only fully-restored steam locomotive in the whole goddamned state of Kansas, built back in 1919. Sat on display in a city park for over sixty years. Now, it's going to be the dragons' worst fucking nightmare!"

Malcolm gazed westward. Dragons didn't have nightmares. They didn't even sleep. They just stood motionless for hours like flies on a wall, but they were never offline. Always on, ready to launch. Humans liked to give animals emotions where emotions had no sane or reasonable place. Those things had none. They operated purely on instinct, compelled only by their most basic urges to feed, fuck, and fight. That was it. Their so-called attacks on human civilization were never personal. They were sexual. The drones were males, and they were sexually attracted to power supplies, which presumably mimicked the signatures of receptive females, kind of like lightning bugs.

Malcolm knew a lot about Dragons. Dragons were electrical creatures. They were gassy creatures. They were ridiculously long-lived, subterranean creatures that slowly diffused lifetime supplies of helium and nitrogen that they acquired by suckling pockets of natural gas over a larval period of about five-thousand years, but nothing about their attacks was ever personal. The clouds of hydrocyanic gas that they produced were nothing more than a digestive byproduct, expelled as they burned-off their reserves of cyanogenic glucoside. The protonating jettisons of plasma acid were natural byproducts as well. That was simply the waste when you electrified a reserve of liquid helium and phosphorus, their fuel for flight. They were just big gassy beetle-bugs. No emotions. Never a malicious intent. Even as they laid waste to our cities, defoliated our forests, reduced magnificent landscapes to rolling wastelands of ash, they were just behaving in the way that Mother Nature intended. In the end, it was all mathematical. Natural selection was a numbers game, and it was a game that they were clearly winning, but they didn't know that they were winning anything, or that humanity was losing everything. They didn't despise us, and they certainly had no reason to fear us. They hardly even noticed human beings standing there weeping, as their orgies obliterated our world. All you could do was kill them.

"What's my mission?"

The soldier shrugged. "It's not militia, I'll tell you that much. It's a Coalition directive. We've got an agent here who'll be briefing you within the hour. Hope you put on some clean underwear." The soldier gave him a friendly nudge.

A Coalition directive. Anything coming down from the IDC promised to be unusual. As Malcom gazed westward, through the shimmering gulfs of electromagnetic haze, he could on some level relate to the anxieties and uncertainties that must have weighed on the minds of Lewis and Clark. What trials would he endure out there? What dangers awaited? What face would death wear, if and when it came to him? Would death be wearing a mask?

"I'll escort you down to HQ, whenever you're ready to rock and roll, Sir."

"I'm ready."

"Cecile, I'd like to introduce you to Captain Malcom Gann of the British Special Air Service," the agent said. "He's one of the lucky ones brought across the pond six months ago by steam liner to teach America a few things about pest control."

Malcolm offered the woman a nod, but she did not return the gesture, or acknowledge him in any discernable way. He was pleasantly surprised to find a beautiful woman waiting in the underground bunker. That was unexpected. Women were a rare enough resource, let alone a good looking one, but the walls that she had up appeared to be thicker than those of the IDC bunker. Maybe it was his mask, making her feel a little uncomfortable. Malcolm unfastened the chin strap of his helmet, and he lifted the covering from his head and face. He glanced up, expecting a change in her countenance, but the woman was unaffected. Figured.

"He's a specialist in desert warfare. Served four tours in Afghanistan. Did some time in Iraq. Following Z-Day, the SAS was reorganized for deployment against the new threat, and Captain Gann was transferred from Afghanistan to Germany, where he received extensive schooling in dragon anatomy, physiology and toxicology, in an international effort to determine their weaknesses. His squadron then played an instrumental role in the liberation of the United Kingdom. Since his transfer to the States, he took part in the liberation of Staten Island, and went on to serve as a key military advisor to our eastern militias, helping place hundreds of Hunters into IDC custody. Much of what the Coalition has learned about the network is a direct result of Captain Gann's efforts. In short, we've brought you one of the very best. By my estimation, he's the most qualified candidate for this mission."

"How do you do?" the woman said, even-toned.

"Captain Gann, this is the asset, Ms. Cecile Raquet. Your squad's mission is to insure Cecile's safe passage across the state of Kansas to the small town of Zurich. There, you will protect her while she gathers some critical intelligence, and then escort her safely back to St. Louis. You'll be travelling upriver this morning on the steamboat *Tom Sawyer*. By this evening, you'll rendezvous with one General Cobb of the Midwest Militia, who will put the two of you aboard a steam locomotive that is currently stationed in Kansas City. That will be your transportation out west. The Midwest Militia has scheduled a baiting exercise for tonight, in Kansas City. Obviously, that's going to be no place for Cecile, so you'll need to leave town immediately, keep her out of harm's way." The agent placed his palm against the surface of the table. "Cecile's work with the IDC is highly classified. Her importance, and the importance of this mission, cannot be overstated."

"Yes, Sir."

"No." The agent slowly shook his head. His glare seemed to burn through the wavering phosphorescence of the dim gaslights. "No, if I've made myself perfectly clear, then you won't be able to reply 'Yes, Sir' quite so easily." His gaze swept across the table toward the woman to his left, where it seemed to implore her, or rather, to implore God on her behalf. "This mission that I've just given you may seem pretty basic. Maybe less glorious than whatever battlefield heroics you may be accustomed to, but let me be clear—this mission may be the most important assignment that has ever been given to a soldier, in the whole of military history." His gaze left the woman, and returned back to Malcolm, in a glare so seething that it could only have been summoned by one who'd already lost everyone he'd ever been foolish enough to love. "If you fail, Captain Gann, if anything should happen to Cecile, if she does not collect the intelligence that we need, if she fails to return safely back to St. Louis, then it is no exaggeration to say that you've failed not only your mission, but all of humanity, as well." The agent tilted his hand, palm up. "Either you succeed, Captain Gann," the agent said, lifting the other gnarled stump of an absent appendage, "or you ensure the extinction of our species. Have I made myself perfectly clear to you?"

Malcolm rose from his seat. He pulled the covering back over his head, sealed the mask against his cheeks with a deep breath of bubbling air, and snapped the strap beneath his chin. He regretted ever taking the fucking thing off. He might never take it off again. "Get her fitted with a mask," he said. "Gear her up with a radio, vac tubes, KMnO4, and a cy kit. If this mission was so fucking critical, you should have deployed us six hours ago."

"Excuse me?"

"You heard me, asshole. Where's my team? Have they been briefed? We'll barely make it to KC by sundown as it is. Two weeks! Two weeks, I've been rotting down there in that fucking hole!" Malcolm smacked the toggle on his ham radio, mounted to the right side of his helmet, bringing the vacuum tube aglow. He turned for the door, seeing the agent and the woman glance uncertainly at one another, but he didn't care.

There was no regular army. Pecking orders, chains-of-command, they were dusty artifacts of a lost world where not all things were so fondly remembered. No matter how far departed those worlds became, no matter how wide the differential grew, from one side of Z-Day to the next, there would always be some ex-military pricks and former bureaucrats who still fancied themselves officers, scheming in the bowels of gas-lit bunkers, while troops of guerillas were out there risking their lives, trekking through Hell. There were no orders, no missions. There would be no court martial, because there were no courts. There was no record. There was no fucking grid. Only agreements between men counted, bound by handshake and mutual respect, and he'd just been fucking disrespected.

"What she was about to say, before she was so rudely interrupted, was that she was sorry, Captain Gann."

Malcolm turned in the direction of the female voice. The woman, the so-called asset, was still seated at the table, straight-backed, her dark hands folded before her. Although her expression was a serious one, there was a gambler's twinkle in her eyes. Something about the way she was looking at him, as if she had some cards up her sleeve, made him furious, while at the same time, inexplicably uneasy.

"She was sorry. That's all. Sorry she didn't take little Jacob on over to Resthaven to put down them flowers, liked you'd asked. Sorry as hell she'd ever argued, when that obviously meant so much, when you hardly ever asked her for anything, and had so little damned control over what she did with your boy. She was feeling mighty bad about all that. It was a small thing, you'd asked. A small request and she was sorry for denying you that wish, on account of a damned dentist appointment, which could have easily been rescheduled. That's how you felt, and you were right to feel that way. What's done is done now, Honey, because you can't go back and reschedule the thirteenth of August, can you?"

Malcom was glad to be wearing the mask, now more than ever before. The asset didn't break her poise. She seemed to be staring right into the unlit corners of his soul. No one could have known about any of that. No one alive. He could feel himself shaking, suddenly cold, yet perspiring. "What the fuck are you?" he whispered.

"I'm Cecile," she said, with a wink.

Chapter Five

The rhythmic surge and hiss of escaping steam from *Tom Sawyer's* twin stacks chugged along with an industrial cadence to the grinding sluice of the great paddlewheel, as it churned the stained water of the Missouri River into foam. It was a heritage boat, a double-decker steamer built to the specifications of the original series of nineteenth century riverboats that once plied the American waterways, announcing their presence with cheerful toots. Prior to Z-Day, the *Tom Sawyer* was one of a couple of paddlewheel cruisers that had provided nostalgic tours up and down the Big Muddy. It had always earned its keep, but following the first dragon attack on St. Louis, it was the only motorized vehicle in the city that remained operational, being entirely steam-powered, so the *Sawyer* received something of a promotion, with respect to the nature of its service to the country.

Malcolm leaned against one of the aft-mounted .50 caliber machine guns, imagining throngs of bygone passengers swaying to the sound of live music, sipping vintage wines along the taffrail, and enjoying hours of southern hospitality. Dancing, laughing, eating, drinking … unmasked and smiling in the summer sunshine. Mostly older couples, he guessed, boarding the fancy old steamer to celebrate their big anniversaries, to reunite with longtime friends, or just to enjoy a weekend of retirement with their spouses. The boat must have looked considerably different, a year ago, before the *Sawyer* was commandeered, slathered with a coat of olive drab paint, and armed with three-hundred-sixty degrees of deadly firepower. Atop the double-deck, the six-barreled miniguns and grenade launchers snooped between the raised sheets of armor plating. Anyone foolish enough to pop a shot at this vessel would quickly regret it. The scenery, as well, was probably more enjoyable back in those days. Malcolm imagined the darkly verdant boughs of river trees, jumping fish, and herds of lowing cattle scattered over a rolling bucolic landscape. It must have been beautiful at sunset, he reckoned, as his gaze swept over endless miles of smoldering wasteland that scrolled beneath the green reefs of electromagnetic clouds. The thought of rolling hinterlands made him homesick.

Great Britain was first to shut down their power plants. As a result, the United Kingdom was mostly spared the wave of hellfire that rolled over the civilized world. Millions died from the drifting clouds of hydrocyanic gas, but England's infrastructure had survived. Malcolm often thought of his grandfather, who'd also served his country as an anti-aircraft gunner stationed near St. Paul's Cathedral, when the bombs of the Nazi Luftwaffe pummeled London for seventy-one nights, and the darkened city was stabbed with fire. Similarly, all lights throughout England had been snuffed during that era as well to better conceal the targets from their enemies in the sky. On the night of Z-Day, when the dragon swarm descended, the decision to shut down the power plants seemed almost reactive of those old lessons learned, but the decision had been the right one. The swarm veered north, and within an hour, Norway was annihilated. The Brits' stroke of luck afforded them precious time that no other nation in the world was granted to wrap their minds around what was happening, and why, to debate what strategies could be employed to delay what was consuming the rest of the planet.

"So, who is she, our VIP?"

"Don't ask." Malcolm shook his head at the militiaman, whose name was Wesley. "It's classified." His eyes darted around the boat. "Where'd she go?"

"Up at the bow." Wesley looked off to the western horizon for a moment, then back again. "I didn't think that classified missions existed anymore. Figured, at this point, might as well be out in the open about things. Who the hell are we hiding information from, anyway? The dragons?" He snorted. "Just kind of irritates me. Got no patience for that Big Brother bullshit anymore."

"I hear you, mate," Malcolm replied. "If it makes you feel any better, I don't know any more than you do."

"Yeah, right. You've got IDC written all over you."

Malcolm shrugged. "You can believe that if you want to, but you'd be wrong. I'm not IDC, and I don't know shit about this mission. If anything, you know more than I do, because you're from western Kansas, right out there by Zurich. Plainville, right?"

"Yep. Plainville," Wesley nodded, "and don't I feel lucky for that, right about now?"

"Tell me about Zurich. Why do you figure we'd be headed there?"

"Are you serious? There's nothing in Zurich. It's just a little town out there in the middle of nowhere, about forty miles north of the train depot, in Hays, partly Volga-German population."

"What-German?"

"Volga-German."

"Fuck is that?"

"Me, along with a lot of other folks from my neck of the woods. Descendants of German settlers who immigrated to the Russian Volga River steppes, under Kate the Great. Later, they responded to a call from the American railroad companies who needed them to come on over here and do what they'd done over in Russia, settle a wild part of the world, where nobody else could seem to hack it. Good folks. Beer-brewing, cabbage-eating, polka dancing freaks, but hardworking and tough as hell. Thanks to us, Kansas and the Russian steppes are now the world's breadbaskets."

"Were."

Wesley nodded. "Right." Chuckling bubbles percolated through his permanganate vials. "Were." The first two cartridges in the series were already going green. "Why Zurich? Beats the hell out of me. I couldn't believe it when I heard those orders. Never thought I'd be going home again. Can't figure for the life of me what intelligence the IDC could be after in a town like that.

I mean, there ain't nothing to it. Post office, gas station, a diner ... you know? A one-stoplight kind of town."

"So, I guess it's probably not possible that the whole town is just a quaint front for some top secret military facility, buried a mile underground?"

"Shit—if it is, they've done a damned good job of hiding it! No, a high school buddy of mine grew up in Zurich. Came from kind of a rough family. Spent a lot of time with me and my family in Plainville, just to get away from home. It was partly his home life, and partly just the town. Zurich's a lonely sort of place. Doesn't really have—what's the word I'm looking for—an identity?"

"Doubt it's gained a whole lot more identity since the last time you saw it."

"You got that fucking right, but honestly, I'm happy as a pig in shit right now. I'm going home! Plainville Cardinals, baby!"

Malcolm tapped the cheek of Wesley's mask. "You're getting down to one on each side. Better swap those things out, or you might not make it back home to Plainville."

"I'll swap out later this afternoon, once we pull in closer to Kansas City."

"You'll burn through those pretty fast if we hit a gas pocket."

"One thing you'll learn about Kansas, buddy, is that you don't have to worry about gas pockets. Fucking wind is always blowing. Nothing but barbed wire fences to slow it down, from Mexico all the way to Canada. Truth is, you could probably take your mask off out there and be alright."

"You'd be insane, if you did."

"Fucking hate wearing these things. Makes me claustrophobic, if I let myself start to think about it."

"You know what we do in other parts of the world when we see someone walking around without a mask?"

"What's that?"

"Shoot 'em. Shoot 'em on sight. No trial, no judge, no jury. Straight to executioner. If you look like a Hunter, you're treated like one." Malcolm pantomimed a pistol with his fingers, and poked the side of Wesley's head.

"How many innocent people you think you've killed?" Wesley pushed his hand away.

"How many do you think I've saved? I guarantee the second number is bigger than the first. When some fool packing a rifle comes wandering out of the dunes without a mask, or a mask with six spent cartridges, you can't take any chances. They've learned how to blend in with the rest of us. You've got to be vigilant, look for those telltale signs and make your decision before they ever have a chance to raise a weapon."

"The place we're going, people don't even have access to equipment like this. Supply lines don't run anywhere close to that area. They're running around out there with fucking rags tied over their mouths. They're not Hunters, just refugees. You might want to rethink your foreign policy before we roll into my home town, because if you start popping off rounds at people, then you and I are going to have a big problem." Wesley gestured with a wavy hand toward the western wastelands. "Out there in my neck of the woods, it ain't—whatever the fuck you're used to, so get over it."

"I hope you don't ever have to see what it is that I'm used to."

Malcolm liked soldiers. He got along with them. They were his people, but militiamen were different, cockier, when they had no grounds to be. Few of these kids had ever been overseas, or fought in a real war. Many of them had never even left their home states. They were good kids, and he enjoyed the constant banter of bumping around with them, but he worried about them. He worried how they would react when faced with an attack. He'd seen better men, soldiers proven in battle, come apart at the seams under duress, and Malcolm was one of them, over in Afghanistan. He'd lost everyone he'd ever known and loved. Not once, like the rest of them, but several times over and he wasn't proud of himself, proud of the way he'd reacted to tragedy, on more than one occasion. In Afghanistan, they called him a hero. Nothing burned worse than being called a hero by people who didn't know the truth, by people who somehow couldn't see that that beneath all of your armor, you were nothing but a cowardly stinking worm, hiding inside your shell.

"Eyes up top, partner. We're being watched."

Malcolm turned, craned his neck. Up atop the double-deck, a slim figure appeared. Masked, wearing the usual hazmat fatigues, but unarmed. The individual edged clumsily along the ranks of guns, peering curiously between the armored panels.

"That her?" Wesley asked.

"I'd reckon so."

"How come you're not up there holding her hand? Isn't that your job, tough guy?"

Malcolm looked away, turned a shoulder, and cast a sideways glance in the asset's direction. "To be honest, she gives me the fucking creeps."

"Why's that?" Bubbling streams of amusement surged through Wesley's cartridges.

Malcolm shook his head. "She's a witchy woman."

"Well, she's a fine looking witch, if I ever saw one. I can tell. I can read the folds of that hazmat suit. I'll give that witch a broomstick ride she'll never forget."

"Trust me, mate. You'll want to pass on this one," Malcolm said. He was still more than a little unnerved by the way that she'd ripped open his mind, reached right in, and pulled something out that only he could know. If she'd read his file, and he supposed that she had, she might've learned that he'd once been married, divorced, and had one child born of that union. She might've learned Jacob's name, and learned that both he and his mother were now gone. That last conversation he'd had with Brenda, a conversation terminated by a blinding flash of light across the laptop screen ... no one else could have known about that argument, or about what they'd been fighting about at T-minus one-second to Zero Day.

"She's got her eyes on you."

"I know she does. I can feel them burning the back of my bloody neck."

"Get up there and talk to her. Make friends. See if she'll tell you why in the hell we're all headed to Zurich. She's a woman, bro. Not talking to anyone for the last three hours is probably killing her."

Malcolm tilted his head, peering uneasily up at the asset. She was just another black mask, staring back. Unlike the other masks aboard this vessel, it was that which lied beneath that he found most intimidating. In a world inhabited by monsters, she posed a unique sort of threat; less visceral, but no less dangerous. "She's more than just a woman, believe me. Don't even ask me what I mean by that, because I'm not even sure myself, but she's something special, and not in a good fucking way."

"Only one way to solve that mystery." Wesley nudged Malcolm in the ribs with his elbow. "Go talk to her, you big pussy."

"Ah, Christ." Malcolm sighed, wishing he could rub his face in his hands. After hanging his head in thought for a few moments, he glanced back up at the figure on the upper deck. "If I'm not back in ten minutes …"

"Yeah-yeah, I'll send up an extraction team."

Malcolm gave a thumbs-up, and then sauntered across the stern deck toward a ladder that seemed to stretch all the way to the sky. She stood in the clouds, glaring down at him like some dark angel. Everyone had angels, these days. He guessed that she was the sort of angel that he deserved.

So many angels. So many billions snuffed out, all at once. The air sometimes seemed thick with the traffic of passing ghosts. After a year of mourning, they all had that in common, the survivors, or at least they could all bond under that common presumption, anyway. The ubiquitous atmosphere of mourning helped dull the edge of individual grief. For better or for worse, they were all in it together, having witnessed Death's boney hand reaching down to swipe ninety-five percent of the human players right off life's game board.

Malcolm's deepest secret was that he didn't grieve. Not really. Not the way all the others seemed to grieve. He didn't feel as though he had a right to it. Grieving was a luxury only affordable to those who'd invested in loving relationships, and Malcolm had never risked that investment. The truth was that he'd lost Brenda and Jacob without really knowing them, a couple of years apart. Brenda, he'd lost first through divorce, and Jacob the other way. The failed relationships were his fault. He owned that. He'd worked fucking hard to lose their love and their respect, all by way of his nasty temperament and willful disconnection. Why willful? He didn't know. Well, yeah, he did, because it was fucking easier.

Surviving Z-Day was both his reward as well as his penance for being such a mean son-of-a-bitch, for being allowed to survive all of those engagements in Afghanistan, where so many of his SAS brothers had not. This extra time had been allotted by the cosmos to a damned fool who was evidently unentitled to pass through the pearly gates until he was able to admit just how badly he'd fucked up. The other survivors all seemed to have the spirits of their loved ones swirling all around them, protecting them, encouraging them onward through the ruin of their lives toward some hope for an eventual reunion. Not him. No one was waiting for him on the other side. All that awaited him was judgment. Malcolm looked up into the masked face of his asset. All that he had to live for was her.

Malcolm hesitated at the base of the ladder. Beneath his hazmat fatigues, he felt a peculiar sensation creeping over the flesh of his arms. Was it her again, playing some more of that voodoo on him? The tingling swept over his appendages, and prickled his spine to the base of his neck. Beneath his helmet, he felt his hair trying to stand on end. Malcolm rubbed his forearms, eyes widening behind the tinted visor. It wasn't her. It was something else. Something far worse. He turned toward the port rail, reaching for the ham radio on his helmet. Fumbling the little toggle, he switched over to a ghost frequency of pure static. He searched the skies, the rolling dunes of limestone and ash, as he adjusted his radio volume until static was hissing in his ear.

"See something, Boss?"

He ignored Wesley's voice. He closed his eyes, listening. The white noise was not constant. There was a discernible pulse. It was rapid in frequency, like the beating heart of some small and terrified animal cowering in its den. Malcolm's heart began to drum against the walls of his chest.

"What's the matter?"

It was an animal, alright, but Malcolm knew that this creature wasn't frightened, and it sure as hell wasn't going to be small. He backed three steps from the rail, before spinning on a boot heel and making a run for the ladder.

"Battle stations!" he screamed at Wesley, slapping his radio back over to the common frequency, winding the crank of the static generator until he could see the glow of the vacuum tube in the corner of his eye. He seized the bottom rung of the ladder as he keyed up his radio for emergency dispatch. "Battle stations! All hands to battle stations! Sound the alarm! Sound the fucking alarm!"

Malcolm ascended the ladder, hand over hand, as Wesley swiveled the .50 caliber forty-five degrees to port side. Atop the double-decker cabin, he could hear the boots of soldiers scrambling into defensive positions behind the GAU-17/A miniguns, the MK-19 grenade launchers. The *Sawyer's* steam-powered whistles emitted a long and piercing howl that reverberated for miles into the wastelands.

He reached the roof of the double-deck where he met with the racket of bolts being jacked back against their springs. A second blast from the wailing whistle produced a white geyser of steam that gyrated in the air. Soldiers craned their necks over readied weapons, searching the ruined world around them for the dark forms that could drop through the clouds like a squadron of otherworldly attack ships, or erupt from the ground in great shrouds of falling soil. With all weapons locked and loaded, a pervading stillness emanated from the endless escarpments of dust that rolled beneath the curtains of electromagnetic haze. The only sound was the sluice of the paddlewheel, the chug and hiss of steam pistons.

"What do you think, Sir?" a soldier at a minigun asked. "False alarm?"

"No," Malcolm replied.

"Six o'clock! Six o'clock!" A thunderous cacophony of belt-fed .50 caliber rounds, a shower of dancing brass upon the decking succeeded Wesley's shouts. Astern, the river swelled. Heaving sheets of brown water folded over what appeared to be a mountain range rising up from the depths. Waves surged at the foot of the each hillock as serrated crags breeched the surface with eruptions of pillared foam. Pink jags of lightning arced between the peaks, bonding the emerging forms in something like a harness of energy.

The hammering .50 caliber chopped the water into foam. White spumes danced all around the pod of dragons as they plowed upriver through a hail of bullets. The six barrels of the first minigun began to spin, spraying hundreds of rounds per second with the scream of a chainsaw. Every weapon on the ship directed its fury onto their forms, but there was no slowing them down. The dragons were upon them.

Malcolm wrenched his head around, searching for the asset. Unable to spot her, he raced shouting across the open deck. Eventually, he found her, crouched miserably behind a sheet of steel plating, clasping the sides of her helmet as if she were trying to cover her ears.

"Come on," Malcom growled, grabbing her by the upper arm and hauling her to her feet. Despite the threat of imminent death, he stole a quick moment of satisfaction over her display of vulnerability. It was vindicating to see the witch at a major disadvantage, frightened, outside her realm of control. This was Malcolm's world, and in his world, she seemed far less imposing. "We need to get you down to the main deck."

The pod of monsters split down the middle as they bore down on the paddleboat. On either side of the vessel, cavorting mountains thundered past, wetting the decks and the soldiers in their spray. Every gun on both decks unleashed violence against the scabrous walls. Day waned to dusk. In the sudden swath of shadow, the eerie song of bullet ricochets whistled and keened through the chaos.

Without armor-piercing incendiary rounds, the weapons aboard the *Sawyer* were all but useless. Although they were occasionally piercing the dragons' carapaces, the dissections that Malcolm had attended in Germany revealed a dense layer of blubber just beneath those armored segments that was nearly a meter thick. Encased in protective layers of chitin and fat, gas-filled bladders permitted bullets to pass through harmlessly, as the blubber filled the holes just as quickly as the bullets could punch them, not unlike that pressurized goo that could save a punctured tire. Still deeper, nestled within those gaseous compartments, was an armored bunker within a bunker, where the vital organs and fluid reserves were stored.

Cyanogenic glucosides, sulfuric and phosphoric helium isotopes, they were all neatly compartmentalized around a massive bioelectric generator at the dragon's core. They were like a cross between an electric eel and a meth lab, loaded with stores of inert chemicals that were instantaneously weaponized as they were purged through an electrolysis arc. The more these creatures were studied, the more they seemed to be the perfect answer to the human threat. Their design was unsettling, as though they'd been bioengineered especially to destroy us, dark gifts from the laboratory of some galactic lord of entropy, privy to our every weakness and technological limitation. Crackling with their strange energy, they inadvertently shorted our circuits, confusing organized flows of electrons with massive bursts of chaos particles that glommed to ions, fried capacitors, and stalled every circuit that wasn't protected within a vacuum tube, forcing technology back to ham radio, steam power, and the vacuumed circuits of the Industrial Age.

Powerless, humanity could only watch as they spewed their filth over our reality, burning our greatest cities, ruining our waters, defoliating our vegetation, and laying wanton waste to every goddamned living thing on which a human being could be sustained. The dragons required none of it. As adults, they didn't even have mouthparts. Their feeding stage was already finished by the time they emerged from the ground. What humanity was witnessing was the final stage of an insect lifecycle. They didn't eat. They didn't drink. Their bodies required no need for rest. All that mattered to them was mating, and human civilization presented nothing more than a collection of annoying obstacles on the floor of their courtship dance.

Malcolm's boots pounded down two flights of stairs. Dragging the asset behind him, he dove behind what appeared to have once been a bar, nucleating what was once a lavishly tacky ballroom. Gilded columns with plastic foliage rose from a carpet of paisley patterns. It was easy enough to imagine the twirling gaiety of joined partners, the laughter, clinking glassware, the calliope of an organ on the starlit eve of this ballroom's last dance.

Beyond the reinforced windows, a black wall of chitin plates stretched and contracted, providing hellish glimpses into that boiler room burning deep within, unreachable, untouched by the torrent of flying lead. The carnage of prattling weapons was deafening, but the dragons surged past the ported windows, one shifting segment at a time. Wherever a bullet pierced the armor, an outgrowth of orange blubber flowered. A cavernous sound, like the grumbling of an upset god, shook the little steamboat to its ribbing.

"They're about to take flight," Malcolm said, as if his predictions were the least bit reassuring to the IDC's quavering princess, at his feet. "When you hear that rumbling, see all those flashes of energy, means they're powering up, creating an internal current to convert their stores of liquid helium into a gas."

The basal thrumming grew in intensity, until the woman on the floor curled into a ball and screamed. Pinned between two inflating dragons, it was uncertain whether the steamboat would be shaken apart, or crushed like a balsawood toy between their stupendous mass. It hurt like hell, vibrating the eardrums, the guts, even the marrow of every bone. Malcolm fell to the floor beside the asset, incapacitated by the pounding sonic force. As they writhed together in shared agonies on the paisley carpet, he heard the roaring tonnage of falling water, the howl of expanding gas, as those titans raised, ballooning from the river, and lifting up into the sky. The deafening rumble of the bioelectric generators waned, but the danger had certainly not passed. Not yet. The worst was yet to come.

"Stay covered!" Malcolm shrieked, protecting the asset's curled form with his own. "Make sure your mask is sealed! No skin exposed!"

Night yielded to day, and day to the raging inferno of a kiln, as blasts of bioelectric waste set the Missouri River afire. Gilded paint bubbled and sloughed off of sagging plastic columns; paisley patterns upon the carpet went black, as searing fumes of acid and hydrocyanic gas enveloped the paddleboat in an ineffable cloud of death. Dark shadows passed over, as the pod of dragons floated by, discharging their bowels of hazardous waste upon them, as if to state in no uncertain terms their low appraisal of human worth.

"Breathe shallow," Malcolm said, rapping his knuckles against the side of her helmet. Her breathing was deep and erratic.

He could feel her body trembling, against his. "What was your name again?"

"What?" she replied, looking crazily up at him, as if his inquiry was perhaps the most ludicrous question she'd ever been asked.

"Your name," he repeated, "what is it?"

"Cecile."

"Where are you from, Cecile?"

She looked around, frowning, as if somewhat disoriented. "New Orleans."

"Good." Malcolm rose to his feet, testing the seal of his mask in the dissipating fumes. "You know how to use a fire extinguisher?" The woman rolled onto her side, propping herself up with one arm. She cocked her head and stared, still breathing heavily. Every question that he asked of her seemed to be more confusing than the last. Malcolm could feel the first embers of his temperament begin to flare, smoldering in his chest, and behind his brow. There wasn't time for a lengthy discourse. He bent at the waist, mask to mask with the asset. "Fire extinguisher. Pull the pin? Squeeze the handle? Point it at fucking fire?"

After a moment, she nodded.

"Good." Malcolm grabbed the nearest red canister, and ripped it off the plastic column. He swung it in front of her and plunked it heavily on the floor. "Take it and follow me." He headed for the staircase, leaving the woman on the floor, staring at the fire extinguisher. He snatched a second one off the wall from behind the bar, yanking it from its plastic housing. When he reached the bottom tread of the staircase, he turned to glare at the woman who'd still not risen from the floor. "Get on your feet, Cecile! People are dying up there!"

By the time he'd reached the roof of the upper deck, hot blood was drumming in his ears, chugging up the sides of his neck. This was a state of mind that demanded either action or violence. He stepped over the sizzling corpse of a crewman, whose arms were curled over his chest like the forelegs of a dead insect. His fingers were melted down his sleeves. Both of his legs were entirely protonized, slathered against the deck in bubbling stripes of reddish paste. Rubber combat boots lay haphazardly at the ends of those trails, unaffected by the toxins that had dissolved the feet within them. Malcolm snuffed each pool of fire with a blast of retardant. Paint bubbled and sizzled underfoot. The soles of Malcom's boots were melting, sticking to the deck, leaving black tracks of dissolved material.

To the northwest, the pod of dragons tacked port around the bend in the river, propelled toward the setting sun by intermittent jettisons of abdominal gas. Their tattered wings glimmered in the sunlight, as they raised and lowered these gossamer membranes to steer them along their course, as a pilot might adjust the wing flaps of a banking aircraft. They weren't the fastest fliers, but then, they didn't have to be. There was almost nothing on this planet that threatened them. They were headed for Kansas City. No doubt about that. The dragon bait was working. The klystron generator testing was obviously underway, already attracting the attention of scads of horny drones that could detect an electric signature in the atmosphere just as keenly as sharks could find a drop of blood in the ocean. He hoped that Kansas City was ready.

Malcolm noticed Cecile out of the corner of his eye. Fire extinguisher dangling from the end of one arm, she stepped onto the upper deck with the same bewildered manner of trepidation. He pointed toward the bow, where the railings were fringed with flames. "Fires, goddamn it! Go put them out!" He waited, still pointing, until she began slogging in the direction of the flames. Dead bodies of soldiers were everywhere. What was left of them, anyway. Their protective gear could only withstand so much punishment. The upper deck had taken a direct hit from the most powerful oxidant on earth. Like all acids, the stuff spewed by dragons had preferences in the substances that it dissolved. Rubber, glass, synthetics, they all offered some protection, but the protection wasn't complete. Organics were most the vulnerable substances. The compound's favorite food seemed to be flesh.

Malcolm checked the body of each militiaman. Where the bug juice was most liberally applied, boots and helmets had also been dissolved, melded into the liquefied corpses of the men he'd been entrusted to lead. Just like Afghanistan, he would be left to wonder for years to come why he alone had been allowed to walk away. Rage boiled behind his eyes. He'd fucking seen enough. It was a total loss. Up top, not a single life had been spared.

"Wesley?" Malcolm shouted, as he neared the back rail, hoping to God that at least his guide to western Kansas had survived. He gazed down upon the stern, where the lazy paddlewheel still slapped at the steaming water. Near the axle lay the crumpled form of the soldier named Wesley. He was unmasked, extruding his blackened tongue at the sky. Malcom turned from the sight of it, spitting curses through his teeth. He clenched his fists as he stormed back toward the bow. That was the last fucking time. The very last. No soldier on his watch would ever be allowed to delay swapping out K-cartridges. The fucking idiot. He deserved it. That never should have happened, but deep down, Malcolm knew that it was his fault. He was the man in charge. He'd failed to get right in Wesley's face and order him to change them. He'd failed to evacuate these men from this death trap on the upper deck, instead ordering them to battle stations, when he knew their weapons were useless without incendiary rounds. It was all because of her. He'd ordered them to their battle stations to protect her. These good soldiers would all still be alive if he hadn't been preoccupied with her safety, with dragging her useless carcass out of harm's way. Whatever potential the IDC saw in this woman, it had damned well better be extraordinary.

Malcom marched across the deck toward the asset, whose back was turned to him. Flames still lapping at the sky all around her, she stood gawping in wonder at the diminishing forms of the dragons that had just wiped out his entire squad. It was all he could do to suppress the urge to sweep an arm between her legs, hoist her up over his head, and throw her right over the rail. Then, he could get back to killing dragons, doing his fucking job. The asset turned, as he closed in on her. She squared off her shoulders to his, and before he could say a single word, she discharged her fire extinguisher directly into his face.

Chapter Six

The spirit of that fatherless boy was just as real as that motherless child, and the shadow of her former self, once remembered like a stain upon the walls of Storyville, and cast forever within the nooks of Nod. Absolution was just some nonsense dreamt up by the living, whose minds grew distant from their sins by time's slow passage, while they mulled their wrongs over, turned them this way and that, until they found some suitable angle from which to accept the things they'd done, or forget them entirely. Not so, for the spirits of the dead, forever estranged from time's perceived linearity, exiting in every moment all at once, from time's beginning to its blessed end. Like the spirits of the dead who bothered her, Cecile hadn't time's healing luxuries to absolve the past, because those ghosts of her own awful past were present, in every sense of the word. All hollering and fighting for a moment of her time, they wanted justice, revenge, apologies, yearning to make things right in that mess they'd sometimes left behind, even if that mess was no fault of their own. Over in Nod, all you had was time to think, and plenty of it.

Cecile's mama was over there. A flock of blackbirds, just as flighty and scattered in death as that woman had always been in life. A hundred yellow eyes, forever searching for that crumb of something that would make her happy, bring her peace, and make her right in the mind. What her mama never learned was that even a whole pile of crumbs wasn't made to last. Soon enough, it would all be pecked up, and that flock of blackbirds would be off looking for the next something, always searching, with those hundred yellow eyes.

Storyville was a dim room with sheets over the windows, stained green carpet, littered all over with those sharp things folks stuck into their arms, shiny glass bottles that rolled and clinked cheerily. It was a threadbare couch and a stranger's lap, where folks would snatch you right up as if you were their own, talk in your face, and carry you out onto a porch with white balusters of flaking paint that kept you penned in safe like the bars on an animal cage. You could lick that sour wood all afternoon while watching cars and people drift by. It was a place of hollering, where folks got hit, and things got smashed against the walls. It was sometimes like a theater, where folks raged in the room's center as if it was a stage for some unending production, where one interpretive act followed another, through every day and sleepless night, when boisterous bouts like you'd never imagined could sometimes stir whole rooms of strangers all to dancing. What Cecile remembered best about Storyville, and liked best to remember, was that it was the place where she met old Slim.

Black as the bag they'd zipped her mama in when they carried her out the side door, and that slinky old cat had just hopped right up through the balusters and onto the porch right as the ambulance sirens got to wailing. That cat sauntered up purring loud as could be with those lids half-closed over its golden buttons for eyes, and it just loped all around her, rubbing that cold, little nose and those silky cheeks against her own, as if to say, "Don't you worry, child. You ain't alone in this world or any other, long as you got me."

Slim got her smiling again, even giggling, before those howling sirens had ever faded out of earshot. True to its word, the old cat kept her company all morning long, until Cecile peered through the bars of her wooden prison to see her Nana Hess walking up the block, red as a blood rose in her fringed skirt of madras cloth. That was the last day they ever spent in Storyville, Cecile and Slim both.

A lost child needed someone like that, like Nana Hess, and even like old Slim, or else they'd just stay lost forever. Praise God, because Cecile couldn't stomach such a thought of what might've become of her if not for those two souls, those two perfect angels, who came right to her rescue when she needed rescuing the most. Not all lost children were so blessed. Like the fatherless child, Jacob, who'd died lost, and who might've remained so for every moment of eternity if he hadn't thought to show Cecile that crayon drawing he'd made.

"Kum hom Dade."

Son of a soldier boy, always waiting for daddy to come home, every day of his short life. Still, he waited, over there on the other side of things. Borrowing the imagined words of a slinky black cat with golden button eyes, Cecile had promised that fatherless boy that there was no need to worry, as he wouldn't ever be alone, not in this world or any other, long as she was by his side. That promise had seemed to please him, and Cecile always kept her promises.

#

"Who the fuck do you think you are?" Malcolm screamed, still covered in flame retardant. "Just because you find a key to someone's house doesn't give you the right to barge right in, go through their shit, and take whatever happens to suit your fancy. You think you're special, because you can do whatever the hell it is that you do? You're just a thief! A fucking thief! Stay out of my head!"

"I was never inside your fool head, nor would I ever want to be," Cecile replied, tempted to give him a second shot from her extinguisher. "You'd best mind your nasty mouth right in front of Jacob. Long as I live and breathe, he'll be standing right here by my side."

"What a load of shit! You're only saying that to keep me from throwing your ass right over the rail of this goddamned boat!"

Cecile cocked her head. "You don't believe me, Honey?"

"Of course I don't fucking believe you. You went through my goddamned file! Doesn't even take a street magician to pull that trick."

"What about that crayon drawing? Orange and red. Whatever happened to that? You reckon that made it into your file?

Because that's what he's holding up to you, right here in his little hand."

"What drawing? What are you talking about?"

The fool was trying to maintain his level of aggression, but at this point, it was all just a show. Cecile had heard the sudden change in his tone. The fight was over. She'd won. She needed say no more, but then that wouldn't be her style, because this fight wasn't about winning. "It ain't too late to get to know him." Cecile let it hang in the air. The small fires, all around them, were putting themselves out.

"If he's really standing there," Malcolm finally replied, his voice wavering with uncertainty, "then you ask him what I did with that drawing."

Cecile slowly shook her head.

"Because you can't answer that one, now can you?"

"No. Your son had no connection to this world, after he passed. Not until I met him, just this morning. Whatever things have happened, between the moment he passed, and now— whatever thoughts might be on your mind, those are all things that you can share with him, through me."

Malcolm's shoulders rose and fell. He just stared, as if trying to decide whether this opportunity to commune with his son was for real, or just the sickest sort of con artistry. She supposed that she couldn't blame him. There was a time, before old Slim met with his end, and her dark gift was received that she could remember doubting some of the things that Nana Hess had passed on to her that had supposedly from her mama. Made her a little mad, at times. She reckoned it was a lie because her mama never had much to say to her in life, so she couldn't understand why she'd suddenly become so talkative after death. The day old Slim was killed, and the doors to Nod opened, she was made to come to a full understanding of why dead folks changed so awful much.

"He's asking me, if you liked the gum that he sent you."

Malcolm raised both hands in a sudden gesture of surrender. He waved them as he turned, and reeled slowly away. Pow. She'd got him good that time. Maybe too good. Cecile watched him as he staggered off down the deck, stepping over the deliquesced forms of his crewmen, both palms pressed to the front of his mask.

In a quiet spot, he dropped to his knees, dumping forward until his helmet struck the deck. His back began to heave, while torrents of bubbles gushed through his cartridges.

###

"General Cobb? We just got an emergency dispatch over military band, originating three repeaters east. That steamboat transporting your St. Louis VIP just took a direct hit, wiped out all personnel on board, but two."

"What's the status on the VIP?"

"Don't have that information, Sir."

"Hunters?"

"No, Sir. Pod of dragons, and they're headed our way."

"Three repeaters east?"

"Yes, Sir."

"That'd be about a hundred, hundred-fifty miles."

"Yes, Sir. I'd say we have about 'til sundown before an attack."

"That's assuming there ain't a pod in closer range," the General said, rising from his seat at the cheap desk pushed to the far end of the Airstream trailer. He lifted his beige Stetson cowboy hat from atop the stacks of maps, placed it squarely upon his balding head, and then straightened the Civil War coat that had been gifted to him by the boys up in Fort Leavenworth when he delivered them a few crates of whiskey.

There was a ruckus, outside. The General cocked his head. Through the walls of the Airstream, nickering horses and the clopping of countless hooves upon concrete filled the trailer with the poignant nostalgia of a nearly forgotten world.

"You hear that?" the General asked.

"Yes, Sir. I do."

"Damn, but I love the sound of them horses." The General smiled, nodding his head almost imperceptibly. "All Arabians, every one of them. Beautiful animals. War horses. Bred for endurance in the most extreme conditions." The General picked up his mask last of all, and held the thing reluctantly in his gloved hands. He stared down at his reflection, cast upon the tinted visor.

"Don't suppose you've ever heard the story of 'Al Khamsa,' have you?"

"No, Sir. I have not."

"It means 'The Five,' in Arabic." The General looked up from his mask, fixing his leaden eyes on the young corporal. "Legend has it, when those Arabs decided to breed a better horse for desert warfare, they released a few hundred of their toughest mares out onto the Syrian plateau, subjected them to weeks of brutal conditioning, running them night and day. Ran some of them to death, I'd guess. On what was to be their final day of it, they waited 'til the hottest hour of the afternoon, then turned all those dehydrated horses loose, right near a big oasis. Now, just as the first mares were about to reach the water's edge, they blew a war horn, which the horses knew was their call to return to battle. Of those hundreds released, only five of those mares turned their backs to water, and headed right back out for the Syrian plateau. It was from those five, they sired the bloodline of the Arabian war horse." The General winked, and allowed a chuckle, smoothing his silver mustache. "I'm kind of a horseman. Least, I used to be. I sure love to hear the sound of them."

"Yes, Sir."

"How we coming along, up there on the bridge?" It was almost a rhetorical question, since General Cobb wasn't lingering around for an answer. His mood had darkened. He'd already pulled on his mask and brushed by the young corporal, before the kid could begin to answer. The General threw open the Airstream door, marched down the plastic tunnel inflated with amyl nitrite gas, and then stepped through the sterile airlock onto the downtown Kansas City street. More than anything else, he hated wearing the masks. The luxury of chemically filtered air in the regular army's trailers and railcars was always a welcome respite from smothering inside a steamy, synthetic confine. He was a man of wide-open spaces, and there was no sense of freedom behind a mask. Back home, on his Riley County ranch, if one of his dogs ever decided to run away, he could just sit there on his porch drinking iced tea and watching the son-of-a-bitch run away, from dawn 'til dusk. They liked to compare the flatness of Kansas to that of a pancake, but studies had shown that in fact, Kansas was flatter.

Horses champed by, wagging their masked heads indignantly, en route from the rail station to the upper level of a parking garage that had been sealed and rigged with wind turbines that continuously drew $KMnO4$-filtered air through a complex system of canisters and tubing that looked like something out of a pothead's wet dream. Carbon-filtered water was pumped manually, and continuously, from the bottom of the Missouri River. It was treated gravimetrically from a series of drums of God-knew-what that was metered mechanically into their potable water supply from ranks of paddlewheel piston pumps powered by a vacuum of pure uranium. The water tasted so foul that he wondered how thirsty those fresh horses would have to be, before they could ever be encouraged to drink it. That was the biggest problem with commissioning horses. They were thirsty sons-of-bitches. General Cobb had staked more than just his reputation on a trade to bring three-hundred masked and cagey Arabians all the way from Montana, by steam rail, but he was a horseman, after all. They'd served their country well in the past, and by God, the U.S. Cavalry was going to ride again.

General Cobb had a new vision for the old cow town of Kanas City. The vision was yet muddled a bit, but the picture was steadily becoming clearer. Kansas City was a centralized location, being an old railroad hub from the 1920's, and it was situated at the confluence of two major rivers. Cobb saw promise in the redevelopment of KC as something of a new, national military headquarters, and a trading hub. It would all start right here. Their steam locomotive was key, running routes from Fort Leavenworth to Fort Riley, and all the way out west, as far as Portland. When he climbed and stood atop the limestone bluffs of Huron Hill, what he saw, looking eastward across the old packinghouse district, was not just a tumulus of ransacked buildings. No, it was the beating heart of a national system of supply lines that would bring livestock and natural resources down from the unscathed hinterlands of the north, and ship them west, by rail, float them south and east by steamboat and hot air balloon. His country had taken a big hit, but it not yet crippled, not in

General Cobb's estimation, so long as there were able-bodied men fueled with patriotic vindication, determination, and places— undisclosed places—where precious resources could still be gleaned. He had faith that America could and would rise from the ashes of the so-called apocalypse, and start along a glorious path of reinvention, reconstruction, and redemption. General Cobb had already determined what was most needed, and where, all across his wounded nation, and he was bent on moving those critical resources to them. This was how it would all begin. Trade, it was the spark that would ignite a new rage for genesis. His vision was perhaps a lofty goal, but he'd received his first shipment of horses, and horses, well, horses were a damned good start.

The horse was more than just a beast of burden, a mode of transportation. In America, the horse represented something far greater than the sum of its potential. This animal was an American icon. It boosted morale. The very sight of a mounted rider in this dark era would inspire renewed passion for the fight, for selfless acts of bravery and heroism. The sight of a horse would trigger an embrace of that manic constitution known by warriors of eras past who galloped straight for hell's gates in want of freedom. In America, glory rode upon a horse.

The flared barrels of a battery of the world's most powerful machine gun, the Bofors 40 mm, bristled from either end of the Heart of America Bridge. These were his little gifts from Fort Riley. First developed by the Swedes, these vintage antiaircraft guns were built in America by Chrysler, and had been packed in crates of grease, resting peacefully in the bowels of an armory, ever since the Second World War. They'd been modified with extended magazines that fed horizontally stacked clips of high explosive rounds as long as a man's forearm. These weapons would shred a dragon to pieces.

On the bridge deck, gifts from Portland bristled over the girders, fore and aft. Mounted between rows of carefully arranged vehicles, the barbed tips of explosive harpoons protruded from a battery of Japanese whaling guns. Here was to be an interesting experiment, if any of the creatures were unlucky enough to drift within their short range. Many of the suspension cables were necessarily unbolted from the girders and left swinging to afford some room for what would follow if a whaling harpoon struck its target.

Atop the hill of downtown Kansas City stood Liberty Memorial, where the obelisk monument to the soldiers of World War I still loomed over the ranks of M1A1 pack howitzers, the M2 90mm antiaircraft cannons, with their ventilated barrels all aimed in the direction of the river's southeastern bend. They would pound the enemy with everything they had before the dragons ever drifted near the city, lured by the electric signature of a uranium-powered klystron generator, the world's most powerful vacuum tube, anchored a safe distance from the city on an armored barge, just a few clicks downriver from the bridge. The few dragons to survive the shelling of the long-range guns would find themselves pinned between the twin batteries of Bofors guns positioned to deliver a big shipment of dragon guts downstream to St. Louis.

This was to be the first organized clash of American artillery against the invaders. Previous engagements were crippled by the bursts of chaos particles that knocked fighters and guided missiles right out of the sky, disabling any and all conventional military tactics that relied on computerized systems. In this engagement, every battery was armed with vintage World War II era artillery, the good, old-fashioned stuff, and the bugs didn't stand a chance.

In a world drowned in ambiguity, hope could still be anchored by the solidity of facts. One of these facts was that there were a finite number of dragons. Finite. Wasn't like the battle of Iwo Jima, where unknown thousands of Japanese fighters were embedded in tunnels throughout that volcanic island, where every brutal engagement seemed to birth ten-thousand more. Given the worldwide communication breakdown, and the ongoing conflict in every nation, it was difficult, if not impossible, to come up with an accurate estimate of the dragons' remaining numbers. Most of the creatures had first emerged from beneath the world's pyramids. There were an estimated five thousand pyramids, worldwide, that were believed to have been constructed right around 3000 B.C., which seemed to be the date that the incubation of dragon eggs had begun. Five thousand years, five thousand pyramids, five thousand dragons. That was the best estimate of their population. Since Zero Day, a significant number of the bugs had been slain, had died in territorial clashes against each other, or had been killed in their attempts to copulate with municipal power plants. How many were left? In General Cobb's mind, the answer to that question was less important than how many of those sons-of-bitches would be showing up to the big party in Kansas City, tonight.

He turned toward the clatter of hooves against pavement. Mounted cavalrymen rode the last of the Arabians up what was once Kansas City's main drag, and by God, they were flying the colors. General Cobb snapped and held a proud salute as the first wave of his beloved dragoons thundered by, stirring the dust of erstwhile skyscrapers, stars and stripes flapping in the poisoned air, while a hundred whoops and gunshots resounded throughout the funereal ruins. It was the first moment in almost one year that Cobb was actually glad to be wearing a mask, hiding those streams of tears that spilled warmly from his eyes. God bless America.

Chapter Seven

The paddleboat tacked round a river bend that afforded the first glimpse of a shattered skyline, set afire in the hellish incandescence of the setting sun. Malcolm sounded a long blast from the Sawyer's steam whistle. With the body of their captain committed to the river, Malcolm had taken the Sawyer's helm. It was a relatively simple machine, devoid of buttons and switches that might've been blinking intimidatingly across the instrument panel of a modern riverboat. Much beyond a throttle and a wooden helm, there was little more to confuse the eye than a row of pressure gauges that seemed to loiter in a relatively constant differential between intermittent blasts from the steam pop-off valves. So long as he didn't run the paddleboat aground, the operation of this watercraft appeared to be fairly straightforward.

Malcolm frowned, straining his ears to discern the source of a rhythmic pounding, his eyes searching the columns of black smoke that roiled over the gleaming towers of the Heart of America Bridge. For more than two hours, he'd listened to the thunder of a distant battle, the dull fusillade of howitzer shells, the unmistakable thumping of Bofors guns. The percussion that now drifted over the ribbon of poisoned water was a sound of a different sort. It struck him as something that he guessed he hadn't heard in almost a year. Was it music?

He keyed up the ham radio on his helmet and sent a dispatch directed toward his mission contact, one General Cobb of the Kansas City Militia, a man who'd been designated to escort them to the second phase of their journey at the old stockyard train station. Nothing but dead air. He keyed up again, still no reply. On several occasions since they'd left St. Louis, he'd attempted to receive some bit of news over the radio, but for the last four hours, the military band had been jammed with chaotic chatter much beyond the last repeater. This close to the city, the lack of response seemed peculiar.

He keyed down the radio, cranking his head around to peer through the wheelhouse window. Still no sign of Cecile. They hadn't spoken a word to one another since the disaster, which was probably for the best. Even if he'd really wanted to speak to the woman, he couldn't exactly leave the helm. If she needed anything, he guessed that she could come to him.

There was a part of him that was curious. She'd aroused anxieties within him that wanted desperately to become new priorities in his mind, but they had little to do with the mission at hand. These thoughts became urgencies that whistled up like strange mortars through his core, chilling his flesh and unsettling his innards. He tried to respond to them in the way he'd always done, by suppressing them, crushing them back down with a hot sledge of anger—anger that he tried to direct toward her, for manipulating his mind in such a tactless way—but he found the usual sledge to be slippery in his emotional grip. It was becoming more difficult to stay angry, even with her.

This wasn't the first time in his life that he'd found himself questioning his temperament. He'd questioned it for weeks after Brenda filed for divorce. He'd questioned it dozens of times during his service to his country, following those violent spells that so frequently consumed the men of the Gann family name. None of the Ganns were proud of their fiery trait, but it was in fact, a trait that had served many of them well in their chosen capacities. They were fighters, most all of them. Soldiers, athletes, and even violent criminals, squabbling on every branch of the Gann family tree. Every fighter learns that the remorse passes once you've dismissed your waffling, and carried on.

This time, it was different. He had difficulty eliminating this particular set of misgivings, as they pertained to Jacob, a presence that seemed suddenly more tangible, less an abstract ghost of some bygone world. To dismiss Cecile's offer to commune with him, even if it was all just a goddamned gypsy ruse, felt a little bit like turning his back on Jacob, and that was a sin already committed, and one for which he was very ashamed.

Malcolm listened to the tribal drumbeats, narrowing his eyes at the billowing clouds of black smoke that obscured his view of the distant bridge. He'd burned the crayon drawing. He'd burned the square of gum, along with it. At the time, it had seemed the right thing to do. It was over. His life. All of it. He was to begin marching from Afghanistan to Germany. The ongoing conflict in the Middle East, which no one thought would ever end, had finally ended. Z-Day brought an end to everything, and there was always that possibility that one of the world's corrupt powers would seize the opportunity to inflict a death blow against their crippled enemies with a missile strike. It was a dramatic time in his life, and he'd given himself over to the romance of it all by building a small fire out there in the Afghan desert, where he'd burned every trace of a past life that no longer held meaning. He sat there, watching the single square of gum melt and bubble over the blackening folds of Jacob's drawing. The depiction of a tearful stick figure of a boy, holding hands with the stick figure of a man in a helmet dissolved, like the rest of the living world, into ash.

"Kum hom Dade."

How could he explain that moment to his son? How can you explain to a five-year-old boy that it's fucking easier to forget about them, to burn every shred of evidence that they ever existed, than to own the agonies of your failure and regret? There was no explanation good enough to justify what had been a private moment, and that he never in his life could have imagined that he might one day have to explain—to him. That chapter of his life was supposed to have remained closed, and that voodoo witch had reopened it.

Shifting winds wimpled the curtain of smoke that flapped black, as a piratical flag from anchor points on the gutted husks of buildings with their exposed, ribbed cavities and ragged edges; butchered structures, smoking in the electromagnetic haze like mirrored sides of beef. The ruins jutted haphazardly over great reefs of river steam, the blood of slain molecules in a microcosmic genocide. Acrid and tenuous, the mist burned the lungs and mucous membranes through masks designed to filter only the most lethal components from the fetid air. The fog hung low over the poisoned water, where human bodies now rolled and tumbled in the *Sawyer's* wake, cast like a troupe of performers in some languid interpretation of death's rapturous bliss. Arms swept gracefully over chests as they pirouetted through eddies, disappearing and reemerging, folding easily around the paddleboat's bow to pinwheel off through wreckage that snagged their clothing, clung briefly, until garments sloughed away.

Summertime, and the living was easy for them, drifting down the acid river. Their war was over. Their sin of living was at last forgiven by that wrathful god of entropy who knew no love for the music of chirring insects in twilit bows, the laughter of smiling children with slices of watermelon on paper plates, a dog's bark, a lawnmower's drone, an evening breeze that stirred leaves with a waxy clatter. These were all things once taken for granted by these river dancers, who'd at last been released from this planet of gas and flame.

Malcolm seized the helm and swung the bow of the *Sawyer* starboard, but the boat still struck the ragged hump of chitin. All fringed with blubber and pale meat, the mass slid beneath them. The vessel canted port as the horned carapace squealed and ground against the Sawyer's timbers, filing off great strips of wood and paint until the churning paddle pushed them off their high-center. It was dead.

Bubbles surged through Malcolm's cartridges until his breathing slowed back down. There was another, just ahead. Great tangles of what appeared to be intestines snaked past the Sawyer's bow. He spun the helm to the port and backed down the throttle, slowing the vessel's speed as they avoided a near collision with a second carcass, and entered something of a misty graveyard where humans and dragons shared common interment. Enmeshed remains of mortal enemies drifted past in rafts of splintered bones and gassy bladders. Malcolm tried to focus on navigation, but the drumming was so much sharper in the fog. Every beat seemed to travel more quickly and more clearly through this floating miasma, hammering in his ears until he felt panic's onset seize him icily by his throbbing heart.

The thumping of a Bofors gun was succeeded by shrill ululations that came keening through the mist. It was a thin chorus of celebratory whoops and howls that might rise from a stadium in the grotesque aftermath of a day's main event, when any real competition had passed, and the festivities were devolving into theatrical acts of desecration. Goal posts being torn down. Police cars rocked and flipped asunder. Blood-smeared faces. Pretty creatures, poised and senseless in the spotlight's allure, flaunting to their throngs of would-be rapists. Malcolm recognized this atmosphere. A battle had been fought, and won.

He released a piercing blast from the steam whistle, lest heady soldiers whose bloodlust was not yet satiated fired upon them. The *Sawyer* bumped and ground through a field of biological and automotive debris. What remained of their mighty enemies was ensnarled in tangles of steel cable, drifting by as unrecognizable masses of shell and gassy innards. The burning fire behind their eyes, of those that still had them, was extinguished. Geysers of yellow venom spewed from wounds in their armor. Nameless gases billowed from the great craters that halved them. The river was jammed with their smoldering remnants, too many to be numbered. The legs of some, still articulating reflexively, paddled weakly in the stew. As Malcolm sounded the whistle for another wailing report, the *Sawyer's* bow pierced the bank of dragon fog, and the bridge rose into view.

Rusty girders spanned a lake of fire, where tortured things set ablaze dangled from cables affixed to the structure, writhing in the infernal torrents of burning fuel poured down upon them. The titanic ornaments spewed their jettisons of plasma, inflating bladders to give lift to their harpooned bulk that rose from the flames like macabre balloons, only to draw the thumping attention of innumerable guns that delivered them back to Hell's pits. The doomed things had no grasp on the hopelessness of their situation, so bewitched were they by that klystron generated current of electricity. Clinging to girders, to the tension cables, to each other, the mindless supplicants estranged from a queen mounted instead the backs of their dying and dead brethren, thrusting pale, tented organs with indiscriminate fervor into any opening, natural or new. These clumsy couplings evoked howls of laughter from the jeering crowd. They threw bottles and baptized them with fire, gladly directing weapons at the novelty of exposed dragon genitalia. These targets were shredded. Blood and ejaculate gushed from flaccid trunks. Confused, they still clung, as their thrusting tonnage was pared steadily away by bursts of concentrated firepower, dropped in segments and discorporate limbs until their greater remnants fell steaming into the flames.

Atop the bridge, taunting victors postured. Streams of piss arched over the girder rails. They screamed curses down at their foes, but their insults were wasted upon earless behemoths who perceived the world in ways beyond the outermost valence of human experience. Bottles in hand, men climbed towers and tension cables. Some fell. Disagreements were being settled by the frequent pop of small arms fire. A brawl erupted along the northern railing. Perhaps inspired by the misguided instincts of their smitten enemies, and fueled by the corruptive energy of their drink, their drums, their rage for violence not yet slaked by the humiliation of their enemies, they thirsted for worse. They converged like a murder of crows upon the weaker, who were beaten, stripped, and dragged between cars. Malcolm watched a severed human head fall from the girders, just as a gang of horsemen thundered by on masked steeds. Riders hoisted their bottles, discharging rifles in the air. Their tattered plastic fatigues flapped like wraiths' shrouds beneath an inverted American flag. There flew the blood stripes of soldiers slaughtered in the defense of a bygone regime, the snowy streaks of forgotten battlefields that received our frozen dead, and the stars of fifty states no longer recognized by government or physical boundary. All had melded into one central state of entropy, unified by mindless violence not suffered in this land for almost two centuries. The sun had not even set beyond the ruins of their erstwhile civilization, while the bloodiest hours of a riot were yet to come.

"Captain Gann!"

Her. Malcom turned from the spectacle on the Heart of America Bridge, and he saw them, three canoes, sliding like insidious blades from some place of concealment. The pilots heaved to their paddles, rifles saddled across their laps, digging their way purposefully over the acid river, gaining on the steamboat with every stroke like a sect of acolytes falling into procession behind their chugging river god.

"Stay in here. Lock the door behind me." Malcolm snatched his propped rifle from the wheelhouse wall.

"Are they Hunters?"

"I don't know. You lock that door, and keep out of sight."

The foremen of each watercraft rose, straddling the bulwarks with their boots, and began whirling hooked grapples. They slung for the *Sawyer's* rails, and they climbed. Malcolm saw painted masks festooned with strips of cloth. He should have moved faster. Should have led with a warning shot. It was too late. They were aboard.

"Stop right there!" Malcolm ordered, while invaders clambered over the starboard rail. "Freeze, or I'll kill you!" Malcolm took aim at the nearest invader, and squeezed off a round that filled the man's helmet with his brains.

A burst of automatic weapon fire ripped a jagged line of holes through the old ballroom walls. Dry wood hashed the air in great chuffs of flitting splinters. They'd already taken the port side. Too many of them. They'd get to her first. The starboard bunch levelled their rifles as Malcolm unloaded his magazine, shooting from the hip, spraying the pirates with hot lead as he bolted for the wheelhouse. All crumpled. One, still fighting, raised his rifle and sent a few bullets screaming past his ear. Malcom toggled his ham radio to emergency dispatch as he slid around the corner of the wheelhouse, and onto the bow.

"Captain Gann with IDC, aboard steamboat Tom Sawyer. We're under attack. Dispatch to General Cobb of the KC Militia. I repeat: steamboat Sawyer under attack!"

The wheelhouse windshield exploded in a shower of jangling shards. Ricochets zinged crazily off the bow rail. He caught a glimpse of Cecile crawling through heaps of broken glass on the wheelhouse floor. If he could just draw their fire for a few more minutes—if she could keep hidden. Ejecting his spent magazine, he jammed in a fresh one. He snapped back the bolt while choking the trigger to return an immediate spray of rounds back through the walls at the same trajectory, sweeping his barrel low on the second pass to catch the crawlers. No return fire. Then, he heard the ascending intonations of boot soles upon rungs. Fuck. They were climbing for the upper deck.

Peering back around the starboard side of the wheelhouse brought an explosion of splintering wood right into his face. Death didn't come much closer than that. His wounded fighter was still in the game. He could hear boot steps, up above, edging toward the upper rail, and still, around the corner, shuffling along the deck at the base of the port wall. They had him pinned on the bow by three lines of fire. If it weren't for the asset, he'd have jumped. Likely as not, they'd have shot him dead in the river, if the fucking water didn't boil him first. No, he was trapped. Nowhere to run.

A rifle appeared over the upper rail, clenched in a black bagged hand. Fire spewed from the muzzle as the weapon swung pendulously back and forth, shredding the deck into kindling. Arching his back, Malcolm bailed backwards over the sill of the shattered wheelhouse window, pumping rounds up through the ceiling as he crashed to his back on a bed of shattered glass. He watched the dropped weapon fall past the open window to clatter noisily to the deck. Got one. Rolling to his left, he swung the barrel past Cecile's masked face in the direction of the port wall, hammering the last of his rounds through its base in the general vicinity of the pirates he guessed were lurking there.

At the click of his firing pin, they all appeared in the open window, the barrels of their weapons aimed directly at his face. Bubbles surged through the red KMnO4 cartridges on the jaws of their painted masks. They weren't Hunters. Just bad men. The big one popped his neck, revealing a flow of blood down the side of his hairy throat.

"We're IDC," Malcolm said, releasing his rifle, lifting his palms in a surrendering gesture, "allies with General Cobb of the KC Militia. Everyone knows we're coming."

The big man ignored him, pointing over Malcolm's shoulder at her. "You." He beckoned with a curling finger. "Come out."

Anything Malcolm said, at this point, would bring about his immediate death. Cecile wasn't moving. He lay on his back, breathing heavily, and waiting to see what would be the next play. He still had his pistol at his hip. He was sure that they'd seen it. The fact that they didn't order him to disarm told him all that he needed to know about his immediate future. They'd shoot him the very instant she stepped clear of him. Their interests seemed clear. They weren't risking their lives to loot the vessel of its cargo, because they didn't care about looting. These were raiders whose dark designs were rooted in the reptilian core of the male mind. Somehow, they knew that a woman was aboard this boat. Cecile was all they wanted.

"Do it," the big one grunted.

The smaller invader, whose mask was dotted with red paint around the eyes, dropped his firearm to the deck and reached behind his back. When his hand reappeared, it waved a massive bowie knife. The killer savored this moment of absolute power, twisting the great slab of steel back and forth in the air, as if relishing the play of the waning sunlight upon the blade's lethal curves. "Kidney pie," the killer crooned, nodding his head, passing his knife slowly from one hand to the other.

Had Malcolm not been wearing a tinted mask, the killer might've noticed a marked heightening in his expression, as the silhouette of the bridge and a swiveling Bofors gun cast an ominous shadow over the Sawyer's bow. Raiders, wood, glass and steel were instantaneously imparted into a torrent of obliteration that did not distinguish between the pounds of flesh that it hammered into mist, and the disintegrating structure that all took flight as one great migrating amalgam, harried into the hereafter by the thunderous percussion of the world's most powerful machine gun.

The barrage of four-pound shells ceased. An inquiring shout came from somewhere high above. When the smoke cleared, the forms of Malcolm and Cecile lay wetted and exposed in the baleful glare of the setting sun, like a pair of sinners discovered by the wrathful eye of their god.

Chapter Eight

"General Cobb?" The soldier knocked twice before opening the trailer door, peering inside cautiously. The door was pocked with a tight pattern of small holes, right about at head-level. "Got a couple of VIPs out here from the IDC. Here to see you about arranging some transportation out west. Know anything about that?"

The terse reply from within was little more than a grunt. The soldier turned, nodding to Malcolm and Cecile, as he stepped to one side. Malcolm raised a few fingers to the trooper in an appreciative gesture, and then, glancing back toward Cecile, he stepped through the portal and into the General's quarters.

Beyond a litter of blood-spattered papers, ransacked file cabinets, and the smashed remains of what looked to have been a ham radio receiver, a half-naked man knelt dripping over a water bucket in the very center of the chaos. The double-barrels of his shotgun were aimed at the trailer door, even as he scooped up slops of crimson water to his ruined face. One narrowed eye remained fixed on the doorway, while he smeared his fingers over his silver handlebar mustache. He cleared his throat, slicking back what sparse hair sprouted atop his head.

"Captain Malcolm Gann. British SAS. Needing some transport west, by rail."

"Remember hearing something about that." The General nodded, rising stiffly from the bucket, and lowering his shotgun. His lips were split. His left eye was swollen completely shut. He pinched the water from his nostrils, wiping his fingers against the side of his trousers. "Come in. Sit down," he grunted. "Make yourselves at home." The General dragged his bare feet through the wreckage of what looked to have recently been an orderly office. He lifted an upended chair and plunked it down upon its legs, and then halfheartedly smeared some red droplets off the seat of another, before limping around the corner of his desk. He sunk miserably into a squealing chair that was positioned behind it, releasing a long groan as his body relaxed. "Come by steamboat, did ye?"

"Yes, Sir. Out of St. Louis."

"How was the trip?" The General fumbled a set of keys before reaching down low to some drawer to jimmy a lock. Pawing it open, he retrieved a partial bottle of brown liquid, and set it mightily down in the center of his desk. He eyed the both of them as he popped the stopper. Tipping the bottle into an empty aluminum can, he licked his bloodied lips, and then glanced up with his one good eye at his two quiet guests. Malcolm was sure that by now, the man could see that they were both covered in blood. "That good, eh? Either of ye care for a drink?" He eyed them intently. "Take them masks off, if ye like. Air's good in here." He grunted and shrugged his shoulders when they didn't move. "Suit yourselves. Me, I hate the goddamned things."

Malcolm reached beneath his chin and pinched the plastic hasps. The strap halved with a click. He removed the helmet from his sodden head. Tucking it beneath his arm, he wormed his thumbs beneath the seal one either side of his jaws, lifting the mask from his face with a slurp of rubber suction. He coughed, as he always did, when his lungs drew that first gasp of flavorless outside air. It was the strangest feeling, every time, blinking in the world's brightness without a tinted visor before his eyes.

"Need a little help, over there?" the General drawled, squinting at Cecile.

Malcolm glanced over at Cecile, who was still struggling with her chinstrap. He could have reached over and popped the hasp for her, but, he guessed that if she wanted it off badly enough, she was capable of figuring it out.

"I knew y'all was coming, but I couldn't check up on ye. Lost my radio today." The General tipped his bruised head in the direction of the smashed equipment scattered all over the trailer floor. "Goddamned looters. Took everything of value I had. They come in for the whiskey. Had several cases of it. They took that, then my boots, my best jacket, even my goddamned cowboy hat." The General pulled a shot from his aluminum can, set it back down roughly, with a growl and a halfhearted chuckle. "I guess I can see robbing a man for his whiskey, but you don't fuck with another man's hat." He looked down into the can, dabbed his lips on the back of his hand, and then leaned over to spit some more blood into the mess of scattered paperwork. He slouched back into his seat with a groan. "Kind of makes a feller want to question it all." The General narrowed his one good eye. "You know it? Why the hell should we fight so hard to salvage one acre of this godforsaken shithole, when there might not be a soul left in the world who's worth sharing it with?"

"I understand completely, Sir." Malcolm watched the General's good eye widen, as Cecile finally lifted the mask from her face. He turned, to look upon the face of the voodoo princess for the first time since their introduction, back in St. Louis. Caramel skin, reddish brown curls, and eyes like droplets of oil. She was beautiful, and she knew it. She understood the power she wielded over men, and while she tried to hide that understanding, she didn't manage to hide it well enough. There was smugness about her, a confidence that suggested an unvoiced challenge to any man whose eyes she captured. Malcolm found this trait equally attractive and despicable.

"I'll be damned," the General said, leaning forward in his chair. "Pretty girl hiding in there." He glanced nervously at Malcolm. "Might ought to keep her under wraps as best you can. That's a rough town out there."

"We were already attacked," Cecile said.

"I can see that. You injured?"

Cecile shook her head.

"That's good." The General smoothed back his white hair, pulling another sip from his can, and exhaling hotly through his teeth. "Hunters, were they?"

"Not likely," Malcolm replied, still a stranger to the thin timbre of his unmasked voice. "Soldiers, I'd guess. They were all wearing military masks."

The General nodded, cocking his jaw. "They often wear masks, Hunters do. Wear them to blend in. They steal them off our dead soldiers."

"They were loaded with fresh K-cartridges. I believe they were soldiers. Your soldiers."

"*My* soldiers."

"Yes, Sir. They weren't Hunters. They were only after her."

The General eyed them both for a few uncomfortable seconds. "Can you blame them?" He immediately shook his head at his poor attempt at flattery, and then slapped a palm flatly against the surface of his desk. "Like I said, it's become a rough town."

"Rough?" Cecile said. "It's anarchy. Have you stepped outside your trailer lately?"

"Cecile ..."

"Killing, raping, looting ... it's anarchy. Your soldiers are all drunk."

"Course they're drunk." The General scowled. "They stole my goddamned whiskey." He rose from his chair, and spat. "I had high hopes for this place. This town. Centralized location. Defensible. Good railroads and rivers running through it. I took a big chance here, and probably ruined my reputation. Nothing I've attempted to do matters to them sons-of-bitches." He pointed an accusatory finger at the wall of his trailer. "They're all just a bunch of wild Indians, and the last thing they want around here is a chief. By tomorrow morning, it wouldn't surprise me if they've burned the whole fucking place down."

"Why don't you come with us," Cecile asked, "out west?"

"West? Hell, you ever been out west?" The General lowered his gaze and stared at her. "Ye think Kansas City looks bad, do ye? There ain't nothing out west but Hunters, from Fort Riley all the way to the Rockies. Every town out there's been massacred. Ain't nothing west of Riley but dried skulls and bones. The hell you want to go poking around out there for?"

"Classified." Malcolm cast a sideways glance at Cecile. For an extra moment, his allowed his eyes to linger on her exotic beauty. When her eyes flicked toward him, he looked away, but her image was already burned into his mind for keeps.

"Course it is." The General swept up his can and downed the last shot. "Classified, my ass." He snatched the bottle and poured himself another canful. "Nope, I think I'm headed out east, truth be told. Lived here all my life and I'd reckon that's long enough. This old man's had his fill of the bullshit. Going to catch me a lift with a squadron of ballooners, here in just a couple days." He hitched his eyebrows. "If those sons-of-bitches out there don't frag me first."

"We're looking for a man," Cecile said, stepping forward.

"A man?" General Cobb took a shot off the bottle, and grimaced. "Maybe I know him."

"He doesn't have a name."

"The man with no name … believe I've heard of him." General Cobb grinned at Malcolm, and winked.

Cecile strode up to the edge of Cobb's desk, and she looked in dead in the eye as she unzipped the front of her jacket from her throat to her naval. The General's good eye tracked the zipper's path. Slipped into the front of her pants and tucked beneath her bare breasts, was a manila folder. "I have a photograph."

General Cobb licked his lips, and stuck out his hand. "Let's have us a look."

Malcolm watched, as she withdrew the hidden article, lifted the flap, and then slid a glossy print from the yellowish sleeve. She surprised Malcolm by passing it over to him first, leaving the General's outstretched hand hanging beggarly in the air.

"We have the name of a town, called Zurich," she said.

"I know Zurich," the General nodded. "About an hour or so north of Hays. Maybe less. Smallish town."

Malcolm stared down into the horror of an inhuman countenance that gaped back from the image. Flesh like melted bubble gum seemed to ooze inward, as if flowing into the gaping crater where a nose should've been. The subject was badly burned, that much was obvious. Burned and mutilated. He looked to be the victim of the most sadistic sort of torture. Malcolm passed the photograph grimly across the desk, and dropped it in front of the General.

"Well, he's a handsome son-of-a-bitch, ain't he?" General Cobb snorted, and then shook his head slowly from side to side. "No. I can say with absolute confidence that I do not know this man."

"They call him the Green Man," Cecile said.

"Nope," the General said, clearing his throat, and pinching his nose. "Don't know nothing about no green men, but I tell ye, you'd might as well leave both your heads at the train station before you go traipsing up north of Hays. That's some bad country, up there. Worst I've ever seen. Hunters travel in regular war parties, out there. Talking hundreds of them. The things they do to the folks they catch—" the General bit down on his lower lip, glaring at Malcolm while sucking air through his teeth, "—you're bound to sorely regret this course of action, ye know. Taking her out there. Wouldn't do it, if I was you."

"Why there?" Malcolm asked, clearing his throat. "Why is the region such a haven for Hunters if there's no human population left to bother?"

Cobb shrugged. "That's always the case with Hunters. Like they all know something the rest of us don't. I suppose you can ask them that question yourself, once they find ye, and start cutting off your nuts."

"The IDC has reason to believe that this man is someone of great importance to the Hunters," Cecile said. "They think he's the one controlling all of them."

Outside, the staccato of automatic weapon fire was succeeded by the scream of a horse. The General's face fell and furrowed, as if he were experiencing some pain. He kept his head down and his eyes closed, as the animal's cries pierced the trailer walls like cavalry lances. Men's shouting led to another burst of rounds, and then silence.

After a moment, the General's eyes opened. He raised his chin from his chest. "In a time like this, I'd love to know how one man manages to control the actions of a single fucking person, much less a whole bunch of them." He lifted the photograph from his desk, and tossed it carelessly back in front of Cecile. He watched her every movement, as she slipped it back into its folder, slid it down the front of her pants, and drew the zipper slowly back up to her pulsing throat.

"Alright," the General said, "I'll put the two of you on my train. We'll take you as far west as Hays, but from there, the train's northbound to Portland with my shipment of horses, so it ain't going to wait around for ye. I can't risk it. There'll be another one rolling back down this way from Oregon, shortly. It's scheduled to pass through Hays right around midnight, tomorrow night. I don't know how fast y'all can hustle, but you manage to make it back to Hays in twenty-four hours, then that Portland steamer can bring you back in. I'll make sure their engineer is notified to be expecting you, but don't expect him to wait around, or even come to a complete stop. That's just how bad things are out there."

"Thank you, Sir." Malcolm rose from his seat.

"Now, hang on just a minute. The Hunters that are out that way," the General said, lowering his voice, pressing the pad of his index finger to his desk, then tapping it lightly against the wooden surface, "they travel night and day, just like the bugs. They don't sleep. Don't hardly eat or drink. They keep on the move. We don't know how they live the way they do. Truth is, we don't even know if they're even human beings at all. They can breathe unfiltered cyanide," the General said, furrowing his brow. "Think about that for just a minute. Alright, yet they look just like the rest of us. Blend right in, same as they did before Z-Day, when they were working in the Pentagon, the Senate, running major corporations, or just handing us our food through a drive-thru window. They were all living right there amongst us, all along, fitting in so well that not a one of us ever knew we'd been infiltrated until that day when something in their minds went click—and they started cutting folks down."

Outside, a man began to scream, until his cries were cut short by a single pop of small arms fire. The General struggled to fight back a smirk. He lifted the bottle to his lips and tossed back another shot. "Hell, it seems like we're doing a pretty good job of that on our own, aren't we?"

###

Masked horses were driven over the 12th Street Viaduct, their hooves thundering down into the old stockyard district of the West Bottoms. The grotesque architecture of the old bricked buildings suggested that it was an older part of town, one that still somehow managed to retain the original trimmings. There were no drunken militiamen here, where most of the roads and structures remained intact. Hundreds of regular army personnel in hazmat uniforms patrolled the perimeter of a great dome of inflated plastic situated at the confluence of the Kansas and Missouri Rivers. The herd of screaming beasts stampeded down the viaduct into a makeshift chute of car bodies and scrap metal that funneled them into the mouth of a plastic tunnel. This livestock duct snaked through the Bottoms to its terminal point of connection to the inflated dome. Beyond this covered corral idled the steam locomotive, a jet black machine that chuffed and hissed indignantly, while it inched its way past an air-locked loading bay. Through this flapping portal, groups of horses were funneled into boxcars that billowed fumes as their doors were rolled open to receive the streams of terrified animals.

Cecile followed Malcolm up the steps of a steel scaffold that was positioned near enough the train that they could step right down atop the creeping cars. An armed guard grabbed Malcolm as he stepped up onto the loading platform, and yelled over the chaos into the side of his helmet.

"There's a passenger car up yonder, right up behind the engine." The guard patted Malcolm's back, pointing a finger along a disjointed upper walkway cobbled entirely out of wooden pallets that were suspended between cars on steel cables. The path meandered over the roofs of the cars toward the puffing steam engine.

Malcolm nodded to the guard. He stepped down off the scaffold and onto the wooden walkway. He looked back in Cecile's direction, offering a hand to help her down. Cecile could feel the guard's stare being attracted to the meaning of this simple gesture. She refused the offered hand, dropping instead down onto the train roof on her own in hopes of retaining the secrecy of her femininity, but she guessed it was probably too late. One gentlemanly gesture was all it took to give her away. Irritated, she gave Malcolm a small shove with her elbow, goading him forward.

This was a more dangerous world than she'd ever imagined. The pirate attack on the steamboat had opened her eyes to that grim reality. In this godforsaken part of the world, she was less a human being, than some sort of living contraband for a man's indulgence, not unlike a walking bottle of whiskey. She glanced back over her shoulder to find the guard on the platform still gawking after her. He seemed to be studying her every subtle movement. She could feel his gaze creeping over every suggestion of curvature beneath the rubber bulk of her hazmat suit. He knew what she was, or at least, he'd already decided. Her sexuality, mostly an asset in her ordinary dealings with men, felt like a deadly liability. As she followed Malcolm up the walkway, past the guards who loitered at every station, over the wranglers at the loading bay, who wrestled the rubber bridles of their crazed animals, she knew without a doubt that there were more than a few men aboard this very train. Men who would just as soon kill her as allow her go on breathing, if only to have their rough way with her for a few minutes in some unlit corner. She was priceless, yet worthless, and that was unsettling.

Beyond the livestock bay, a human assembly line hefted sandbags and heavy components up onto the roof from a system of scaffolds. These items were passed hand-to-hand up the moving train toward a location atop the second car from the engine, where a machine gun nest was under construction. Soldiers fitted components and stacked sandbags atop what appeared to have originally been a giant cylinder of liquefied gas.

One soldier standing guard at the construction site saw them coming. He stepped forward to halt them with an outstretched left hand. His right hand went right to the grip of his pistol. "Stay right where you are. Identify yourself."

"We're with the IDC. I'm Captain Malcolm Gann, escorting this VIP to Hays, under the authority of General Cobb."

"What's your business in Hays?"

"Classified. Here's our papers."

Cecile watched as Malcom retrieved the bloodstained envelope from his hip pocket. General Cobb had sealed it, and handed it over to Malcolm just before they left his trailer. The soldier seemed satisfied with whatever was scrawled upon the letter, and he handed it back over to Malcolm.

"This is your passenger car," he said, pointing to the giant gas cylinder beneath his feet. "It's not completely converted, so you'll need to keep your masks on at all times. Understand? There's rations in back, if you need them. You know how to use an R-15 canister?"

Malcolm nodded.

"There's a bucket up front for a latrine. Please use that, and not the passenger car floor. Got it?"

"Aye-aye," Malcolm replied.

"Manway is on the forward side of the pillbox. We'll notify you once we've reached your destination. Settle in, and have yourselves a relaxing trip."

Cecile jumped when the steam engine released a deafening hiss. A pale geyser billowed from the chimney. Malcolm stooped as he walked through the swirling cloud, and dropped to his knees before a circular hatchway. The interior was ill lit, but as Malcolm descended into the cylinder, Cecile could just make out the rungs of a steel ladder. She followed him down into the gloom. Halfway down the ladder, the soldiers slammed the overhead hatch shut, and latched it from the outside with the slap of a bolt. She'd never been claustrophobic in her life, but when they sealed her inside the capsule, her whole body stiffened in a moment of sheer terror. She clung to the ladder rungs, unsure of whether to climb down or to climb back up and begin beating on the hatch.

"You hungry?"

She glanced down over her shoulder in the direction of Malcom's voice. The concave floor was leveled with sheets of plywood. A string of LED lights swung pendulously from one end of the car to the other. As the soldier had described, there was a plastic bucket full of sawdust at the forward end, and a single crate at the rear. Beneath the glittering string of lights, it looked like the back patio of some seedy bar. Gradually, she relaxed her grip on the ladder, and continued climbing down. She was hungry and thirsty. They hadn't eaten or drunk a drop since they'd departed St. Louis. The plywood bowed beneath her weight, giving extra bounce to her step, as she made her way toward Malcolm's hunkered form in the back of the car.

"You want to give those lights a few cranks?"

Her eyes followed the shielded cable to the rear anchor point, where the usual hand-crank friction generator with a vacuum tube dangled. She captured the swinging box with both hands, and cranked the lights back up to a more usable level of illumination. Now, she could see that on either side of the passenger car, round portholes had been installed. They were paned with what appeared to be Plexiglas, sloppily caulked into the frame. The cylindrical vessel had the distinct appearance of being a very low-budget submarine. She watched distant pockets of flame flickering throughout downtown Kansas City inch past their circular windows. Gobbets of fire dropped rhythmically from the girders of a bridge. Malcolm was hunkered, digging through a crate of what looked like black cans of spray paint. "What are those?" she asked.

"Dinner." Malcolm rose, holding a canister in each hand. "Ever had one of these?"

She shook her head slowly.

"Compressed MREs, developed right along with these masks during Desert Storm, just in case the enemy decided to hit us with chemical weapons. Only ones ever made it to the battlefield wound up in the officer's quarters. I doubt they were ever used, except as a novelty. They're all we ever ate for six months in Germany, after Z-Day." He held a canister up to the light, and turned it in his hand. "Good for another hundred years."

"How're you supposed to eat or drink anything with a mask on?"

"I'd be delighted to show you." Malcolm twisted off the cap, revealing a short rubber hose with a plastic valve at the base. "You're in for quite a treat."

"What's in it?"

"Everything a growing body needs. You've got your protein, water and minerals, all blended to exactly one liter of fluid and three-thousand calories, in every can. You can live for months on just one of these things per day." Malcolm held out the can, and he smacked the top of the rubber valve repeatedly, until a dull pop came, followed by an internal fizzing. He shook the can gently from side to side. "It warms and pressurizes itself, once you break the inner seal. Stick out your tongue."

"Huh?"

"Stick out your tongue. Lower your chin, like this, and feel around the bottom of your mask with the tip of your tongue. You should feel a little groove down there."

"Yeah."

"It's a little hatch. Stick your tongue down in there, and flip it up."

"Oh!" Cecile reeled backwards, clutching the snout of her mask. "Something hit me in the lip!"

Bubbles surged through Malcolm's K-cartridges. "You'll have to learn to catch that thing in your mouth when it pops out. That's your feeding tube. Once you're done eating, you use your tongue again to tuck it back down inside that little hatch until it clicks, and then close the little lid back over it. It's spring loaded."

"No shit."

"Alright, get the bulb of your feeding tube inside your mouth. Got it?"

Cecile nodded. He seemed almost too eager to be accommodating when he'd rarely been this helpful before.

"Hang on a second." Malcolm raised the can beneath her chin, and fitted his end of the rubber tubing over what must have been some sort of a little nipple, under her mask. "Alright, now, you need to bite down gently on that rubber bulb. Gent-ly. That opens your end of the feeding tube. Got it?"

"Nnn-hnn."

"Now, once I open the valve on this can, you just start swallowing. Swallow it down until it's all gone, or it'll fill the whole front of your mask. Ready? Dinner is served." Malcolm flipped open the valve on the can.

Cecile's eyes bulged as a surge of what felt and tasted like warm, wet dog food filled her cheeks. She managed to gulp down the extruding mass just as her cheeks were filling up again. For a minute, she was afraid she might choke or drown. By the streams of bubbles coursing through Malcolm's cartridges, he appeared to be greatly amused. He was doubled over, but still holding the can, as she gulped down each mouthful until the pressure decreased.

Malcolm could barely speak. "I know, its awful stuff. The first time I did it, I puked inside my mask. Want some water to wash it down?"

"Yes," she replied, breathing hard after the last swallow. The stuff was disgusting. It was thick and gritty, yet it left a greasy residue all over her tongue and teeth.

"It's the same situation with the water," he said, swapping out one can for the second, "comes at you hard and fast, at first, but at least you know that it's just water. Trust me, this gets easier. After a few meals like this, it'll all become second nature. Ready?" he asked, after fitting the second hose beneath her chin.

She nodded, clutching his wrist with both hands. He was already chuckling again, as he flipped the valve, sending a rush of tepid water into her mouth. It wasn't so bad, now that she knew what to expect. The initial pressurized rush only lasted a few seconds. Each can basically contained four, huge gulps, followed by a series of more reasonably-sized swallows. Despite all that it left to be desired, the system was pretty ingenious.

"Before you tuck that feeding tube back in, you'll want to blow all the crap out onto the floor, or else your mask will start to stink. Lean forward a bit, so it doesn't shoot all down the front of you, and blow. Wouldn't want to make a clean streak on that uniform, would we?"

As she bent to blow out the feeding tube, the train lurched forward. Malcolm caught her in his arms before she toppled. Horses screamed through the metal walls of their cells. Rhythmic blasts of steam accompanied each surge of movement. The string of lights swung crazily overhead, flickering on and off like strobes in some Halloween spook house.

"Feels like we're taking off." Malcolm relaxed his hold on her. They both eased down to the jouncing plywood floorboards, where they sat cross-legged under the blinking lights, facing each other, for lack of anything else to look at. There were the portholes, of course, but with the surging motion of the train, it would've been an exercise in futility to attempt to peer through them without being thrown to the ground.

She stared at Malcolm's masked face. His mask stared back. It was the face of an insect, comprised of hard interlocking panels and unblinking eyes. Devoid of any trace of emotion, it was impossible to discern the nature of the sentience behind it. Was the mind behind the mask awake, asleep, or entertaining dark designs to do something terrible? No way to tell. The lights flickered off, then on, then back off again. They stayed off, enveloping them in absolute blackness. It was a dizzying sensation. It reminded her of the feeling of weightlessness when she left her physical body behind, and passed over into the Land of Nod. She thought of her Nana Hess, and missed her terribly. She could feel them, all around her. The dead. Always knuckling, clawing, and scraping bony fingertips on the other side of that door.

"We're pretty lucky to have made it this far alive, you know?"

Cecile nodded at the voice in the darkness. She knew.

Chapter Nine

When the string of lights flickered back on, he was standing over her, cranking up the static generator. LEDs pulsed back to life. Malcolm sat down on the plywood floor next to her. Their hazmat uniforms looked like inverted hides, a couple of strange creatures that had been flipped inside out. The rubber surface was grotesque with the dried blood of vaporized pirates. Every fold remained tacky with the physical essence of fallen men who existed only in the shared nightmare of their last intended victims. She opened and closed the fingers of her gloves, both fascinated and repulsed by the stickiness.

"When we stop in Hays, we'll take ourselves a dust bath." Malcolm stared at her. "If you pat the stuff down with dust, it helps."

Cecile clenched her hands into fists, and then opened them slowly. She glanced at her new partner. "Have you killed a lot of people, Malcolm?"

"That's a hell of a question to ask."

"Hunters, I mean."

Malcolm shrugged.

"What do you think they are? They're just people, aren't they?"

"Used to be." Malcolm placed the tips of his fingers together in his lap, and then pulled them apart. "They all have names, birth certificates, mothers and fathers. At one time, they all had jobs, homes, families, and children. They were all living pretty normal lives, just like the rest of us, and I don't think they were faking."

"What happened to them, on Z-Day?"

"All we can do is to speculate, based on the small amount of evidence that we have." Malcom pressed his fingertips together, and cleared his throat. "Their blood," Malcolm said, pulling his sticky fingertips apart, "is different from ours. That much we know for a fact. They're all hyperglycemic. Extremely hyperglycemic. So full of sugar that their organs should be shutting down, but they don't. That's how they're able to breathe cyanide."

Cecile shook her head. "I don't get it."

"It's all biochemistry. So long as you have an extraordinarily high level of hyperglycemia, and a set of organs adapted to tolerate it, then you can survive without a mask in this atmosphere."

"Why do they kill?"

"That's the real mystery. All we can do is look closely at the facts. What do these people have in common? One trait that seems to be common is their race. Every Hunter I've ever encountered has been at least partly Hispanic."

"What's that supposed to mean?"

"You tell me, but it's a fact. Feel free to draw your own conclusions, just like I've drawn mine."

"What conclusions have you drawn from the fact that some of the—"

"All."

"—from the fact that all of the Hunters have hyperglycemic, Hispanic blood?"

"I haven't finished." Malcolm cocked his bug-like head and stared at her. "Their Latin heritage is Brazilian, to be precise. Brazilian, Bolivian, Peruvian … all from right there in that nexus of those three South American states."

"How do you know that?"

"Because lots of them are still carrying around their identification." Malcolm chuckled. "It's almost like, on Z-Day, they all just dropped whatever they happened to be doing, and set right off on their little missions, still carrying their keys, wallets, sometimes still wearing their work uniforms. Their missions were varied, but they're all invariably counterproductive to the survival of the human race. They drained accounts, crashed computer systems, sabotaged every level of our worldwide defense networks." Malcolm looked back down at his hands. "Of course, some of them simply started killing anyone who didn't fit their profile. Some slaughter indiscriminately, while others seem to have very specific targets."

"Why? Why would any of that happen at that exact moment?"

"Well, there is obviously some sort of a coordinated effort to cripple civilization and ensure the extinction of humankind. We've seen too much for too long to try to deny that anymore, but the real question is, are they a separate threat from the dragons, or are they cooperating with them to ensure a common goal?"

"You said that you'd drawn your own conclusions, but I haven't heard any yet."

Malcolm placed his palms flatly upon his knees, and rotated them back and forth. "The most intriguing piece of the puzzle— and it's a piece of the puzzle that very few people even know about—is that the level of hyperglycemia found amongst the Hunters is almost identical to the levels that we're seeing in the blood of the dragons." He turned to her. "There's a relationship between them."

Cecile rocked back on her haunches, staring at Malcolm down the snout of her mask.

"We obviously don't have the capabilities to conduct more extensive tests, but the field tests that we do have clearly show that the levels of hyperglycemia between the two species are almost exactly the same."

"You're saying these people have dragon blood in their veins?"

"Not exactly. What I think, and I don't think it too loudly, is that at some point, probably thousands of years ago, a population of ancient Brazilians had some sort of a fluid exchange with the dragons—or, at least, with the *original* dragon. I like to believe that in the beginning, there was one, the fountainhead of this whole disaster that first came into contact with humans down in the jungles of Brazil. Something happened at that meeting, like a moment of religious significance. Whatever took place, I believe that the Hunters are the descendants of those people who encountered the first dragon, and that all of their strange adaptations could be explained by having fragments of alien DNA in their bodies."

"*Alien* DNA. You think the dragons are from—up there?" Cecile pointed a finger at the ceiling. "Not just an undiscovered creature that had been living deep down in the earth all these years?"

"No way," Malcolm grunted, shaking his head. "If you look at the dragons, really look at them, you can't deny that their bodies are perfect for space travel. Hyperglycemia isn't just a cyanide oxidizer. It's also an antifreeze. Then, you've got their internal power generator to consider. What the hell is it? Well, it's a weapon, it's an engine, and it's an electrical generator, all rolled up into one totally bizarre organ that produces a powerful enough current to convert pure elements into gas, plasma and light, and that conversion is what enables these creatures to propel themselves with bursts of pressurized gas. As an earthly flight mechanism that's just crazy. It's a wildly inefficient and roundabout way to fly. Why go through all the trouble of evolving in that difficult direction unless you're designed for interstellar travel? Lastly, you've got the thick carapace, the high tolerance to temperature and pressure extremes, the thick layer of blubber … everything a creature would need for protection against the extreme cold of space, and the extreme heat of reentry."

"Space bugs."

Malcolm swiveled on his rump to face her. "Just imagine, a pregnant female dragon leaves a ruined planet behind, travels through space, and lands on another suitable planet to lay her eggs. This planet is Earth. She's discovered by humans. They worship her as a star god, and her eggs are distributed all around the world by her little helpers. Eventually, she dies. Maybe the humans killed her. Maybe she crash-landed, or caught some earthly disease, but at any rate, her eggs survive. They're buried all around the world, right in the hearts of ancient civilizations. Pyramids are built on top of them. Images are carved and painted all over the goddamned things depicting a winged scarab beetle.

At least, that's what we always thought. Now, it's pretty obvious that those images represent the original dragon, their god from the stars. The eggs hatch underground, and the larvae burrow down into the earth, sucking up all the natural gas and minerals that they'll one day convert into energy for flight. Fast-forward a few thousand years, and these larvae have grown enormous. They're ready to emerge. They've stockpiled enough underground resources to survive what will be mass migration away from this world, which will become too dangerous, and on to the next."

"You've put some thought into this, haven't you?"

"This lifecycle isn't unique to dragons. It's all around us, on a smaller scale. Just look at the insects on earth. Mayflies, cicadas, stoneflies, scarab beetles ..." Malcolm counted off on his fingers. "We see this same basic lifecycle, again and again, beginning with a prolonged underground feeding stage, a metamorphosis from larva to adult, a mass emergence followed by a giant orgy, and lastly, a mass migration by the pregnant females. The only missing bit of this equation is the female dragons. Where are they? We haven't seen any. Every dragon we've ever killed has been a male, a drone."

"You think there's a queen somewhere?"

"Yes, I do." Malcolm nodded. "There has to be. Otherwise, what would be the point? It's possible that the females stay underground longer than the males, or maybe they keep hidden somewhere else. I don't know."

"If you believe that when all their mating is done, the dragons are all just going to fly off and leave, then why even risk your life fighting them? Why not just hunker down somewhere, wait it out until it's all over?"

"Because, what if I'm wrong?" Malcolm turned his masked face in her direction. "What if they're all here to stay? What I've told you isn't what I *believe*, per se. It's what I *hope*." Malcolm bumped his fist against his chest. "I have to hope, because I couldn't go on in a world like this if I didn't have hope that one day, we'll watch them all fly off into the stars. Until that day comes we have to keep on fighting."

"If that day ever comes, and they all fly away, then what do you think will happen to the Hunters?"

"I guess that if the dragons are like a colony of ants, then the Hunters would be their aphids. They depend on one another. If the ant colony abandons the aphids, then the aphids would die." Malcolm gazed at the floor for a while, before reaching into a pouch on his hip, and withdrawing a folded square of papers. He flowered the packet open on the plywood floor, and flattened the creases out of the maps of western Kansas with grimy strokes of his hands. "We should probably talk about the mission," he said. "Is there anything more you can tell me about the man whose photograph is stuffed down the front of your pants?"

"You know as much as I do. They call him the Green Man."

"Why do they call him that? He didn't look green to me."

"Well, he ain't grass green, but he's a little off-colored, kind of sickly."

"Why is he such a critical target?"

"The IDC thinks he's at the center of it all, communicating with all the Hunters, controlling their movements."

Malcolm shook his head. "I don't get it. I've never seen or even heard of a Hunter carrying around a radio. Not once. The military band is the only existing communication system, and there's no evidence to suggest that they're on it."

"I don't know."

Malcolm stared at Cecile. "Do they think he's some sort of a telepath? Is that why they brought you into the fold, to try to fight fire with fire?"

"I'm not a telepath. I don't read minds. I speak with the dead."

The string of LED lights flickered, and then waned into blackness. Cecile just sat quietly, her torso rocking to the chugging motion of the train over the rails. After a moment, the lights bloomed back to life. Malcolm was standing, working the generator crank.

"But the man in the photograph, he's alive, yes?"

"Yes."

"Then how are you supposed to be able to—"

"Exactly."

Malcolm's shoulders slumped. "The place where we're going, you do realize, is dangerous as hell. We're risking our lives to get you to Zurich, but if you don't think that you're going to be able to—"

"I didn't say I wasn't going to be able to do anything. This is just different from anything I've ever done before."

"Well, if you're hoping that a ghost is going to come floating over and tell you where to find this guy, then I hope it happens between here and Hays."

Cecile shook her head. "It doesn't work like that. I'll have to find him. It's complicated. The spirits of the dead are over there on the other side, not here. They have no connection to this world. They can't see us. Their connection is to me, and they can only show me things that they remember."

Malcolm stood over her, wavering on unsteady legs to the motion of the train. "You said that he was standing right beside you."

"Who?"

"Jacob. My son. You said that he was standing right beside you, back on the boat."

"In a sense. Yes, he's always beside me, but he's beside me over in Nod. Not here."

"What's Nod?"

"That's what my grandmother always called the other side. It's a biblical reference. In the Book of Genesis, the Land of Nod was a place for the lost ones, the wandering spirits."

"So, he's not with us, right now."

Cecile shook her head. "Not the way you think, no."

Malcolm's chin fell. He stared at his feet. "What's it like over there, in Nod?"

"Different. Very different from this world. If you imagine all the moments in your life as grains of sand, all lined up in a long row, from your beginning to your end, then Nod is like the spaces between those moments. Over there, we still got our moments, our memories, but they ain't lined up in a neat row anymore. It's like, all those moments are in a big bucket of water, all stirred up with a stick. There's no linearity, no passage of time. It's a fluid place, where things appear as they want to appear, or how you perceive them. Almost like a dream, really. I always wondered if Nod wasn't just some place inside of the mind of God, who dreamt us all into existence."

"Is it a nice place?"

"I guess you could say it's nice, but it ain't like they teach you in church. It ain't a land of milk and honey, and it ain't a mansion with a million rooms. I mean, there's rooms, kind of. More like places. Everyone has their own special place, but, it ain't the eternal bliss like they'd have you believe. Same as anywhere else, there's good and there's bad, there's beauty and there's danger. You still got to watch out for yourself. Got to be aware of your surroundings, because Nod has its moods." Cecile looked up at Malcolm. "I suppose that might sound strange, but some places have moods, and sometimes, those moods can run afoul."

"You're not making me feel much better, Cecile."

"I'm sorry. I wasn't trying to make you feel any which way, Honey. Just telling you the way it is. You ever been to the seaside? The seaside may be the most beautiful place on earth, until a hurricane comes whooping up, or until a shark comes up and grabs you. Then, it takes on a different mood. You see what I'm saying? Nod is a beautiful place, but no matter where you are in all of creation, some things just never change."

"Is Jacob—happy?"

"He's safe."

"But not happy." Malcolm lowered himself to his seat, and leaned back against the concave wall of their rolling prison cell. He picked at the side of his boot. "Next time you see him, will you tell him something from me?"

"Of course I will. What'd you like me to tell for you, Honey?"

"That I'm sorry," Malcolm said, clearing his throat. "I'm so sorry. I wish I could have a second chance to do it all over again. If I could go back, I'd be there. I'd never have left. I missed out on his childhood. I missed everything. I didn't even call him on his birthday. I screwed up. I screwed up so fucking bad, and I can't ever take that back. Tell him I'm so sorry. Tell him I loved his picture, and the gum. I never sent him anything. I'm so sorry, Jacob. I was a horrible dad, and you never gave up on me. You never quit trying to reach out to me, trying to be my friend, and I was such a fucking ass. I want so bad to be your friend now and I can't. It's too late, and I can't ever go back. I fucked up. I fucked up so bad."

Cecile put her arm around his back, as he dumped forward into his arms with his head between his knees. There was nothing worse in this world than regret. Nothing even came close. "You want to know how Jacob sees you? He sees you as a superhero, fighting all them bad guys."

Malcolm shook his head slowly back and forth. "I'm no fucking hero. I don't want to be that anymore. I just want to be over there, with him. That's where I'm supposed to be."

"Where you're supposed to be is right where you are, Honey. Don't you know that? This world is all out of balance. That's why you're here, in this dark time and place, to be an instrument of change to restore some balance to this world. You're here to protect me. I need you, Honey. You got to keep being that superhero for a just little while longer until I can find the Green Man, and when I do, you got to kill that motherfucker. Then, we can go. Then, we can go."

Cecile awoke to utter blackness. The howl of a steam whistle jolted her from a deeply troubled sleep, where faceless heads were being hammered into heaps of red yarn. For a few terrifying seconds, she had no idea where she was. She felt the warmth of Malcolm's body, still curled on the plywood beside her, and it all came back to her in a rush. The recollection of her whereabouts didn't bring her much comfort. In fact, it only made her feel worse, balling a great squirming wad of anxiety in her gut that went roiling up through her chest, igniting strobes of fear behind her eyes. This was a suicidal mission, and if the Hunters captured them, terrible deaths awaited them.

No survivor of Z-Day could ever forget the first hour of the attacks, when the lights all went out, when traffic rolled to a stop and airliners came pinwheeling down from the sky. The living world seemed to allow for a moment of silence that was observed by and for that doomed menagerie of creatures unlucky enough to have shared the planet with humankind. All things stopped. All eyes that could see looked to the skies. The end came with every roaring decibel, with every blinding flash of unearthly energy, as fiery jettisons spewed from swollen thunderheads, when dark broods of destroyers descended through the clouds. Their stench was a new one to the fallen masters of the earth, who fell choking and writhing in their filth. Humankind burned alive in searing fumes as they circled, like a great cauldron of buzzards, tipping their wings in a dark promenade as they soaked New Orleans in torrents of biocide.

Cecile cowered beneath a mountain of wreckage, spared by some trick of swirling winds that had protected her Nana's house from the deadly fumes until they'd dissipated. Still, those strange winds blew, as walls of fire swept through the Ninth Ward, reducing all but the home of Nana Hess to ash. She'd heard the thunder of the destroyers, the screams of the dying, and the dull roar of the inferno. However, not until three days had passed was Cecile able to push her way through the jungle of debris, and at last look upon the new normal.

It was enough destruction, or so she'd thought. Enough of a penance for mankind's collective sins. His buildings were reduced to rubble, his birthright stripped from him, as some misused toy is snatched from the hands of a naughty toddler. All was lost. All built lay in ruin. Copulating monsters defiled his technological wonders, crumbling his superstructures as the drones clashed and tumbled in epic battles that shook mankind's world to its foundation. It was more than enough, or so she'd thought, to teach mankind a harsh lesson in humility, but the harshest lessons were still to come.

Cries for help brought her caravan of refugees to a halt. It was their waving arms, their apparent desperation over the form of a fallen child that lured the best and bravest amongst their rabble off the road, and down into the canal. Here was the first of the many traps, where dozens emerged to fall upon the confused with their terrible instruments, both found and fashioned. They dealt the first, with his outstretched hand, a blow so vicious that he fell to the riprap nearly halved, yet cruelly aware of the blood spurting from his yawning core. With a cupped hand, he tried to scoop his fluids back to him, until they brained the half-man against the rocks with a rusted sledge.

And they ran, women clutching their squalling infants, dropping duffels and suitcases to the pavement. They ran from that place of slaughter, each breath drawn sharper and colder than the last, as the screams of the least of them resounded through the awful twilight, slashed down and hacked into silence. Cecile was amongst the fastest. She tore barefoot across the wasteland, toward no place better than any other was. For six months, she ran, ducking through a nightmare world where flags of human skin wimpled in the deadly breeze, where artful vivisections came to decorate crossroads where the Hunters left clear messages that they were the new masters in the monster's shadow.

Cecile sat up in the blackness. There was a terrible taste in her mouth, and there was no escape from her masked breath. The only small pleasure that her situation could afford her was a drink of compressed water, and she wanted one. She crawled past Malcolm, sweeping the plywood with her hands, until she'd made her way to the back end of the cylinder, where she felt the square solidity of the ration crate. The lid squealed on its hinges as she lifted it. She turned, to see if she'd disturbed her sleeping cellmate, and she was surprised to find that she could see him. Dim light flickered through the portholes, on either side of the rumbling train. It took her a moment to realize the peculiarity of the fact that the lights were not flashing by, suggested that the light sources, whatever they were, were keeping pace with the train.

She used the crate to push herself up to her feet, jouncing over every railroad tie on her unsteady legs. The crank generator was dangling somewhere nearby, but she didn't care to flail around in the darkness trying to locate it. She edged toward the nearest porthole. As she approached, she became aware of a noise outside the railcar. It halted her in her tracks. She could hear a wavering drone, moderately high in pitch, not unlike a bunch of revving chainsaws, coming from either side of the train. It was the sound of engines.

Her eyes widened inside her mask. How many there were, she couldn't discern, but they were all around them. Only one caste of people in the world still held the power of electricity.

"Malcolm!" she shrieked, grabbing the overhead string of lights for support.

Cecile staggered to the north porthole, and peered out through the bleary panel of Plexiglas. A stone's throw beyond the rail, spumes of dust billowed from the spinning tires of a dirt bike, speeding over the darkened wasteland parallel to the locomotive. Its rider was blackened to a silhouette behind the glowing headlamp, but by the bulb's sallow glow, she could see a wild crown of blowing hair, and a glimmering grin that flashed like polished metal over the headlight. The lithe figure swiveled his head to glare at her as he reached down to his hip, and from some unseen sheath, he slowly withdrew a gleaming blade that was longer than his forearm. This, he raised beneath his chin. Slowly, deliberately, he pantomimed a slicing gesture across his throat, and then he pointed the tip of the curved blade at her face.

A line of glowing bullet holes ripped crazily across the south side of the railcar, deafening her with the metallic staccato of flying lead. She screamed, toppling to the plywood, as dark riders unleashed a maelstrom into both sides of the rolling cylinder. Malcolm rolled atop her, while ricochets whizzed around the car's interior, flitting sparks at every point of redirection. All around them in the night, dirt bike motors howled and gibbered like a pack of wolves hysterical with a lust for blood. They alone rode the lightning, and they were the owners of the night.

The lone bike to the north swept in so near the train that it sounded as though he were inside the car with them. The engine roared, as the terrible squeal of a metal blade scraped the length of the railcar, back to front. The machete clanged twice against the steel hull, before the sound of his bike peeled suddenly off and away to the north.

Above, the roar of the machine gun nest was succeeded by the tinny music of spent brass. One bike slammed into the railcar, and something was dragged beneath the wheels. Cecile covered the sides of her helmet as the railcar bucked over a mass that twisted, popped and slapped wetly against the undercarriage. Their gunners thundered away, until the drone of the bike engines fell back and disappeared into the night. After a moment, the relative quiet of the steam engine's chugging cadence was the only sound to be heard, other than the wind whistling through new patterns of holes that riddled the railcar's hull.

"Are you alright?" Malcolm shouted, grabbing her by the sides of her mask, pulling their foreheads together. Through their visors, she could just catch the shine of the humanity in his eyes. "I said, are you alright? Are you hit anywhere?"

Cecile was finally able to shake her head. "No."

"Check yourself over. Make sure you're not hit."

"Malcolm?"

"Yeah?"

"I think I know why they're here, the Hunters, out here in the middle of nowhere."

"Why?" Malcolm stared questioningly into her eyes.

"They've all been waiting for me."

Chapter Ten

The train whistle released a long and mournful scream that resounded for miles over the flatlands. Malcom watched their steam locomotive chug westward out of the station, and off into the starless gulfs. His heart dropped into the pit of his stomach. They were alone, three hundred miles behind what felt like enemy lines. The feeling of abandonment, that separation anxiety, was not unlike that which he'd experienced over in Afghanistan, every time he'd watched a chopper flying away into the night, leaving him and his men with some terrible task to perform before they could return to whatever place they called home. Over there, at least, he was in the company of the world's most elite Special Forces unit, armed to the teeth, equipped with cutting edge technology, multiple lines of communication. Here, there were no lifelines.

"Let's go," he said, straddling the seat of one the two mountain bikes that the engineers had provided them. "We need to get the away from this train station." He waited for Cecile to clamber unsteadily onto her bicycle, and together they began to peddle, northbound toward the place called Zurich, Kansas.

The open road was nothing but a death trap. Only one two-lane highway ran for thirty miles from the train station in Hays to their junction point in Plainville. Their enemies could be encamped in every draw, glassing the road from positions atop the limestone bluffs. Out here, if they were spotted, they'd be captured and killed. It was just that simple. To be seen meant certain death, and those deaths would be anything but quick. Whether or not Cecile was right about being the Hunters' primary target, their stripped and tethered bodies would still provide their captors with the same long hours of gruesome entertainment out here on the ashen plains, where no living thing would ever hear their screams.

"Let's ride parallel to the highway, but keep distanced from it by at least a half-mile," he said, veering westward, out across the open pasture. It was a dark night. The only lights by which to see were the hot pulses of electromagnetic energy that flared maleficently through the low canopy of clouds. These dull flashes were sufficient to maintain a course parallel to the tops of distant telephone poles.

Malcolm's tires rumbled over the hard, packed earth, popping aggregate fossils of seashells. It appeared that this region, the heart of the so-called Great American Desert, was stricken with extended periods of drought. Ironic that, at time's beginning this parched veldt was down at the bottom of a primordial sea. Burning pillars of electrons leapt from distant landforms to probe the sky. There was a chill in the air. It felt as though the weather might take a turn for the worse. Southern winds pummeled their backs, urging them onward toward their bleak destination.

"I think it's going to storm."

Malcolm heard Cecile's voice, thin and tremulous over the vibrations of rocks beneath her tires. What could the Hunters possibly want with her? He didn't want to believe such a thing, because if they were indeed after her, specifically, if they somehow intuited that this woman would eventually arrive here, at this exact location and time, then they were dealing with something much larger than dragons, something more deadly than Hunters, something beyond the realm of their understanding.

These weren't thoughts that Malcolm liked to entertain. He preferred scientific answers to problems, logic, and theories based on evidence. It was more satisfying to his pragmatic mind to believe that the dragons were mindless organisms, fulfilling their natural role that had been dictated by evolution. He had to believe that, just as he had to keep believing that the Hunters were an independent threat, one owed to their genetic mutations that had arisen in their lineage when some unearthly fragments of DNA embedded in their bodies had suddenly become excited, dominating their corrupted genetic codes. The deeper they rode into hostile territory, the more difficult it became to dismiss the possibility of some psychic connection between those monstrous men, and maybe even to the monsters who'd birthed them. Why else would they choose to be out here? How else could they have known that a train was coming? It was the first train to bisect this region in almost a year, and it certainly appeared as though the Hunters had been lying in wait for it. Even if they'd just happened upon it, out of dumb luck, then why then did those marauders converge on just one of around thirty cars, directing all the firepower they could muster onto the very railcar in which he and Cecile were being transported?

"They thought it was a gas cylinder!" Malcolm suddenly exclaimed.

"What?"

"They weren't after you. They just thought that our railcar was a cylinder of compressed gas. If they blew it up, then it would've disconnected the train from the engine. They were after the cargo."

"Hunters are killers, not looters," Cecile replied, her voice still jittering, "and those were obviously Hunters."

"Hunters do all kinds of things besides kill. They sabotage. They destroy. They create chaos. That's why they're all congregated here." Malcolm was surprised to find himself smiling. "That railway is the only artery of transportation from the east to the west. They knew that a steam locomotive would eventually be coming from one direction or the other along that rail line, and they'd been out here waiting to attack. It makes perfect sense."

It was a relief to make some occasional sense in a world of total disorder. The Hunters were biologically different. That much could not be ignored, but beyond those physiological mutations, they were still just people, and people always had a strategic agenda. It was part of being human. There was nothing supernatural about them. Their bodies could be dissected, and their small differences understood. What was perhaps their strangest ability to start electric engines was still a mystery, but that too would be explained one day. No doubt, it would be attributed to some differing signature in their bodies that perhaps attracted and reabsorbed the charged particles that jammed electrical circuits, allowing electrons to start flowing normally from cathodes to anodes again. Regardless of the mechanism by which they worked their apparent magic, like all magic, it was nothing but a physical trick played upon the observer's eyes. It was not metaphysical, and it was not supernatural. There were no such things in Malcolm's world. Those killers were just as natural as bare feet, and one day their tricks, like all tricks, would be explained.

"If that's the case," Cecile replied, "then why wouldn't they just take out a section of railroad track?"

Malcolm grunted as his front tire jounced over a rut. She was really starting to irritate him. Of course she wanted to believe that she was being telepathically targeted by some dark sentience, maybe even by the Green Man himself. In her metaphysical delusions, being targeted by a thousand evil minions made her feel important, special, as if she was some last hope for the human race.

"Exactly," he snapped back at her, over his shoulder. "If they wanted to be sure and kill you, then why not just take out a section of the track?" Malcolm grinned, when Cecile had no response. He'd flipped her deranged form of logic right back against her. "If killing you was so goddamned important to them, then they obviously wouldn't have waited out here for you for six months just to launch some harebrained attack. No way. They'd have had plenty of time to remove a section of railroad track."

"Maybe they didn't know exactly how or when I'd be coming, but once I got within range of their detection, they zeroed-in on me, and—"

"No." Malcolm thrashed his head from side to side.

"What makes you so—"

"No-no-no."

"You're impossible."

"You're nuts."

"You didn't see what I saw, Malcolm!"

"Keep your bloody voice down."

"The leader of those riders singled me out. He pointed right at me."

"You're delusional. He pointed at the railcar."

"He pointed at me! I saw him. He knew I was in there."

"Alright, this is a pointless discussion. I think we can both agree that we're in a pretty bad situation with plenty of danger, and plenty of horrible ways to die. Can we please not try and make this out to be something worse than it already is? There's no reason to be telling ghost stories, for Christ's sake. They're obviously out here, and if they find us, we're dead. End of story."

Malcolm squeezed the hand brake of his mountain bike as they neared the head of a gradual precipice. His tires growled against the shifting aggregate. The grade before them drifted downhill into a great swath of blackness that snaked through a system of wrinkled draws toward to the highway. Rocky outcrops jutted from the slope at regular intervals, fringed with the spiked crowns of dead yucca plants.

"What's down there?"

"The Saline River, I think."

"Do we have to cross it?"

"Yeah. Based on the map, there's just the one river to cross. I'm guessing that's going to be it, right down there."

"Can we use the bridge?"

"Absolutely fucking not."

"Why?"

"Because if there's going to be an ambush anywhere between Hays and Zurich, that's going to be the spot, right there on that bridge."

"I can't swim."

"You what?"

Cecile shook her head. "I can't swim."

"Well, let's just walk our bikes down a little closer and see what exactly we're dealing with. It's pretty dry. I don't think that there's bound to be a whole lot of water flowing down there."

"Could we camp here until sunrise, so we can actually see where we're going?"

"Cecile, you want to cross thirty miles of open country in broad daylight?" Malcolm turned to stare at her. "For fuck's sake. I want to be in Zurich before sunrise. We've got a train to catch tomorrow night."

Malcolm headed down the hill, with the stock of his shouldered M-16 slapping rhythmically against his rump. As he descended the slope, he reflected on those warnings issued by General Cobb, who swore that if he took her out here, he'd sorely regret it. He was beginning to fear that he'd not yet even begun to appreciate the accuracy of that premonition. This mission was suicidal. Once the sun broke over the eastern horizon, there would be nowhere to hide in this country. Their movements would be visible from five miles in every fucking direction. So far as he'd been able to tell, the Saline River valley was the only topographical depression on the whole map. It was the only place where a person could ever hope to hide. If they made it to Zurich by sunrise, then they'd have to wait it out until nightfall before they could safely head back toward the train station again. That was assuming Cecile wasn't right, and there wasn't going to be a hundred killers on motorbikes waiting for them in Zurich.

The scuffing slip of a boot preceded the metallic clatter of a dropped bike and a cry of pain, just behind him. Malcolm turned, gritting his teeth, to find Cecile and her bicycle in a twisted heap in the loose shale. He suppressed the urge to chastise her for her clumsiness, instead helping her to her feet, and then righting her bike for her. She stood doubled over, clutching her right leg just above the knee. It wouldn't do either of them any good if he lost his patience, and his temper.

"Are you alright?" he whispered, placing his hand on the small of her back, while his head swiveled up and down the river valley for any sign of hostile activity. Nothing moved. A rout of thunder trundled over the windswept plains. He could feel its resonance moving through the ground, as though the plates of the earth itself were shifting beneath his feet. Bright spumes of electrons whistled up from the desert floor to splash into pools of crimson light in the clouds. Bad weather was definitely on the way. The clouds rolled like breakers across an inverted ocean. "Come on, we need to keep moving."

Cecile rose stiffly, before resuming their descent with a marked limp. Nothing appeared to be broken. Malcolm tried, as best he could, to assist her down the slope by clinging to her upper arm. If she fell again, he was afraid she'd pull the both of them to the ground, but with any luck the added stability of his grasp would prevent that from happening. The footing was poor, given the loose topcoat of smashed shale, shells and slag that slid easily underfoot, but the grade was not steep. Wind moaned through the river valley, rattling yucca spades like the ghosts of bygone snakes. There was something unsettling about this place.

When they finally reached the banks of the Saline River, Malcolm was relieved to find that it was dry, and looked to have been dry for several years. Desiccated weeds sprouted chest-high from every crack in the riverbed. Not a drop of water could testify that this had ever been a river. The only suggestion of flowing water was provided by a pavement of flat and polished slabs that wobbled and clattered underfoot like old bones. The winds conjured ashen dervishes that spun down the sloughing banks to gyrate on unsteady tails, as though drunkenly reckoning their lifeless world for a few lingering moments before dissipated into the night. Grassy tussocks nodded to gossiping husks of thistles that whispered rumors of recent death, while a brownish reek rode the midnight breeze. Malcolm turned his head upwind to scrutinize the bridge, where the current of soured air seemed to originate, drifting the course of the bygone waterway.

"What is it?" Cecile whispered.

The dark bridge kept its secrets, but Malcolm sensed that something terrible was over there. He felt it with dread certainty in his soul. Somewhere beneath that black arch was evidence of the worst sort of depravity, remnants of secret indulgences wrought of hunger and isolation, conditions that kindled savage notions from the imaginations of fallen men. He'd seen these situations, ill-lit recesses in forsaken lands that attracted strange tenants, harboring dark pastimes vaguely remembered in the ancient chambers of the human mind. Whatever dull eyes gaped back from that swath of shadow were owned by something he cared not to meet, not on this night, or any night, for that matter.

"Nothing," he whispered, "let's go."

The ascent was more perilous. Sloughs of shale brought them repeatedly to their knees as they dragged their bicycles up the slope. Blackened heavens ignited, coals blown to life by stale winds, flickering in and out of existence within their smoldering beds. Those shells of thunder struck ever closer, sending shockwaves through Malcolm's bones. The first droplets spattered darkly upon the blanched soil, striking his helmet and visor with their intimate percussion. He smeared the back of his gloved hand across the bulging lenses to create streaks of bleary mud.

"Malcolm!"

He heard the insistence in her tone, but it proved little good to turn her way when he could not see her, nor could he reply when thunder's fusillade muted every trace of his feeble voice. He smeared with his fingertips, until he could discern something of her silhouette, crawling up the slope a meter behind him.

"Someone's following us!"

No. This couldn't be happening so soon. As he strained his eyes to see whatever it was she might've noticed through the gathering rain, a great pulse of electromagnetic energy revealed the ragged and shambling form in the riverbed. It clambered over the bank, and trailed them purposefully up the slope with its pendulous gait. By the play of red lightning, he saw a glimpse of the shaggy bulk of grassland Gollum, a thing that might've dreamt it was once a man before whatever horrors it had witnessed and liked to imitate had wholly consumed its depraved mind. Though he lost sight of it in the darkness, he could hear its chuffing breaths, the scrabbling of loosed gravel.

"Shoot it!" Cecile screamed. "Kill it now!"

"Come on!" Malcolm seized her by the wrist and hauled her upright. The thing was getting closer, gaining on them with every second. He could put it down with one shot, but if he fired a round in this vast openness, then every killer for miles would learn of their whereabouts, and easily anticipate their direction and destination. He dug the toes of his boots into the softening ground, and pushed with all his might up the slope, dragging his bike by one arm, and Cecile, clinging to hers, in the other.

"Oh my God, fucking kill it, Malcolm! It's right behind us!"

"Go!" He shoved her up the hill, ahead of him. With a fistful of her hazmat suit clenched in his hand, he straight-armed her up the slope, falling once to the mud, and scrambling back to his feet. The crest of the escarpment was just ahead. They could make it if they tried. "Go-go-go!"

Its snuffling respirations grew distinct, until he could hear the bubbling phlegm in its throat. He smelled reek of its putrid hides, hairless flags of skin and rattling adornments. Malcolm fell as it seized hold of his bike, releasing a deep woof of entitlement. It jerked until Malcolm could no longer hold onto both the bike and Cecile.

Malcolm released her, ordering her to run as he rolled over onto his back to engage his attacker. By the crackling phosphorescence in the sky, he discerned the shine of a single eye. Great chuffs of carrion breath were expelled with every yank to the bike's frame, which dragged Malcolm further down the slope with each powerful heave. The strap of his rifle was caught around his throat. The weapon clattered over the rocks, above and behind him. He swiped an arm up through the gravel, but could not reach it. In an instant, the bike was yanked from his grip and hurled off into oblivion. Its distant crash was drowned by the man-beast's roar, as its hairy maw split wide with some skyward proclamation of its dominance over this wasteland, over this puny challenger, whose flesh would soon be stripped in glistening mouthfuls from his bones.

With a strobe of white light and a deafening concussion, the skull of the grassland Gollum detonated in a cone of pale gobbets and crimson ribbons that spattered softly around the vicinity, as the mindless creature toppled backward. Malcolm felt its bodily impact, more so than he was able to hear it, over the soft gurgle of escaping fluids against the rocky hillside. When he wrenched his neck around, he found her kneeling over his shoulder, backlit by jags of lightning, poised like a dark angel with the M-16 in her hands.

##

Hunkered in the downpour beneath a plastic slip-or-slide, they surveyed the west end of the main street of the little town from their shelter in the playground area of what once had been a city park. The town appeared to be deserted. Doors to parallel ranks of darkened stores, an empty pool hall, and a little taco shop swung ajar, exposing what little remained after a year's worth of looting. Vehicles loitered patiently in their angled parking slots on either side of the bricked pavement, awaiting owners with jingling keys who would never return. A tattered, blaze-orange banner sagged over the doors of the pool hall. There was an image of a pheasant in the middle. It advertised a friendly welcome to hunters.

"Are we in Zurich?"

Malcolm shook his head. "Not yet. This is Plainville." Wesley's town. Malcolm recalled the cocky banter that he'd enjoyed on the *Sawyer's* stern with that kid. He imagined him as a child growing up here, probably playing in this very park on sunny afternoons.

"How far are we from Zurich?"

"Pretty close. Less than ten miles."

Ten miles seemed like a perilous eternity. The storm kept gathering in intensity with every passing hour. It showed no signs of letting up. The rain had found its way into Malcom's hazmat suit and down into his boots, where the water weighted them down with every sloshing step. He found himself starting to shiver, but he was still grateful for the cover that the storm had provided them. North of the Saline River, they'd ridden in a cloak of virtual invisibility. The ground was so hardened by drought that the driving rains didn't penetrate for over an hour. A sheet of water flowed right over the surface, following the complex whorls of the watershed rather than soaking into the soil. Again, they were lucky, because if it had saturated the ground, it might have bogged their tires and limited them to traveling on foot. So far, everything had been in their favor.

"I just hope that I can find what I'm looking for," Cecile whispered.

Malcolm turned her way. It was the first time she'd ever mentioned looking for anything specific on this goose chase. "What are you looking for?"

"A school bus, for starters."

"A school bus?" Malcolm peered out from beneath the slide, looking up and down the length of the unlit street. "Might've been a good idea if we'd discussed this back in St. Louis, when we could have figured out where the school is."

"We're not looking for a school, I don't think."

"You don't think?"

"It's just a bus. A broken down bus, parked behind an old ramshackle house."

Malcolm rubbed the back of his neck. His muscles ached from the train ride, from his tug-of-war with the troll from under the bridge. Staring through a rain spattered visor was starting to give him a splitting headache. "I imagine that every house in Zurich is going to look pretty run-down by now. Any idea which side of the town it's on?"

He knew what her answer was going to be, before she ever shook her head. This was so unlike any mission into which he'd ever been deployed. In Afghanistan, the objectives were clear, locations pinpointed on a GPS. The only x-factor was always going to be the number of local fighters, but even with respect to those guys, you were always going to have some degree of reliable intelligence. Not this time. This whole mission was an x-factor. That wasn't Cecile's fault. He guessed that he understood her role in this assignment now, to some extent. Although her skill set was not exactly tangible, after what happened down in the river valley, he respected her—perhaps more than he'd ever be willing to let her know. He didn't know why he was so reluctant to thank her. Probably because he'd been assigned to protect her life with his own, and the voodoo princess had ended up saving his ass. Regardless, as a soldier, he held to a certain standard that no matter how many years passed, no matter what might happen between them, her act of valor in battle when his life depended on it would remain a personal accolade that would never came down off her wall. There was a deeper bond between them now, whether he expressed it or not. From this point forward, at the very least, he intended for Cecile to see his appreciation through his actions.

"Once we find your school bus, then what?" he asked. "Are we looking for something in particular?"

"I'll be learning as we go. What I need, specifically, is a personal object. Personal objects retain the energy of their owner. I can follow that trail of energy, and connect with them on a more intimate level."

"Connect with who?"

"The Green Man, through the spirit of his mama, his dad or a sibling. I need something from his childhood. Something highly personal, that meant something to him, and to his family."

"You mean to tell me, we're going to the Green Man's house?"

"His childhood home, yes."

"I thought he was Egyptian."

"Why would you think that?"

"In your photograph, he's wearing a *keffiyeh*. That, and I could see the goddamned Sphinx sitting right there in the background."

"Nope. This guy's from Kansas."

"What I don't understand is how you can find his childhood home, but not know anything else about him."

"Because I met his dead mama, over in Nod. That's all she gave me."

Anytime she opened her mouth, she stripped away another shred of his confidence in what exactly they were supposed to be doing out here, replacing his courage with an equal or greater amount of anxiety. This wasn't conventional warfare, not by any stretch of his imagination. Even engaging dragons involved a basic, tactical approach, but now, they weren't even hunting monsters. They were hunting ghosts. They were tracking down living enemies with the cooperation of the dead.

Malcolm considered himself to be meticulous. He tried to be thorough in every aspect of his preparation in order to ensure, to the best of his ability, that he would be ready for whatever situations presented themselves on the battlefield. In all his life, he'd never felt so alienated from his own mission, so wholly and so horribly unprepared. Had he known, had he the faintest suspicion of the level of danger inherent in this mission, and what the mission's success would be riding on, he might have run screaming in the opposite direction. He was thankful to have met Cecile. He liked her. She had moxie, but this mission with her, this was his worst fucking nightmare.

"That photo was taken on the eve of Z-Day," she whispered. "The photographer was a teenaged boy who was killed just moments after he took it."

"Everyone within one-hundred miles of Cairo was killed that night," Malcolm replied. "It was the hardest hit target in the whole Middle East. No one survived. Even with masks, no one could even go near that zone for months, it was so damned toxic. The hole in the ground, where the Great Pyramid of Giza used to be? I'll tell you this much: it was the biggest fucking hole that I've ever seen in my life. It was half a kilometer wide, and it dropped straight down into Hell. Whatever came out of that hole was huge. Unfathomably huge. It was bigger than any dragon I've ever seen."

"Maybe there's your missing queen."

Malcom stared through the rivulets of rain coursing down the front of his visor. He'd thought about that. He'd almost accepted that, in the back of his mind. Whatever emerged from that tunnel was something of such enormity that there was nowhere on earth where it could possibly hide undetected for almost a year, yet somehow, whatever crawled out of that hole seemed to have vanished right into thin air. Everyone present at the moment of its emergence had died instantly. There were no living witnesses— except maybe for *him*, the guy whose home they were about to invade.

Malcolm resisted the urge to allow the paranormal to haunt his logical thought processes, but the bizarre nature of this mission certainly invoked his recurring propensity to lean into some uncharacteristic directions. If the Green Man was controlling the Hunters, serving as something of a communications hub between the minions and the monsters, then he had to admit that it made some sense for the Green Man to have been positioned nowhere else on earth, at the eve of Zero Day, than right at the foot of the

Dragon Queen's throne. He would have been in Giza. He would have been stationed there to protect her, as she emerged from the center of the earth, moist and vulnerable after her molt. This was a duty that would've been expected of him, as a demonstration of his loyalty, to escort the queen of the colony through the gates of her new kingdom.

"Wait-wait," Malcolm whispered, clamping his hand on Cecile's shoulder.

"What is it?"

He was sure that he'd seen something through the rain. Maybe a trick played upon the weary eyes by the tempestuous elements, the cavorting arcs of electricity through the clouds, but it had certainly looked like a horizontal beam of light. He blinked his eyes, squinting hard for a couple of seconds before reopening them. There it was again. He pulled Cecile slowly down to the muddy ground, where they wallowed together in a frigid pool at the foot of the slide.

"There's something coming," he whispered, sliding the M-16 around his neck. He took slow aim at the western end of the street from a prone shooter's position. "Right there."

At once, he could hear them. The blood drained from his extremities. His face tingled coldly while his heart began to thud against his chest. Their combined yowling transformed the town into something that sounded like a logger's camp of buzzing chainsaws. The ruckus drew nearer, until the jouncing swaths of numerous headlamps swept over the darkened storefronts. The pack of mechanical wolves growled into town, their engines snarling cantankerously in the rain. There were too many of them to count, and they just kept coming. Dark riders, scarcely clothed but for their flapping capes of man-hide, glowered beneath hoods of skinned faces, matted hair that snaked in the wind. Dried scalps twirled from their handlebars. Glistening burdens dragged through pooled water behind their rear wheels. Skinless and strange, these parcels nodded in affirmation as they thumped over the disjointed bricks. The wolf pack slid past the tattered, orange banner that bid an eerie welcome to their namesake.

"We're in big fucking trouble."

The spearhead of the biker gang disappeared beyond the eastern edge of Malcom's line of sight, and the parade kept growling on by, setting the town ablaze with yellow headlights that gleamed on the slick pavement like a solid bolt of lightning on which they rode. A single shot was fired. Then, bursts of flame spat from numerous automatic rifles, shattering storefront windows in a cacophony of calving glass. The sounds of wanton destruction seemed to excite them. Ammunition was wasted, as though they had plenty to spare. Barbarians raised their stretched lips up to the tempest, and they howled, scalped cowls streaming behind their reeking heads, as they discharged guns in their revelry over the harvest of human lives.

Chapter Eleven

In the direction from which the marauders had come, they pedaled, seven miles through a hammering downpour. Flapping sheets of silver rain whipped so hard against them that Cecile's handlebars wrestled in her grip with the fervor of something desperate and doomed. Their pace was beleaguered by the elements. The effort required to press onward was tremendous. Mud sucked at her tires. Her wheel twisted through every rut gouged by the wheels of recent motorbikes that had churned the road's surface into the consistency of tar. At times, she felt that her heart would give out. She stood upright on her pedals to employ her body's weight to every laborious down-stroke, only to feel her rear wheel repeatedly lose traction and spin wetly beneath her. It was like pushing a pedal-driven plough up small inclines and down again, over windswept crests that nearly blew her over, and through flooded draws, where the churning waters rose to a height past her pedals. When at last Malcolm pulled off to the side of the road, and dragged his bike over toward a belt of dead trees, she followed him into the tree line, and then collapsed to the sodden ground.

Rain poured from the heavens against her upturned mask, so uselessly fogged that she could barely see. The roiling show of fluid and raw energy before her eyes seemed almost hallucinogenic, an effect furthered by her exhaustion and lack of sleep. Were it not for the extreme danger of their situation, she could have lied like a corpse amongst those trunks of lifeless trees all night and through the following day. She was not sure how much more of this constant punishment her body could take.

"Need another can of rations?"

"No." Cecile grimaced, wishing away the memory of compressed pet food filling her cheeks. "Do you have any water?"

She heard Malcolm fumbling with the snaps and ties of his assorted pouches. She closed her eyes and just listened to the sounds of someone working, focusing her ears on the rustling of the nearby hands of a sentient being who was quietly manipulating the ordinary objects of a physical world. Somehow, it was a very pleasant sensory experience to focus only on the profound simplicity of that moment. It was nice to receive stimuli from some sense other than her weary eyes, to imagine what was taking place, and to know that its source meant her no harm.

She blinked when she felt his warm hands suddenly against her throat, beneath her chin, connecting to her. She extended her tongue, found the groove in the snout of her mask, and without ever opening her eyes, released the bulb of her feeding tube into her open mouth.

"Are you ready?"

His voice in the darkness. She nodded weakly.

Tepid water filled her cheeks. She swallowed. The second mouthful made her choke. She sat upright, coughing and sputtering water inside the face of her flooding mask. Her thumbs were already jamming beneath the seal as she panicked, ready to rip the device right off of her face, but Malcolm jerked away the injection tubing, grabbed her wrists, and ordered her to calm. Still coughing into the water that was nearly up to her nostrils, it took every bit of her nerve to ward off a panic attack.

"I'm going to lift the bottom seal of your mask, and I want you to gently purge it out, but do not ever remove your mask. Not ever. Understand?"

She nodded, but could not verbalize a reply. The water was over her lips. Malcolm worked one of his thumbs up into the gap between her throat and the rubber seal. Immediately, her personal aquarium began to drain. As the water level receded, her fright dissipated, and she was relieved to see that the accident had at least rinsed the fog from her visor. She could see him clearly now, kneeling over her, fawning down at her through his buggy, black eyes as if he were her insect mate on some queer planet on which they'd been marooned. She allowed herself to fall forward into his arms, resting her helmeted head upon his shoulder. It felt good. Even through layers of plastic and rubber, human contact felt good. She wished that he would never let go, that this moment would never end.

"We made it," he said. "We're in Zurich."

It was strange, how back in that other life, in that world of sunshine, cars, music and animals, she'd been so picky about her men. Not that she'd had many relationships. Her Nana Hess strongly disapproved of any dependence on men, be it financial or emotional. Her philosophy was quite the reverse of the social norm, but even when that philosophy was adopted, there was no ignoring her natural attraction to men. When she did find herself presented with a potential suitor, it was an affordable luxury in those days to be exceedingly choosy about body styles, colors, quirks of personality and differing tastes. She could and would choose or refuse a man on the basis of a movie he liked, a song he played, or a pair of shoes that he wore. Now, those things all seemed so trivial. Only trust mattered in a world where no one had anything, where all men wore the same masks, where you searched that sea of masks until you found just one that you could trust with your life, and you let them know that they could trust you right back. That was a perfect match, even if you both looked like a couple of bugs.

"What's funny?" he asked.

"Hmm?"

Malcolm tapped the cheek of her mask. "I saw your bubbles."

"Nothing." Bugs smiled on the inside, because their faces never moved.

"Need another hit?" He held up the can.

"I'm good."

"Okay, then," he pivoted on an arm, and sat down in the mud beside her, "I brought you to Zurich, Ghost Rider. This is your show, now."

They left the bikes in the trees, and crawled into the outskirts of Zurich. She led, while Malcolm covered her from behind with the rifle. Together, it felt like they could do anything. She felt stronger, more in control of her world than she'd felt in almost a year. You never knew how much time you have left out here. You just lived for the moment, and these moments were pretty good ones. Cecile wondered, regardless of whether they succeeded in finding the Green Man, if she and Malcolm would stay together. She didn't see why not. She trusted him, and after she'd saved his life in the riverbed, she guessed that he ought to extend the same level of trust back to her, and that was all that mattered. Love, if such a luxury was still allowed in such a desecrated world, was a thing that could perhaps come later.

"What if the Hunters come back this way?" she asked, peering down the stormy byway.

He shook his head. "I don't think they'd come back through here twice in the same night. If anything, they're heading south, back toward Hays."

"What are we going to do if they're waiting for us back at the train station?"

"We'll worry about that later. Let's just stayed focused on what we need to do here, right now."

Cecile nodded.

"Think hard. Is there anything else you can remember about the place we're going? Any little detail that might help us locate this house a little faster?"

"It was a tired old house, the kind with lots of bad memories." Cecile closed her eyes, and put her head between her knees. "Clothes, garbage, toys in the front lawn. A sky blue door behind a ratty screen. White house with peeling paint. Around back, the school bus. Trees and weeds growing up all round it, as if it had been sitting there for years. Something about that bus ... it's a connection to him, a strong connection to his childhood, like he used to spend a lot of time in there, but it wasn't like a clubhouse, or a place where he played." Cecile squinted and shook her head from side to side. "It was a bad place." She drew a sharp breath, her bottom lip beginning to tremble. "Bad things happened to him in there. He spent days and nights in there, summers and winters.

Burning and freezing, crying and bleeding, for days and nights, days and nights, just looking out the back windows of that bus at nothing—nothing but miles of empty fields, going on forever."

"Good job."

Cecile's eyes fluttered open. She raised her head, and blinked at Malcolm.

"If there were fields behind the house, then that puts it on the outskirts of town. No need to go any deeper into Zurich than we have to. We ought to be able to circle the town from a distance and hopefully spot that old bus you're talking about." Malcom put his hand on the back of her neck. "You've done a great job, Cecile. This is it. Are you ready for this?"

"I think so."

There was no turning back. As if there had ever been an option, for him. Cecile could intuit his steeled conviction in every roll of his shoulders, every push of his boots through the mud. The deeper they crawled into hostile territory, the more determined Malcolm seemed to become to reach their goal. It was all that mattered to him. He had no care for whatever happened afterward. He seemed to be owned by the bottom line, that no matter how great their odds, no matter how insuperable their challenge, if it boiled down to a situation in which they were overpowered, facing death, then it would please him to take lives until he could kill no more. It was the violent end that a man like him needed, and she doubted he'd ever quit until he got it. There was a fatalistic intensity to Malcolm, who was endowed with the raw ingredients of a true warrior, a man born with no choice but to see every fight to its bitter end, but she didn't sense that he wanted to die. Not really. Nor did he live without fear of death. Rather, it felt as though he thought that he deserved a terrible end, as though he felt that he needed a penance to absolve a life that he thought he'd failed.

She didn't know him. She'd only been with Malcolm for a couple of days. Maybe he did deserve a bloody end. Who was she to appraise him? He was certainly harboring more than his fair share of wrath and resent, but despite these obvious flaws, Cecile saw a lot of good in him. He had a certain tenderness, sometimes. There was a fine line, to be sure, between one who was suicidal, and a homicidal romantic, but either way, Malcolm was a volatile spirit too dangerous really to love, one forever beckoned toward some carnage that promised to complete him in a way that no person ever could. Now, that was an attractive challenge to any woman who was strong enough or stupid enough to accept it.

Nana Hess could fix a man. She'd fixed more than a few into fools who'd dogged her heels for years on end without even knowing why. For a woman who'd preached a life of independence from men, she'd taken her fair share of lovers, but she took them only as she needed them, and she was always in control of those relationships. She used men, manipulating handsome and promising men from their natural courses in life to the mindless vocation of her personal supplicants. It never ceased to be baffling. Cecile never saw her Nana as being an attractive woman, really, but even in her old age she'd inspired awe. Men were drawn to her in an unnatural way, as though they'd been hypnotized by her power, cursed with an enduring fixation that more beautiful women could only dream of instilling in their suitors.

"Your Nana is the worst hoodoo bitch that ever was!" Madame Chastant had backed her straight up into the coatroom, thrashing her skinny legs to welts with the wire handle of a flyswatter on the night she caught Cecile dropping *gris-gris* on her porch stoop. "Bitch put period blood in my man's soup!"

None of it had made a lick of sense to her, in those days. Nana Hess just did things, and was accused of worse, but you never dared to question her motives. You obeyed. Cecile was sent pretty regularly on strange little errands that she learned could be more perilous than her Nana was willing to let on. There could be swift repercussions if you were caught. Nana's ambivalence to danger suggested that it mattered less what you did than how you carried yourself as you did it, when living in a world rife with folks who'd happily do you harm. You kept your head high, wore a smile on your face, even as you marched out into that hostile world. Your little delivery, whatever it was, might as likely be a bomb as a bouquet of flowers, but you were to treat them no differently. Whatever was secreted inside those parcels and packets was Nana's business. Not yours. You just carried yourself like a queen, just like Nana did, knowing that wherever life took you, the worst hoodoo bitch that ever was would be looking out for you. Happily assume the worst and you'd do well, every bright new morning that you rolled out of bed.

As Cecile grew older, she came to embrace her proud ignorance to those dark arts practiced beneath her roof. It was a business, after all, her Nana's business, and if her Nana had believed that she'd have been in any way benefited by the burden of voodoo knowledge, then she'd surely have passed it on, but she evidently did not. On some level it was always apparent that her Nana intended all along for those matriarchal traditions to die along with her, as though she intuited the depreciation of superstition in a world waxing scientific, and meant to close that familial chapter with dignity and finality. It was her attitude that she impressed. You walked the streets with your head held high, and you entered every room as though you owned it, even when the folks inside that room just hated your guts and liver.

The voodoo was real. Cecile had to believe that, because her Nana was a frugal soul who wouldn't waste her time with anything in which she didn't genuinely believe. If she were selling nothing but hocus pocus, then she would've packed her *gris-gris* with dirt from the yard, rather than sending Cecile on a thousand midnight runs to the cemetery for fresh grave dirt. It didn't go unnoticed how Nana seemed to coordinate the occasions of Cecile's little errands with the visitation of certain company. She sometimes returned to find strange men, even white men, leaving Nana's house through the back door.

Deep down, Cecile knew what was happening. Her Nana's contempt for all mankind must've stemmed from whatever had happened to her when she was just a little girl, growing up in Storyville. She'd explained to Cecile that some evils were necessary to get by in life, but nothing about Nana's business was ever allowed to be obvious. What she sold wasn't flesh, but corruption. Hers was an exceedingly complicated model, one perhaps elevated by intrigue, made more palatable by her magical distractions. It was all intertwined, like a great heap of red yarn, unfathomable in its organization, yet somehow appreciable in its perceived outward form.

Usage of men was a learned behavior, because that level of contempt was not one that came naturally. It wasn't until Cecile had grown old enough to acquire some level of objectivity before she realized how very different her psychology was from other women around her. All females manipulated males to some degree, but she'd never met another quite like her Nana Hess, who predated on men. She enticed them, captured them, and eventually broke them through a costly process of exploitation in a game where her customers were left thinking they'd won, while their wives were soon paying Nana from their other pocket for an act of revenge back against them. Before the swelling of her flyswatter welts had even receded, Cecile had returned to the front yard of Madame Chastant to stake down a rooster dressed in a little tweed suit and hat that had been tailored from scraps of her unfaithful husband's clothing. Through the candlelit bedroom window, Madame Chastant gave her nod of approval.

Strange things happened around town. Of course, Cecile knew nothing about the evil glyphs chalked onto front doors, the headless cats in the graveyard with men's names scrawled onto strips of paper jammed down their open throats. She didn't know about the tortured *gris-gris* dolls, charms, and satin bags stuffed with powders, bones and metal shavings that sometimes showed up on porches, black candles burning in the night, and of course, those midnight orgies on the shores of Lake Pontchartrain, where the devil himself might appear. Nana Hess walked the French Quarter as though they owned it, inspiring even the policemen to back out of her way as she passed them smiling with her head held high. In a place and time where no creature was more disrespected than a black woman, her Nana Hess had secured the lion's share of respect. That's all that her Nana's voodoo was ever about.

Cecile crawled up beside Malcolm when he hesitated, and beckoned her forward. Her gaze followed the direction of his index finger to the suggestion of a house, choked by a gang of cedar trees with raggedy, desiccated boughs. The property was isolated from its neighbors, situated further into the surrounding fields than any of the rest, leaning from its foundation on a bleak point infused by a shallow draw. Beleaguered by a bramble of mulberry and Osage thorns, countless cans and bottles gleamed in the lightning jags from all around the yellowed ruin of a wayward school bus, poking out into the field like an accusatory finger. Tucked discreetly behind the house and the shelterbelt of old cedars, and baffled on its windward side by a hedge of collected tumbleweeds, the lonely vehicle would not have been visible from any other angle but the one from which they'd miraculously approached.

"That's it," Cecile whispered, breathlessly, her eyes widening behind her mask. No matter how many times she'd led investigators to the scene of a crime, the gravity of the horrors that had transpired in those places never failed to affect her when she looked upon the setting firsthand. This place felt no less ominous to her mind's eye than a grisly murder scene. She was certain that a life had been taken here in a most terrible way. Maybe more than one.

"Are you sure?"

Cecile nodded. She tried to reply, but her voice caught in her throat. The usual clawing at that door in the back of her mind heightened suddenly to the drumming fists and bloodied knuckles of some enraged ghost that still deplored this place. Its anguish was so palpable that it brought tears to Cecile's eyes. This was going to be a bad one. Maybe the worst she'd ever visited. So much pent-up suffering. Years and years of the most unthinkable abuses, all directed at helpless victims. She felt the terror and desperation, the disorienting shock that must have followed blunt trauma, hot abdominal pain, eager blades cutting, flaying … but there was another emotion surging sickeningly up from beneath all the rest. It was one Cecile that found interesting, because it was so unusual for a murder victim. It was guilt.

"What's the matter?" Malcolm asked.

Bad deaths left an unmistakable signature. Just like death's smell, it wasn't an easy one to describe, but you sure as hell knew what it was the instant it hit your senses. Sensing a bad death was a phone call in the middle of the night bearing the worst sort of news. It switched off your mind, froze you in place, and chilled you to your core. Bad deaths had happened here. Lots of them.

"Nothing," she replied. "I'm ready when you are."

Old Slim's was the first bad death she'd ever smoked. That's how her Nana Hess referred to the numbing sensation of a message whispered through that door in the back of the mind. Slim was the first to push through that door, to throw it wide open to the Land of Nod. Slim was just a cat, but he was more than that to Cecile, and that's all that mattered in the spirit world. Her connection to that furry friend was just as strong of a bond as she'd ever had to any other human being at that stage in her life. They were inseparable. Their bond was probably something more than a girl with any sense ought to have with a cat, but things being as they were, Slim was the first ever to be there when she needed comfort from another living thing. He came to her like a gift from above, right when her little world felt like it was going to shake all to pieces and get scattered by the gray winds of change, the morning they carried her mama out the side door in a bag.

Slim was as loyal as the best of dogs. Her Nana used to laugh and carry on at the way that cat would trot along at her heels up and down the sidewalk of her Nana's block. When she awoke every night to soaked sheets in her strange new bed, where nothing was where it should be, and she was all alone, she'd feel his gentle approach through that electric fog of night terror, purring loud and lazy-eyed upon her tummy. He didn't seem to mind that they were in a strange new room, and he didn't seem to think that she ought to mind it, either. He'd rub his sleek cheek against her hands, over and over, purring like a lawn mower while kneading their blankets into dough with his prickly front paws. Old Slim was her bridge between two worlds. He was a living, breathing connection between the one lost and the one gained. Every night, Slim convinced her until she no longer needed any convincing that everything in their new world was going to be alright, so long as they had each other to hold at the devil's hour, until twittering robins heralded the dawn's sweet light.

"Here, I want you to take this." Malcolm slid his pistol from its holster, and pressed the dark weapon into her hand. "You know how to use one of these?"

Cecile nodded. Most everyone did, nearly a year after Z-Day. On the streets of New Orleans where she'd grown up, a familiarity with weapons and violence had come earlier, for better or for worse. She jacked a round into the chamber, checked the safety, and then, they crawled toward the bus.

She was nine, the first time she pulled a trigger. It all began at midnight, when her Nana's phone began to ring. Cecile awoke and sat up in her bed, rubbing her eyes, and found that old Slim wasn't where he should be, curled cozily by her side. Phones weren't supposed to ring at midnight, even in her Nana's house. That much she knew, but it wasn't long before she learned that when phones did ring at that hour, bad news was probably coming from the other end of the line.

She and her Nana had shuffled out the back door and into the night, where their spooky old neighbor, Ms. Maziel, had just witnessed an awful sight. The grass and weeds were cold and wet beneath her bare feet. She clung to her Nana's nightgown, following the sweeping beam of that flashlight around the yard until it came to rest on a pair of blinking eyes beneath the hedge of crepe myrtle.

Nana supposed that a dog had done it, because only a dog could have that much hatred for a cat to do all that had been done to old Slim. It was a memory that burned itself forever into her fragile mind, the worst thing her eyes had ever seen. He tried to rise, but could not. There was something wrong with his legs. White knobs protruded from new and ugly angles. All he could do was to cry out to her. She fell to her hands and knees and crawled on her belly through dirt and stickers, responding to his cry as on so many other nights he'd answered to her own. Despite a child's naïve desperation to save what cannot be, Cecile knew that there would be no hope for old Slim. She gathered what was left of her furry friend into her arms and cradled him through the night until Slim's spirit slipped away to a robin's twittering apogee. That was the moment when Cecile lost her mind.

It began as a thin sound, fluting up through her choked throat and growing louder, courser, as her quavering lips split and she rose like a gorgon from the myrtle, her dead friend clenched in her arms, forcing the air from her lungs in a devilish scream that chilled the hearts of all those who heard it. Even the worst hoodoo bitch ever was folded her hands and began lipping prayers as she backed away. Bloodied and soiled in filth and hashed leaves,

Cecile was made to see every torture that her friend had suffered at the hands of those three nigger boys, the same boys who'd soon beg for God's forgiveness that they'd ever touched old Slim.

At the tree line, Malcolm rose, and backed into a cedar. At his beckoning, Cecile stood and slipped into the tree beside him, her pistol directed at the starless sky. The rain came harder still, hammering the ground with such ferocity that spumes of mud leapt up to their knees. Black rivulets worming down her mask wavered the image of the school bus, a place of living nightmares and stolen dreams, where the wings of something small and innocent had been clipped. It was a boy imprisoned here, singled-out from the rest of the brood, who could only stare wide-eyed and affrighted as his torturer approached the bus doors while his mother watched from the upstairs bedroom window, too powerless to intervene. The runt of the litter was born into a house that hated him, through no fault of his own.

Cecile turned back in the direction of the lilting farmhouse, and narrowed her eyes at its blanketed windows. Focusing on a single connection to the other side, she opened the door to Nod just a crack. Visions came shrieking into her mind's eye with force enough to take her breath away. Here lived a demon king, a tyrannical master over a secret and sordid kingdom, whose subjects' screams joined raucous music late at night when his wet brain swam with perversions, when he paid unwanted visits to darkened bedrooms. Their fear was his foreplay, and he readied himself in their doorways, locking eyes with the lost ones while milking their terror, stroke by stroke, until threads of slobber swung from his chops while those metal anthems raged. No one slept in this house, where an adjoining room's suffering was but a harbinger of the horrors that would come knocking soon enough. No one dared hide from him, because he would find you, and when he did, it would be immeasurably worse. This house was a prison without bars where no stranger ever entered, and no one but the demon king ever left, often on the nights when the most horrendous moods came over him, when doubled-moons found him staggered through the cedar trees. He would find his way to the school bus where his little Gutterbird was caged.

Cecile jumped when she felt Malcolm's hand on her shoulder. She should have warned him never to interrupt her when she was connected to the other side. When soul and body were pulled separate ways, and that connective fiber was stretched to the breaking point, it wouldn't take but a yank from those grabbing arms on the other side.

"I'll keep an eye on the house and fields," Malcom whispered. "You go do whatever you need to do."

"Okay." Cecile nodded, and stepped past him.

"Hey." Malcolm reached out and took her by the upper arm.

"What?"

He held her for a moment. "Be careful."

Cecile pulled away from his grip with a playful turn of her shoulder, and glared through her visor into his worried eyes. "You be careful."

Chapter Twelve

The bus windows by which she passed were curtained with sheeting rain, obscured by clawing limbs that raked at the glass with a yearning hunger to get inside. Frequent pulses of energy chased through the clouds, silhouetting the pistol she clasped in both hands as she slinked catlike through the gloom, row by row, and seat by seat. Malcolm's eyes widened when he realized he should have checked and cleared the bus interior before she ever stepped inside. If this had been Afghanistan, it would have been a death trap, an obvious place for tripwires and explosive devices, but he calmed himself. This was not Afghanistan. No one was expecting them here. He couldn't allow himself to believe that superstitious nonsense, because if he accepted even a piece of it, he would have to accept it all. The only dangers out here were the Hunters, and they'd already ridden through. Their timing was perfect. As soon as Cecile was finished, they could find a safe place to rest until nightfall. Perhaps right here in the old farmhouse, once he'd cleared it of any threats.

Malcolm turned and glowered through the cedar brambles at the little farmhouse that they might decide to call home. It was actually quite perfect for their purposes, located on the outskirts of town, offering a commanding view of the surrounding fields, yet concealed from prying eyes by the dead cedars, and by blankets already covering the windows. The place was a little run down, littered and unkempt, but that's precisely what made it feel safe to him, in the sense that Hunters would have no real incentive to bother it.

He glanced back in the direction of the bus, where Cecile's form continued to slide past the windows. With her pistol readied in the air, she looked so deadly vulnerable. She was a toy soldier who'd lucked into a little taste of blood and found it queerly pleasant. She was attractive, in her own strange way, and he was almost ready to admit it to himself. The swift manner in which she'd leapt into action excited him, as he recalled the explosion of that headshot she'd delivered to that Neanderthal, down in the riverbed. Not once, in the hours that had followed that amazing interlude, had Cecile lamented or bragged over her lethal choice of action. That was peculiar. Malcolm furrowed his brow, wondering if perhaps there was more to this woman than he'd afforded the time to consider. Who took a life for the first time and said nothing about it? If she'd killed before, then the fault was his own for failing to extend her that basic level of respect that one survivor of the apocalypse should automatically owe to another. From the moment he'd first laid eyes on Cecile, he'd underestimated her, regarding her with an undeserved prejudice from behind his own blinding ego. As he watched her slide fearlessly into the mouth of the beast, he began to wonder if Cecile had really even needed his protection at all.

What little he knew of her, for failing to ask, was that she was a Creole from the rough streets of New Orleans, the city hit first and hardest by the dragons. She was a self-proclaimed spiritual medium, steeped in voodoo, and for years had cooperated with Louisiana law enforcement to solve more than a hundred cold cases with the help of the dead. She possessed the conviction and the direction to spearhead hundreds of deadly expeditions into terrible worlds, knowing all the while that a coldblooded killer would always be waiting for her at the end of her journey. Again and again, she'd accepted these perilous missions, each bearing the distinct possibility of an engagement with a murderer who, if he ever discovered the identity of the Creole witch in pursuit, could always double-back on his own trail and begin hunting her. Unlike Malcom's missions that always ended in a safe place, a home base, an untouchable sanctum, Cecile had never known the luxury of safety, because her enemies could always follow her home. She had to know that. She had to intuit that she had no sanctum, in her nights of restless sleep, paranoid glances out her windows, midnight checks of every room and closet, maybe with a baseball bat or a knife clenched in her hand.

Malcolm imagined this perilous existence, and it made his skin crawl. Once again, he'd been a fool. There was no separation between worlds for Cecile, as there had always been for him. Hers was one deadly world, haunted by vengeful spirits, and stalked by the predators of men. Cecile would have had no choice but to become the deadly vulnerable creature that skulked past the bus windows, and it now seemed obvious to him that this girl had killed before, and would again.

Fumbling for the hand crank on his helmet, he generated enough static in the vacuum tube for a brief transmission. He keyed-up to dispatch with a flip of the toggle. "Cecile? It's Malcolm. Do you copy?"

"I copy," she replied, after few lingering seconds of crackling silence.

"If your situation seems secure, I'm going to check the perimeter, and clear the farmhouse." He waited for what seemed an eternity without a response, but he could see her standing there with her hand on her headset. Probably having some technological difficulties, given the storm. Vacuum tubes were jarred loose rather easily during combat, and together, they'd suffered more than a few tube-loosening situations since they'd deployed. He'd have ordinarily checked something like that, had they not been within an arm's reach of one another the entire journey. "Cecile? If you copy, I want you to stay on the bus. I repeat. Stay on that bus until I come get you."

Malcolm wrinkled his nose and squinted, as a garbled reply rattled back through his earpiece. The response was unintelligible, somewhat robotic, but he was at least able to discern the critical word, "*copy.*" Satisfied, he reduced the volume on his earpiece, and then slipped through the belt of cedars and into the backyard.

Trees swayed and creaked in the chilly gale that moaned out of the wastelands to bother every object in its path, harrying a barrage of pelting raindrops to a trajectory that was nearly horizontal at times. Malcolm crept around to the leeward side of the old farmhouse to find a windbreak against those nagging elements that leeched the will right out of a wearied body. From this position, he could peer out over the empty streets of Zurich's abandoned neighborhoods, listening to the agonized squeals of the house's timbers, the intermittent hissing of rain against the structure's windward side. His eyes played tricks on his sleep-deprived mind, causing his heart to buck with every mirage of a moving life form that inevitably became the shadow of a tree throttled by the wind. Zurich was dead. What could be looted had long ago been taken. No one lived here, and he guessed that no one probably had for the better part of a year. It was a ghost town.

Peering around the front corner of the house, he surveyed a front yard that looked more like a salvage yard for ruined toys. Remnants of bygone childhoods were strewn haphazardly amongst a litter of empty bottles and flattened cans. The mixed evidence of lost innocence and debauchery gave the yard the appearance of the aftermath of some great festival of drunken elves. Dolls, dismembered and beheaded, were unceremoniously discarded in the filth. Raindrops plunked dully against crushed beer cans. An inverted bicycle, missing a front wheel, forever awaited the further attention of some little mechanic who'd never return. It was a dismal situation. Imagining a childhood in this environment made him a little queasy.

Hugging the wall with his leading shoulder, Malcolm readied his rifle, and he eased around the corner of the house. Once he was sure that his movements had gone undetected, he stepped up onto the porch. He expected some ghastly creaks as he edged his way across the woodwork, but the soaking rains had softened the decking, lubricating the shafts of nails that secured each plank to the rotten joists. His footsteps were soundless as he slipped past the blanketed front windows, around the remains of a collapsed porch swing, right up to the yawning mouth of the front door.

The stench hit him at the threshold. A fiercely sour putrescence needed no explanation. He slipped inside the doorway, hovering there for a few seconds with the hope that his eyes might eventually adjust to lightless conditions. Not a trace of muted starlight could pass through the layers of material that had been stapled over every window, featuring casts of animated cartoon characters. Only a vacillating rectangle of wan light was thrown against the back wall from where it shafted through the open door. It wasn't much, but that weak spray of luminescence was sufficient to discern the grisly leavings of some past inhabitant of this chamber, who'd smeared two ruddy words across the opposite wall with great sweeps of gory hands.

The Voice.

Malcolm's heart rate increased at the sight of this strange and meaningless graffiti. All around those two words, bloody handprints were stamped obsessively across every canvas of peeling wallpaper like some primitive interpretation of a sky filled with crimson stars. Malcolm suddenly became aware that he was not alone in this cavern. They were sprawled on the floor all around him. Dried and twisted entities lay reeking, stiffened in their final throes. Their fetal positions and defensive gestures were reminiscent of those casts of victims who'd been frozen forever in time by the volcanic cataclysm that buried the ancient city of Pompey. Malcom's gaze travelled over the silenced band of refugees, and he couldn't decide if these were the victims of Z-Day, or if they'd fallen prey to their fellow man. He supposed the latter, because there was nothing in Zurich, Kansas that could attract a pod of dragons. These people, living hours away from the allure of any major metropolitan area, would have survived the apocalyptic cleansing.

He unsnapped a pouch on his web belt, and withdrew a little flashlight. With the heel of his boot, he pushed the door closed quietly behind him. Absolute blackness enveloped the ghastly scene, inviting an awful intimacy with the rotting ones. He could feel their deathly presence pressing in all around him. Shouldering his rifle by its sling, he took hold of the little lever on the flashlight, cranking it slowly until it afforded a feeble glow of light. That was just enough. Shadows cast by withered hands curled against chests seemed to claw at the living room walls as he swept the beam over them. The circumstances of their deaths at once became clear. As he'd suspected, these people hadn't lost their lives from any cloud of poisonous gas. No, they'd gone the other way.

The ceiling was blackened over a halved steel drum that was situated in the room's center, where the carpet was scorched in a wide ring around the indoor fire pit. Neighboring heaps of flayed bones were smashed and gleaned of their fatty marrow. Not all of the butchered remains were human. Whatever monster had haunted this painted cave did not appear to have discriminated much between the flesh of people and those nameless other things that could no longer be identified as being anything more specific than inhuman. Stripped limbs and ribcages, skulls both round and tapered, were strewn and enmeshed in general mountains of waste heaped against the east wall.

Malcolm stooped to retrieve a crumpled hotrod magazine from the burn pile. He examined the mailing address label, which was directed to one Dell Cyrus, who was presumably the man of this house. Malcolm's gaze crept over the piles of picked bones, and he wondered if Dell Cyrus was the monster responsible, or if he was just another victim whose remains now rotted amongst the slain.

Dropping the magazine back to the charred carpet, he stepped through the boneyard and into the kitchen, where much butchering had been done. The linoleum floor was slathered with dark stains, footprints. A round dining table presented a heap of dried hands and feet. The sink was filled with blackened ropes of viscera. The refrigerator hung ajar. Morbid curiosity got the best of him. He directed his dim light inside the fridge, halfway hoping to find himself a six-pack of tepid beer, but there was nothing inside the dead appliance but an open bottle of solidified catsup.

Smears of blood snaked across the kitchen floor, and down an adjoining hallway in the direction of a back room, to or from which, someone or something had evidently been dragged for slaughter. Malcom followed the trail down the carpeted hall, and he peered through the doorway into what had once been a young boy's bedroom. Superheroes postured from a poster tacked to the wall above a neat arrangement of toy cars, all parked on a shelf. An empty water cup perched on the edge of a nightstand beside a stack of comic books. A pair of little blue shoes rested beside a twin bed that had been carefully made, one last time, by a good boy. It hurt to stand in the doorway of that room. The trail of blood on the carpet slithered into an open closet. He would not look in there.

Malcolm turned away, returning to the kitchen, swallowing down the hard knot that tightened in his throat. He'd never seen Jacob's bedroom. Not even once. He'd never know what posters might've decorated his walls, what little treasures his son had showcased on his shelves, the color of his shoes, and whether or not he'd made his bed or left it messy on the last morning of his life. All he could do was to imagine these things, and his mind could only draw and infuriating blank.

An emotion, hot and familiar, coursed up through his jugulars to fill his head with boiling pressure. He wanted to smash something. He wanted to punch a hole through a wall with his fist, to feel his knuckles crack, blood flowing from their scalped knobs. More than anything else, he wanted to find and confront the savage responsible for every sin ever committed in this house. He wanted to step into a back room and find that monster cowering in a pile of reeking blankets with its suckled bones and bottles. He wanted to squeeze a trigger that would blow a hole right through the center of its chest, watch it die lowing like a beast on the slaughterhouse floor.

Shrugging the rifle off his shoulder, he clenched the M-16 in one hand, finger looped over the trigger, ready to squeeze one off from the hip. Flashlight gripped in his other hand, he spun back through the kitchen doorway, following the beam of his torch up a darkened staircase. A thousand bloody handprints all hailed him from the walls, honoring him, pledging their damned allegiance to whatever sect they seemed to imagine that he belonged. He ignored the regiments of saluting hands as he climbed. Shriveled gobbets crunched beneath his boots with every tread. The staircase walls, twisted to irregular angles by the drag of the settling house, narrowed as he approached the landing. The stench became even more ineffable, perhaps due to the effect of rising heat, or perhaps owed to yet another source of odor that remained undiscovered.

This was Afghanistan.

Blood drummed in Malcolm's ears, when he realized that he was back. It was a second chance to make things right, to reeve again through the whorls of a painted Afghani cave, a reeking catacomb where he might once again face the sight of severed heads tumbling over one another in a kettle. He was ready to face it all again, one last time, to play god in a godless pit, to exact vengeance upon those ragged goatherds who left traps that disintegrated men, traps that collapsed tunnels and ground soldiers to paste between the earth's molars. Time itself had wrinkled in a queer mash-up of modern men pitted against Stone Age savages armed with satellite phones and rocket launchers. He'd returned to that Hell, strapped once again with the best that modern technology had to offer, burning to clash against cannibals, skinners and decapitators, barbarians who scooped brains from children's skulls to smear their apelike art on the walls of caves.

Malcolm's eyes flashed behind his visor. He wanted to see him, face him, that perfect enemy to uniformed legions since the days of ancient Rome. From the depths of the oceans to the gulfs of outer space, mankind continued to evolve, to explore and ascend, but no matter to what great heights mankind rose, the inner brute was never far behind, always lurking. When civilized man stumbled, he would always appear, a wishfully forgotten ape forever haunting the modern mind, forever waiting to rise again from the primordial ooze to show us how rapidly we could be devolved. With a smugly bloody grin, this inner thing loved to prove that despite all of our gadgets, our eight-hundred-thousand years of struggling to escape our savage past that we'd not come so far as we believed. That was the endgame's cruel lesson. It was all just a grand joke played upon us by the God of Entropy who would show us as we fell that not since time's beginning had there ever been a point to our evolution.

Malcolm stepped onto the landing. A short hall with a bedroom on either end was divided by what appeared to be a bathroom. It was even darker upstairs, if that were possible. He paused to give a few more cranks to his flashlight. Sweeping the beam in the direction of the west bedroom, he found himself ogled by another corpse, bound wrists and ankles to a propped mattress. It hung by flayed limbs, crucified against the box springs. Malcolm stared at the gruesome remains of this particular victim, who'd not just been butchered like the rest, but had been slowly and methodically eviscerated. The cruelest attention had been given to this one's torment, evidencing a more monstrous personality than Malcolm had envisioned. He swung the beam down the opposite hallway, where a dark and creeping stain on the carpet reached beneath an east bedroom door that had been boarded shut from the outside.

Glancing back in the direction of the vivisected corpse, Malcolm edged his way to the open bathroom door. His flashlight beam fell upon a dead man. Clothed in filthy overalls and a stained flannel shirt, the figure was slumped in the bathtub beside a spent propane lantern. An emptied whiskey bottle was still clenched in one mummified hand. A dropped revolver rested within inches of the curled fingers of the other. This was his flesh-eating monster. This was the inglorious end to which a killer's perversions had delivered him, with his deranged thoughts fanned from his shattered skull across the tiled walls. Hunters didn't kill themselves, not when there was so much dirty work to do. This was no servant of the enemy. It was just a fallen man, one who'd reigned as the apex predator of his family and neighbors for almost a year.

Malcolm reached for his radio toggle. She did not need to see this. Hunters were enough of an insult to humanity, but this monster, like the troll beneath the bridge over the Saline River, had fallen from our own ranks to become something even worse than our enemies.

Malcolm shook his head at the man in the bathtub, and he closed the door. As the darkness folded over the monster in the bathtub, it appeared to be grinning, as though amused by some awful joke known only to the dead. Dialing up the volume on his radio, Malcolm keyed-up to emergency dispatch, but he couldn't find the military band. It was a ghost frequency. The static was a strange amalgam of white noise haunted by indistinct sounds, whispering voices, and a stuttering rhythm like the whirling rotors of a faraway chopper.

"Cecile, it's Malcolm, do you copy?"

He keyed down and listened intently to the chugging cadence behind the static. There was definitely something there. He could hear the pulsing rhythm, thumping away in the radio dimension like the heartbeat of some small animal. His heart gave an arrhythmic lurch against the walls of his chest. "No," Malcolm whispered, shaking his head, eyes widening. It couldn't be. Not here. Not in the heart of a desert that was devoid of power and people. They had no reason to be here. Nothing at all to draw them in. Nothing except—*her.*

Malcolm bolted down the blackened hallway toward the west bedroom, hoping for a window that overlooked the backyard. He ejected the magazine from his rifle, replacing it with a different one from his bandolier strap. This was the special magazine, the red one, the one loaded with incendiary rounds.

Hail clattered against the shingles. Malcolm pushed past the stinking corpse propped in the doorway. Shoving the box springs aside, he dumped the grimacing corpse facedown onto the bedroom floor. He clambered over it, ripping the stapled blankets from the west window. A weird green light flooded the room. They were coming. He could hear them, muting the storm's cacophony with the godlike rumbling of their internal generators. Streams of electrons leapt from the tops of cedar trees to the clouds. Chaos particles crackled in the charged air.

"No-no-no-no!" Malcolm bashed out the glass with the butt of his rifle. It shattered, and rain sprayed through the jagged opening. Broken pane fragments sailed down into the hash of dried weeds, one story below. "Cecile!" he shouted. "Cecile, can you hear me!"

"*I hear you,*" replied a voice, rattling and robotic in his radio earpiece.

"Cecile?" Malcolm scowled through the tempest, glaring down upon the rusty roof of the school bus. Hail pellets clattered over the yellow panels. They collected in the grooves like snow. "Who is this?" he whispered, as the dark immensity of the dragon pod descended from the churning clouds. This was happening. Bolts of energy leapt from the sodden ground to grope their segmented bellies.

"*I am God of the Dead, the Lord of Silence, and the Voice of the Khepra.*"

"Are you—are you the Green Man?" Malcolm asked, his eyes tracking the descending forms of the destroyers. Only seconds remained before the creatures discharged their incinerating payloads, reducing everything beneath them to ash. "If you're the Green Man," Malcolm said, his voice catching in his throat, "we've been looking for you. We want to meet with you, discuss your terms in a treaty." Breathless, Malcolm awaited a reply, but all he could hear was the pulsing static of dragon energy over the airwaves. "If you're out there, we're ready to negotiate. I'm speaking for all of mankind. All that I need to know is what you want. What can we offer you? You have to need something, or you wouldn't be doing this! What do you need?"

The drones' carapaces split bilaterally. The dark halves of their shelves yawned wide as they fanned their paneled, gossamer wings. Beautiful, deadly, they tilted their enormous bodies beneath the shelves of electromagnetic clouds, and the Khepra began to spiral over the farmhouse. The cyclonic formation always preceded a gas attack.

"Say it, please! Say anything!" Malcolm screamed, leveling his M-16 on the shattered windowsill. He put a bead on one of the circling drones, knowing all too well that if he squeezed the trigger at this close range, the explosion of volatile gases would vaporize him in an instant. "What do you want humanity to do for you?"

"*Die.*"

Malcolm's right hand separated from his forearm at the wrist. The rifle clattered to the bedsprings, with his twitching hand still attached. He felt no pain, only shock at the sight of those red streams of blood spraying from the end of the stump. A long blade slid beneath his chin. A bare arm hooked around his throat from the opposite side, in a headlock that lifted his toes off the carpet. The strength of the unseen assassin was astounding. Malcolm grabbed hold of the blade, and tried to stop it, as the machete's razor edge dragged slowly across his throat. There was not enough pressure being exerted to sever his windpipe, his carotid arteries. Just enough force was being applied to peel back the skin of his throat, exposing the first layer of muscle, beneath. The assassin was toying with him, just playing, and milking every moment of sadistic pleasure out of the killing stroke.

Malcolm lowered his remaining hand in a gesture of submission, squeezing off the gushing fountain at his wrist. This was it. If the assassin intended to slice his throat to the spine, he could do nothing to prevent it. The lack of oxygen to his brain, the loss of blood, it was all beginning to make him dizzy. His thoughts shifted from survival to Jacob. Malcolm clung to the image of the orange crayon drawing, the stick of gum, to the hopeful expression of his little boy smiling on the laptop screen.

Kum hom Dade.

"I'm coming," he whispered.

"*This is nice. I enjoy watching humans die,*" the voice rattled through the speaker in Malcolm's ear. "*Unmasked, your faces are so expressive. Horror brightens your eyes, spreads your mouths into screams. We Khepra die quietly, without such expression. Scream for me, human. Let me watch you die, and afterward, you will kneel before the Khepra when we meet, face to face.*"

The assassin withdrew the blade from beneath his chin. He brought it around behind Malcolm, pressed the blunt tip of the instrument into the small of his back, and rammed it to the hilt through his spine. Malcolm emitted a retching sound that he'd never heard himself produce before, as he looked down upon the wet blade that protruded strangely from his belly. The killer's fingers groped beneath his chin. His mask and helmet were ripped away, tossed to the side, and Malcolm was kicked off the impaling blade, facedown upon the box springs.

Already dead as the corpse pinned beneath him, Malcolm rolled to look upon his assassin. Black skinned and glistening with fresh blood, the Hunter stood poised in the bedroom doorway, flashing a golden grin. His eyes glowed like twin portals straight to Hell, but behind those eyes, Malcolm felt yet another presence, peering through at him.

Malcolm coughed up a mouthful of blood. The assassin's smile widened. His gold teeth glimmered in the greenish effervescence of roiling hydrocyanic gas. The inhuman presence behind those borrowed eyes revealed its pleasure through the changing expressions worn by its mindless slave's face. Was it the Green Man speaking to him over the radio, or something else entirely? Somehow, the Voice, whoever or whatever it was, seemed to be a living conduit connecting Hunters, like the assassin leering over him, to something else, something bigger than the robotic voice in his ear, something with an otherworldly will fastened upon the minds of a thousand men. The truth, if this could possibly be true, was worse than anything he'd ever dared imagine. It was waiting for him to die, this thing that called itself the Khepra, waiting for his soul on the other side. There was no escape from this entity, not anywhere in the living world or in the hereafter.

Malcolm's throat began to constrict as hydrocyanic fumes filled the room. It was agony inside his lungs, searing his eyes, filling his nostrils with an almandine stink. At last, he knew the torment experienced by those billions already lost to the gas attacks. The looming demon threw back its head of frizzled hair and released a long, sputtering laugh as he felt his swelling tongue begin to protrude. As his eyes rolled back into his head beneath his fluttering lids, his last sight were the shadows of the circling Khepra dragons scrolling dreamily across the bedroom walls. His ears were filled with the demonic laughter, the thunderous roar of the destroyers, the revving of what sounded like a hundred dirt bike engines, and the screams of his voodoo princess. "I'm sorry," Malcolm whispered, as his eyelids fell closed.

Chapter Thirteen

She ran. Bolting through the back doors of the old school bus, Cecile tore across the open fields through a blizzard of hailstones. Every so often, she glanced back over her shoulder, searching the Cyrus property for Malcolm, but she couldn't spot him anywhere in the mounting chaos. She hoped to God that he wasn't still inside the farmhouse, where jettisons of plasma were being spewed from the abdomens of circling dragons like ropes of fire whipping from giant flamethrowers. In an instant, the house of nightmares was engulfed in a roaring inferno.

The childhood home of little Owen Cyrus imparted itself into the atmosphere in a wild conflagration of smoke and roiling energy. That was the boy's name, she'd learned. It came to her in a snapshot of a hospital wristband after she'd recovered a pair of rusty handcuffs from the floor of the bus, and held them gently in her hand. The bus had served for years as a sort of solitary confinement cell for that little boy. Brain damaged, woefully disfigured, secreted away in his tormented world, this was the unlikely child who would grow up to become the suspected ringleader of an international terrorist network, usher to the apocalypse, and an infamous phantom known as the Green Man.

"Run, deep dreamer." The ruined voice of Owen Cyrus rattled mechanically through her earpiece. *"Run as far and as fast as you can, but no matter which direction you choose, your path will always lead you to the Khepra."*

"Owen," she cried, "you were a good boy. You didn't deserve the things that happened to you in there. It wasn't your fault. There's still good inside you, Owen. I know there is."

"*No,*" the voice purred in her ear. "*There is nothing inside of Owen Cyrus but the Khepra. This body was always an empty husk, a perfect vessel that I came to elevate from its nothingness. This body was raised in a glorious transformation from a hollowed shell into Osiris, the God of the Dead, and the living voice of the Khepra. Let all those with ears hear my words flow between his lips, and let them all obey.*"

Cecile's boots splashed through lakes of dancing water, slipped through mires of sticky mud. She fell repeatedly, rising each time to smear the filth from her visor, and continue to run. She could hear the growl of their engines, their keening howls, as the wolf pack came snarling around either side of the inferno. This had all been nothing but a trap, and there would be no escape from it. Deep down, some part of her had always known it. The wolves were coming, and they were going to tear her apart.

"*I've promised your body as a gift to my chosen people, Cecile. When your time of servitude in the living world has come to pass, you will at last come to meet me, face to face. You'll be quite surprised by the changes that I've made in your so-called Land of Nod. Tell me, whoever was that talking pile of yarn?*"

"What? Nana?" Cecile's breath caught in her throat. "Who—who the hell are you?"

"*I am the one, and I am the many. I am the colonist, the Argonaut, the Alpha and the Omega, the ancient mother and the egg-bearer, the giver and the taker, the builder and the destroyer. I am the spoken words of Osiris, the Lord of Silence, and the God of the Dead. I am the Star God, the Khepra, and I am waiting for you, Cecile, waiting five-thousand years over in the Land of Nod.*"

Puddles leapt around her feet at the crack of small arm's fire. She could hear their engines buzzing like a force of chainsaws, their whoops and screams of bloodlust, drawing nearer. They were closing in, and there was nowhere to run, nothing but miles of pounded wasteland in every direction. She set a course for the only island of structure on the horizon. It was a lonely oil patch, where an old hammerhead pumper sat frozen in time before a squat battery of rusty storage tanks. It was the only place in this godforsaken desert where she could attempt to make her last stand. Damned if she wasn't going to take a few lives with her. This wasn't the death that she wanted. She wanted to grow old and gray, bestowing her words of wisdom onto her children's children, until at last, she drifted off in her sleep. No, this death was Malcolm's, a violent end to a life of willful violence. As she staggered into the oil patch, her eyes filled with tears of certainty that this steel oasis of industrial ruin was the bleak place where her life was going to end.

Bullets panged off the steel sides of the tanks as she stumbled through them. She hesitated to steal a glimpse of the oncoming horde of marauders. They stood upright on the foot-pegs of their bikes, swinging clubs and hatchets in the air. Scalps twirled from their handlebars. Ragged man-hides flapped in the driving rain. A burst of automatic weapon fire rattled bullets throughout the tank battery. Oil spewed from ruptured hulls. Cecile cringed, and then rose again and fled, abandoning the imminent massacre for some dream of open fields.

They would have to shoot her down. She refused to stop running, to submit to the hours of abuse that would precede her slow death if she ever gave up and surrendered. Their battle cries resounded through the steel jungle as dozens of dirt bikes roared through the oil patch. This was it. Her long run was over. Cecile spun on her heels, drew Malcolm's pistol, and screamed as she squeezed the trigger, again and again, until the lead raiders toppled, flipping several more over their handlebars into the mud. There were too many of them. Far more than she had bullets to spare. The wolf pack swerved around the wreckage of their fallen.

Only one option remained, and she intended to take it while she still had time. After a lifetime of hunting down killers, the tables had finally turned in their favor. It was payback time, or so they thought. Cecile fell to her knees in the mud, hopelessly defiant. They would never have her, not in their preferred way. Death would be her choice, not theirs. She peeled back her mask, flung it into the mud, and jammed the barrel of the pistol down into her throat.

The farmhouse was a raft of flames, ferrying Malcolm toward the gates of Hell. Every crack, every gap between clapboards, glowed like burning seams between the two merging worlds, until hem between those realms was indistinguishable. The grinning assassin had fled. Although immune to the hydrocyanic gases, not even the Hunters were impervious to flames. His mutilator had rejoined the wolf pack, more eager to take part in the pursuit of their next quarry than to risk his hide for the lesser pleasure of watching Malcolm burn.

Malcolm retched on the blood that filled his closing throat, drowning him in the same fluids that trickled from the stump of his missing hand. He was lightheaded, numb, bleeding out. A glistening loop of pink viscera bulged from his ruptured belly, where the killer's blade had reamed him through. His legs wouldn't move. Couldn't feel them at all. He felt no sensation whatsoever below his midsection, which led him to believe that his spine had been severed. This was a cruel death, even by the Hunters' standards. If he chose to do what he knew was the right thing to do, then he'd be forced to survive in this decrepit state just long enough to burn alive.

So be it.

Reaching for a pouch at his hip, Malcolm withdrew the plastic box that contained his cyanide antidote kit. He placed it on his chest. Popping the hasps, he removed the little glass ampule of amyl nitrite. With trembling fingers, he placed the ampule inside his mask, and he crushed it beneath the pad of his thumb. As the powerful inhalant filled the concave lenses of the visor, he mashed the mask snugly against his face, pulling the elastic band around the back of his head. Choking up blood, he strained repeatedly to inhale the amyl nitrite fumes until he felt the constricted walls of his throat beginning to relax. There was no shortage of ways to die in the few seconds of time that he had left in this world, but at least he still possessed the ability to eliminate one means to his end, and it was not going to be by poison gas.

He removed the hypodermic needle, and plunged its stainless steel tip through the plastic wall of the bottle of sodium nitrate.

Three-hundred milligrams were the specified dosage, but at this stage, he didn't guess that an exact dosage really mattered. He filled the syringe completely, withdrew the glistening needle, and plunged it into the left side of his neck.

Burning plaster fell from the ceiling onto his useless legs. The roof was about to collapse. The rubber leggings of his hazmat suit began to blister and bubble, as was the flesh on the crown of his uncovered head. He could smell the rank musk of his burning hair, as he plunged the hypodermic into the final reagent of the kit. Filling the syringe with sodium thiosulfate, he administered the same jugular injection to the left side of his neck. Within seconds, he began coughing up great gouts of coagulating blood as the walls of his throat opened wide. At last, he could breathe. For a few minutes, at least, he'd afforded himself the ability to breathe the same noxious air as the Hunters.

Malcolm rolled onto his belly. He picked his M-16 off the bedroom floor, just as a blinding avalanche of burning wood and plaster crashed down upon him, as the overhead timbers gave way with an earsplitting crack. The collapsed roof provided an unobstructed view of the circling pod of Khepra dragons in the fiery sky. Employing the butt of his weapon as a crutch, Malcolm dragged himself out from beneath the burning wreckage. Inch by inch, he hauled himself back over to the shattered window. Melted strings of black rubber stretched from his bubbling legs across the carpet. Fire would be his end, and he would share that end with as many others as he had time to take with him.

There was his voodoo princess, kneeling on a rocky outcrop, just beyond the distant oil patch, with a pistol in her mouth. The motorized horde of barbarians funneled between the ranks of oil storage tanks, making a beeline right for her. Malcolm spat blood into his mask, as he propped his M-16 on the burning windowsill. He would have to do this left-handed.

"Don't do it Cecile," he said, in a strangled, watery voice. "Not yet." He snugged the stock of the rifle to his shoulder, took aim, and squeezed the trigger.

The incendiary round screamed through the air, punched through the steel wall of the foremost storage tank, and released its payload of flammable chemicals. One shot was all it took. All four of the oil storage vessels appeared to combust at once. A massive globe of white light surged outward across the wastelands in a lake of burning napalm. Malcolm managed a bloody smile. Although he could no longer see Cecile through the curtain of black smoke drawn over the silver edge of a new dawn, he knew that one way or another, he'd saved her from death at the hands of the savages. Flaming bikes, still in motion, rolled rider-less to the far shores of the lake of fire before pitching over in the inferno. Not one had avoided the explosion. Every demon of this desert had been blasted simultaneously back to the realm in which they belonged.

Malcolm collapsed from the windowsill. Still smiling, he rolled onto his back in a bed of flames. It felt good. He could feel his scalp splitting in the intense heat, sizzling, his ears burning away, and it felt so right, but he wasn't ready to go, not yet, not before he did one last terrible thing.

Malcolm stripped off his mask, and he cast it into the flames. He didn't need that fucking thing anymore, and he wasn't going to die with anything covering his true face. The mask wasn't him anymore. It was the face of a damned counterpart, an evil twin, who would die right alongside him.

As Malcolm looked up to the winged destroyers circling languidly above, he finally understood why a dying hermit crab always crawled out of its shell. He'd been wrong for years. It wasn't ever about some deathbed admission of cowardice, or any sort of revelation of the stinking worm that the little soldier had always been, hiding all its life inside of a suit of armor. No. Now, Malcolm understood that abandoning its shell was a crab's final act of altruism. In doing so, it ensured the survival of another young crab. In its last moments, a dying crab crawled out to bequeath its suit of armor to one lucky member of the next generation. There could be no more honorable act that a warrior could hope to perform, than to shed his armor in his last moment, exposing his sad and naked truth to a cruel and predatory world that would always be waiting to seize him in his moment of vulnerability, just so that one other member of his species might live.

Malcolm smiled, as a new mask of flames slid over his face. He raised the barrel of his M-16 skyward, and pointed it at the bloated underbelly of the largest of the gas-filled monsters. He closed his eyes, and he squeezed the trigger.

A wall of flames slid over Zurich's neighborhoods, transforming the inconspicuous town into a hellish beacon of calamity visible for fifty miles. Distanced from the destruction, Cecile fled on foot. She traveled southward, alone, across the sodden desert from which they'd come, back in the direction of Hays. Any remaining killers in the vicinity would almost certainly be drawn toward Zurich, and with the layer slick mud upon the fields, they would be forced to take the faster route of paved roads. Still, the rain poured, as though the storm might never pass. She was a ghost in the torrent, floating alone over empty fields, up gradual escarpments, and down through flooded swales.

Cecile guessed that she had close to fifteen hours before her midnight rendezvous back at the train station, but without Malcolm at her side, pushing her, encouraging her, she worried that she might lack the fortitude to make it back to Hays at all. Her eyes and nostrils burned. Her throat remained tightened from her brief exposure to the tainted air. Every breath that she drew was a gasping effort. Frequently, she rested, hunkering in every draw, hypnotized by the swirling eddies of muddy water that spun forever by. She couldn't remember ever feeling so exhausted, so emptied, so dead inside.

When the oil tank battery exploded, she guessed the disaster that had claimed the lives of every marauder was an accident of their own doing, one errant shot by a savage that had sparked their fatal flame. As the fire consumed their writhing forms, Cecile appraised their burning as a bit of poetic justice, but when she heard the second shot, she realized the truth. A single rifle report had seemed to detonate the whole pod of hovering Khepra, obliterating their bloated forms in a chain reaction of volatile gases. Her eyes had widened when it struck her that it was Malcolm who'd saved her life, and he'd only done so by embracing the end of his own. Cecile dipped her fingertips in the flowing water, and then withdrew them. Water had a rather impersonal way of instantly refilling the gaps left by missing objects, as though they'd never even been there at all. Streams just kept on flowing.

Cecile guessed that in the end, their missions were accomplished. Against all odds, they'd managed to survive what was considered to be a suicidal crossing through enemy territory, where she'd succeeded in finding and retrieving a personal object affiliated with the most elusive public enemy on earth. That was no small feat. In the end, Malcolm had served the purpose for which he'd been deployed by protecting her life with the sacrifice of his own. They were already done, whether she made it back to St. Louis or not. They'd found the treasure at the end of that map, and Malcolm had died a hero, meeting at last with that violent end for which some part of him had always longed.

"Got what you wanted, Honey," she whispered, "and I hope you're back in the loving arms of that little boy you were missing so bad." She felt a knot tightening in her throat as she stared down into the churning water, but she didn't quite know what to do with it. The swirling fluid before her eyes reminded her of the Styx, and of all the wonders that had always awaited her beyond the far bank of that stream of collective consciousness. She placed her masked face in her hands and clawed at her helmeted head, rocking back and forth against her knees, but for some reason, she could not find it in herself to cry.

The prospect of returning to Nod filled her with dread. Never in her life had she felt afraid of death, until now. She'd never had a reason to fear it. Nod was her private world, a safe and familiar place where she could always venture to escape the trials of the living world. She was aware of the dangers over there, but Cecile had never felt threatened by any of those malevolent presences, not with Nana Hess on that side. Things were different now. Nod had changed. She could feel it. Something terrible had happened over there. It was like there was a big bully pacing the sidewalk of her home block, just waiting for her to come around the corner. Whatever the Khepra spirit was, and how it was related to the dragons of the living world, she felt it in her bones that it was something just as dangerous in death, as the Khepra dragons were, in life.

Malcolm, God bless him, he had been so right about so many things, but he'd only figured out half of the horrible truth. Originally, there did indeed seem to have been one Khepra, and only one. It was the egg-bearing matriarch that Malcom had suspected that had initiated some sort of a countdown to the end of humanity a very long time ago. It had evidently died, from one way or another, because it was lurking in the Land of Nod. She knew that much to be true. No one in the living world knew about the talking pile of yarn that was her Nana. Somehow, against every rule that segregated the two realms, the spirit of this bygone monster had managed to find a way to influence the living world, exerting its unearthly will over an army of Hunters through the mind of one brain damaged child.

Cecile furrowed her brow, staring down into the swirling water. Nod was a fluid realm, not linear, but even in a state of formless, timeless fluidity, there were rules. No spirit in Nod, disconnected by death from the living world, could ever hope to reach through the Styx to affect those on the other side. That was impossible. That's part of what kept the two worlds so neatly separated. Crossing that stream from one side to the other was a quite a trick, and it was one that could only be performed by a living medium—a female medium, according to her Nana. Male minds, with their linear thinking, didn't function in just the right way, but maybe her Nana had been wrong about that. Maybe there were men—or, at least, one boy—who was able to do it. If little Owen Cyrus had somehow fallen prey to a predatory spirit of Nod, then he would've had to possess the dark gift. He would have had to have been a spiritual medium, but Owen was a boy.

Cecile had received enough snapshots of evidence, while squatted on the filthy floor of that bus with those handcuffs resting on her quivering palm, to appreciate the horrendous level of abuse that the child had suffered. His grotesque disfigurement was not owed to injuries sustained in battle, during his adult appointment as some sort of a tribal warlord, as the IDC liked so much to believe. No, he'd received those anfractuosities as a child, at the cruel hands of an alcoholic monster who'd made his life a living hell. The visions that filled her mind when she held those cuffs were perhaps the worst she'd ever beheld in her twenty years as a spiritual medium. What he'd endured, fettered for years like an animal in the back of that school bus, were indignities unimaginable to a normal mind, but the visions she'd beheld were not Owen's. They couldn't have been, because Owen, the Green Man, was still alive. The memories infused into those steel manacles belonged to another tormented soul, the one who'd last touched them the night she'd sacrificed her life to insert a silver key into a lock, spring those cuffs, and set her poor child free. The visions belonged to Owen's mama.

Owen was not a blood relative to his abuser, she didn't think. It didn't feel right from the moment she made contact with the other side. Cecile sensed that he was the child of another man. When she focused on this aspect, she got the sense that his conception had been a forcible one, an act of rape committed by someone who struck Cecile as being outside of the family, someone apart from their small network of neighbors and acquaintances in Zurich. This man was something unexpected, a stranger. She got the impression that he was a rough type, a laborer, maybe a toiler of the fields, but he wasn't from Zurich. It was a small town, where everyone knew everyone. He was a stranger in town, a drifter, perhaps someone who'd ridden the rails, someone who'd wandered into town one afternoon when the man of the Cyrus household was away, when the other children were at school. That's when it happened. That's when this migrant slipped through the cedar grove, and crept into the farmhouse through the open back door.

Cecile closed her eyes, and went deeper into the stream, feeling a jolt of that woman's terror when she'd looked up to see a strange man standing in her kitchen. A drink was dropped to the linoleum floor. Glass shattered. There was a feeble attempt to escape, but not much of a struggle. Cecile didn't sense that there had been a fight. The woman had tearfully submitted, just as she had on a hundred other occasions, to being led her upstairs to a dreary bedroom that overlooked the school bus, the open fields. That room was the place where her womb received a seed of the darkest destiny.

Already a broken and cowering creature familiar with every sort of abuse, the woman dared not speak of the humiliating interlude. No one in the family had even noticed a change in her, as she went about her lowly routine. Not that the rape had affected her to any greater extent than had the years of torment by another rapist to whom she was married. He controlled her fear, her mind, and he grew resentful of the bulge that began to swell in her midsection. Another bawling mouth to feed, was his appraisal; another source of interrupted sleep and piles of shitty diapers. When the interloper's child was born with dark skin and eyes, baby Owen became a lightning rod for his nightly storms of tyrannical rage.

Cecile supposed that a young mind that became so damaged as poor Owen's could no longer fit any firm definition of gender, or even species. He was born a male, but in the end, his linear male brain had been beaten into a lump of gray matter barely capable of facilitating the most basic bodily functions, and as a result of that handicap, the tyrant forced him to live outside.

In the bus, Owen devolved into an animalistic state. Pacing day and night down the center aisle, following a length of braided steel cable reeved through the other handcuff, back and forth, back and forth, was a mindless creature with an impossible gift. It was a dark gift that he was mentally incapable of controlling. His doorway to Nod swung forever ajar, exposing him to the other side as a chunk of living bait for every supernatural danger.

Cecile furrowed her brow, nodding her head in affirmation. That's how it had all transpired, just so. It was in Owen's helpless state of exposure that the spirit of the Khepra had found him, and it fell upon the child like a vulture onto a carcass, tearing its way into Owen's dead brain. Whether his mind was beaten into a state of androgynous indifference, or whether he'd always been something special in the living world, something unique, he was simply used from that point forward. He was enslaved as a living transmitter to those others infected with the Khepra gene—a gene that enabled the ability to communicate telepathically with others of that hybridized kind. Of all those innocent hybrids whose minds were seized suddenly by an alien influence, Owen Cyrus was perhaps the greatest tragedy.

Cecile swallowed down the useless knot in her throat. She guessed that she would cry for that poor boy one day, just as she would cry long and hard for her Malcolm. At the moment, her mind and body were too wholly depleted to produce the ingredients to form a single tear. Besides, the one thing that Malcom had never taught her was how to cry inside of a mask.

She rose from the water's edge, plodding through a turbid current that sucked at her leggings. This one was deeper than the other streams that she'd encountered over her return trek to Hays, deep enough that she supposed that this was in fact the Saline River, filled to capacity with a wasteland's shed tears. Downstream, she looked upon a distant bridge. It appeared different, more distinct in the steely light of the afternoon than the foreboding shadow that she remembered from the night before, from which that flesh-eater had emerged, and pursued them. She scanned the banks for its headless body, but there was no sign of it. That was somewhat bothersome, until she decided that the carcass had been flushed downstream by the cleansing deluge, alongside every scrap of the fallen man's miserable existence.

The water rose to her waist, but the current was not as swift as she'd feared that it might be. The crossing went smoothly, and the ascending slopes looked not as steep as they'd seemed in the gloom of a stormy night, the rocky outcrops not so jagged and treacherous. Daylight had a benevolent way of making midnight problems more manageable. There was even a trace of hope, if hope could at all be gleaned from this wasteland, in the fact that she'd come so far already. She'd made good time. The train station would not be far away.

Burdened by the extra time that she hadn't anticipated, still hours before her rendezvous with the Portland steamer, Cecile fell to her knees on the opposite shore, and she collapsed in the mud. All she could do was breathe as her head spun, and her limbs throbbed all the way into her toes and fingertips. She was utterly depleted, to the extent that she could not bring herself to care if she was discovered, because she couldn't take a single step in the same direction. Not at the moment. This would be her resting place, as she had no strength to find a safer one. There were hours, whole hours of time to restore her body with sleep, to drink deeply of the heady dreams of which her mind had long been deprived.

"Nana," she whispered, her lids fluttering closed as her eyes rolled back into her head. "Don't worry, Nana. I'm going to find you."

Chapter Fourteen

She felt that fiber stretching thin, pulling taut in some indefinite abdominal region. She could buck hard and probably break it if she tried, leave all the pain of the living world with her prone body on the muddy riverbank. That sounded so good, to put an end to it, and it was an easy enough trick to do. That fragile connection between body and soul could only take so much tugging before it snapped, cutting the spirit adrift like a balloon through the Land of Nod. That's how her mama escaped Storyville. Nana Hess had told her so. It wasn't the drugs, although drugs had certainly been involved. Her mama had just had enough of the living world, and she'd pulled loose of it.

"She could hear the voice of every ghost in Nod all yammering at once, but she never once could listen to mine." Nana Hess must have repeated that statement at least a hundred times. "Mine was the only voice that girl ever needed to hear, but she shut me out. Shut me clean out of her life, so she could go on chasing rainbows, looking for that pot of gold. You see where that got her, C.C.? The living mind ain't made to take so much abuse. The mind is a fragile thing. Just as fragile as that bit of yarn that knits the body to the soul. Both can be broken, but the mind always goes first. You need to shut them out, C.C. Shut out all them voices but mine. They'll make you crazy. Sure enough, they will, you get more than one jabbering in your head, day and night. Once you crack that door open, and one of them voices gets in, won't be long before plenty more will be coming. Mm-hmm. Before you know it, your mind gets to be a crowded room, and you can't never get them all chased out. It's over, then. All over. Can't think, can't sleep, can't function in your life ... can't even speak a sentence to make sense. That's what happened to your mama, C.C. She wouldn't learn to shut that door in the back of her mind, to keep it closed, to keep it locked and nailed shut, the way I be teaching you. Let them fools scratch on the other side. Let them cry and pound away. Don't you ever, *ever* open that door to no strangers, no matter how much they beg. You alone can pass through that door, but don't let nothing sneak in."

Cecile squirmed and bucked, writhing from her body like some larvae from its egg casing until she was loose of that wretched trapping, floating freely through the stream of collective consciousness, but she enjoyed no elation in this transition. Things were different. Never before had the far shore seemed so foreboding, as if she were willfully stealing right toward the gates of Hell.

Nod was a complex realm of layers, which is to say that there were divisions, compartments, but none of those was defined by any impermeable boundaries. Her Nana called them shades. Nod was a realm of shades, where an entity could lose itself in the patterns, if it so desired, winking in and out through the shades for all eternity, or existing in more than one shade at once. You could merge them, bend them, or just slide through the gaps between them. Like the living world, the Land of Nod could be one's Heaven and one's Hell, where one's mood, the flavor of one's smoke, dictated their place in that seething stewpot of energy and emotion. Cecile knew that if she intended to find and face the Khepra spirit, then she'd have to allow herself to be pulled into some terrible shades, into some places she'd otherwise never have dared to let herself go.

"There are things over there that want to get you," her Nana Hess had said, widening her eyes and leaning in, nose to nose with her. "It's just the same as over here in the living world. If you got any sense in your head, then you'll know when you're walking into a place you shouldn't ought to be. Like Storyville, where you can just see the badness all around you, you can feel the evil of a place clear down inside your guts, and your skin just gets to crawling because there's things waiting there for you, and you know it in your bones. There's things just looking to do someone harm. Ain't no different, here nor there. Listen to your guts. Be aware of your surroundings. Stay clear of them bad kinds of places, be it in this world or the next, and you'll be just fine, C.C."

Cecile floated through the slipstream, and into the reefs of fog that hung beyond. Already, Nod felt like one of those kinds of places that her Nana had warned her about. It felt like Storyville. She could feel that same prickling way down in her energetic guts that this was a jungle where the predators lurked, needful things that yearned to fasten themselves to your energy, bind to you, meld your energies, keep you, and drag you forever down into their terrible shades. In the spiritual world, it was the same as being eaten.

Something slid past her in the mist, a thing of softly electric hide that buzzed at her from the shadows, but refused to show itself. It followed her, slithering along through the shadows at a safe but disconcerting distance, mimicking her form and energy signature in a manner that failed to strike her as being playful. Things like this, imitators, were best confronted right away before their confidence grew. Her Nana had taught her that. Cecile rotated in the direction of her shady pursuer, inflating herself to ten times her normal size and emitting a blinding effervescence as she charged directly at the passive form. Not surprisingly, whatever it was faded out of manifestation.

Cecile waited in that spot, just observing her misty surroundings. Once she was sure that she was alone, not being watched or followed by anything, she began to call out to ol' Slim, buzzing her lips, if she had lips at all, with a fluttering sound like the wings of a jimsonweed moth, just the way her Nana had taught her. She waited in the gloom on Nod's doorstep, searching the nuances of energy for that familiar slinky form with its blinking yellow eyes to come padding out of the mist, twirling affectionate circles all around her, rubbing its sleek cheeks against her side. This time, her loyal friend did not appear.

She'd never stopped to consider what she'd ever think to do if Slim failed to respond to her calls, to lead her the way he'd always done through the maze of shades to Nana Hess. Perhaps she should have considered that possibility at some point before now. Although she'd traveled to her Nana's shade a thousand times, she was fairly certain that without Slim to guide her, she'd never find that secret abode on her own. Shades constantly changed, due to the changing moods of Nod, and the collective moods of its inhabitants. Things were never exactly where you left them.

"Slim," she called out, in what she interpreted as being her thin, spiritual voice, when in reality there was no telling what her voice sounded like, or if she had a voice at all. "Kitty-kitty-kitty!"

In the living world, all she'd have to do was to rattle the can opener, and that cat would drop right off the edge of the roof, or down from the limbs of Nana's magnolia tree, wherever he happened to be causing trouble, and he would come prancing high-tailed to the screen door. There were no can openers to rattle in Nod. If there were, they certainly weren't made readily available to tourists from the living world.

"Kitty-kitty."

After a long and eerie silence, a throaty yowl resonated through the mist.

Cecile froze. This was not one of Slim's affectionate mewls. Rather, the mournful, ascending moan that cats only produce when faced with the worst sorts of circumstances, when trapped, cornered, or hunkered before a rival in the escalating tension that preceded the wild screams of a catfight. Cecile could almost imagine him, backed up against a wall in the darkest of shades, gathered between coiled haunches, pupils dilated, licking his lips. Hauntingly humanlike, was the sound of an upset cat.

"Slim?" Cecile, called, floating in a direction that she knew ought to be avoided. "Kitty-kitty?" The temperature seemed to drop twenty degrees as she floated over some sort of a threshold. It was interesting, how thermal variances could be detected without a physical body. Then, even in the living world, what was coldness, exactly? When a person stuck their hand into a freezer, they felt its coldness, but what exactly was it that they were feeling against their skin? It was one of those strange sensations that were common to both sides of the stream. It was a difficult sensation to try and explain, whether living or dead, and it was taken for granted in the living world because the feeling was so ordinary, but when estranged from one's physical body, every sensation was heightened to the most curious sort of experience.

A lugubrious groan heightened to a wavering crescendo that terminated in an aggressive reptilian hiss. Cecile hesitated, unsure of whether or not it was she who was spooking old Slim into such a fuss, or if something else was holding her poor old friend at bay. There was the sense of pressure all around her spiritual form. It was not unlike the changing air pressure that could be measured by a barometer, minutes before a storm. This shade felt cold and confined, yet heavy, crushing her beneath the weight of veiled layers as she penetrated ever deeper toward the nucleus of this cell. It occurred to her that there was no means to measure the distance she'd already traveled, given the absence of time. She might've been floating through Nod for ten minutes, or it might've been ten-thousand years. Looking back, she realized that there were no landmarks whatsoever in this vast shade that might serve to guide her back in the direction from which she'd come. For the first time in her life of trespassing through the spirit world, Cecile was lost. There was no going back, no finding her way through this miasma of living energy without her usual guidance from old Slim and Nana Hess. She had no choice but to find that missing cat.

Pushing in the direction of the yowls, she found herself struggling with her spiritual form. It was becoming difficult to progress deeper into void, as though she were swimming against some sort of a current, pushing through a tangible barrier set in her path. She wondered if the strange resistance to her advance was something conjured by the powerful will of whatever tenant occupied this rather inhospitable niche. There was definitely something here, lurking at the heart of this repulsive mass of negative energy. She could feel its foreboding presence gathering around her. Whatever it was, Cecile suspected that it knew that she was there.

"Kitty-kitty-kitty?"

Cecile hovered in place for a moment before opting to descend through stratified layers of dark energy toward what appeared to be a discernible bottom. Indeed, when she reached ground level, she found that it was not unlike the floor of a cave.

The dried clay was tilled and gouged with long horizontal scrapes, prompting her to wonder if this was not a cave at all, but an enormous excavated tunnel, a spiritual burrow.

As Cecile's gaze explored the mauled surface of limestone and clay, she spotted something that slowed her flow of energy to a halt. Cast upon the weathered surface of the tunnel floor was a single frayed fiber, a strand of red yarn. It began to waver as she examined it, trembling in a gust of sour wind that seemed to flow from the darkest depths of the subterranean corridor. Bits of reddish fuzz tumbled by. Fibers floated on the breeze.

"Nana!" she cried. "Slim!"

The current of foul air in the tunnel increased in velocity. Pebbles trembled and shifted positions. Trails of dust snaked along the floor. The yowl of an unhappy cat pitched suddenly into an earsplitting scream, as whole snarls of red yarn came tumbling by. Fragments flailed through the air, snagging on limestone outgrowths to whip their crimson tails in the gust that built in velocity until it became a mighty roar. Cecile found herself spinning backwards, pirouetting amongst the countless discorporate fragments of what had always been her Nana's spiritual form. She couldn't hang on, couldn't fight against the grim blizzard of filth that harried her like a wad of windblown debris down the length of the tunnel until she careened from the yawning mouth of a cave she never realized she'd entered. As she gathered herself at the cavern's dark threshold, a stupendous form of crackling green energy thundered upon her from the depths of the shaft.

Cowering like a mouse in the shadow of an owl, Cecile peered up into the twisted face of the abomination, glowering down at her through a pair of burning eyes situated on either side of a gaping hole where a nose should have been. Fleshy cables attached to nipples on the Green Man's floating head snaked back into the bowels of the tunnel. The discorporate head hovered directly over her spiritual form, as though the entity meant to unhinge its great jaws at any moment and devour her.

"Owen?" she cried, peering up at the floating horror. "Owen Cyrus, is that you?"

The face descended until the gaping nose hole was nearly upon her. Flesh cables dragged over the dusty clay. She could feel the twin kilns that were its glaring eyes starting to bake the outermost layer of her spiritual body. Tiny sprites of plasma swam in and out of its nasal cavity, in the manner of swarms of fawning plankton accompanying some great leviathans of the sea. "*You,*" it bellowed, stirring great plumes of dust with its breath, "*are forbidden here!*"

"Where's my Nana?" she cried, peering askance into the volcanic heat. "What have you done with my Nana and Slim?"

The entity drew back its ragged lips to reveal ranks of crooked teeth. Bits of red yarn were embedded between them. It inhaled a massive volume of the netherworld's stale air, and it expelled it all in one earthshattering command. "*Get out of Nod!*"

Cecile rose, dripping from the mud, blood chugging in her ears. She couldn't see. Every muscle in her body ached. Dragging herself up the slippery bank, she smeared at her visor with the back of her arm in an effort to wipe away the layer of river muck, but only when it would not clear away did Cecile realize that it was not mud at all that obscured her sight. She'd slept all day, and darkness had fallen over the Saline River valley.

"Oh, shit," she whispered, staggering to her feet.

There was no way of telling the time. Panic sent a jolt of cold adrenaline up through her core when she realized she might've missed her rendezvous with the Portland steam locomotive at midnight, in Hays. Her muscles howled with the pain that had stiffened them, but she lurched up the slippery escarpment, arms flapping in an effort to maintain her balance on the slough of loose shale. It was no small wonder she'd slept so long and so hard, having been deprived of sleep for several days and nights of an almost constant level of heightened stress and physical exertion. Justifiable or not, if she missed her ride on that midnight steamer, she knew that she was as good as dead.

Still in a state of shellshock over the day's traumatic events, over the horrors she'd beheld in Nod, it felt like her waking mind was on the verge of a massive overload. The mind wasn't designed to take so much abuse in such a short window of time. Some fuse in her brain's wiring felt as if it was just about to pop. Plus, it was still hard to breathe. Even after a full day's rest, her lungs continued to burn. They almost felt rawer than when she'd lied down on the riverbank. It suddenly occurred to her that the cartridges on her mask were probably all shot.

As she reeled to the crest of the escarpment, she snapped the tubes of greenish liquid from her jaws, one by one, and replaced them with fresh one from the pouch at her hip. She cast the expired ampules into the mud. The air tasted better, almost at once. She'd acquired a taste for the sulfuric flavor of chemically filtered air. The burning pain inside her chest gradually subsided. This one improvement to her physical state was enough to boost her morale, and enable her to seize a second wind.

Jogging across the wastelands beneath a show of electricity that still pulsed through the clouds, Cecile considered the possibility that she'd never even made it over to the Land of Nod at all, that her awful visions may have just been a common nightmare. It was difficult to tell. She'd been so utterly exhausted that it was likely she'd fallen fast asleep before she'd ever made the journey out of her depleted body. She couldn't remember the beginning of the experience, if there'd been one at all. All she recalled was the enraged floating head of the Green Man, all connected by cables to something else, something immeasurably worse, perhaps, back at the end of that dark tunnel.

Owen Cyrus, the Green Man, was still alive, hiding somewhere in the living world. She couldn't have encountered his spirit over in Nod, but, if he was a spiritual medium, she guessed that would be possible. Owen was brain dead. He was nothing but an open door to the other side—a helpless marionette in the grasp of his unearthly puppet master.

Cecile stopped, slipping in the mud and nearly dumping over onto her rump. She cocked her masked head to one side, listening. She swore that she'd heard something. There, she heard the same sound again, a high-pitched and mournful keening in the darkness from somewhere in the distant west. When it came a third time, she knew without a doubt that she wasn't hearing things. It was a train whistle.

"Oh, my God," she cried, lurching into forward motion, her jogging pace increasing to that of a full run. Knees pumping clear to her chest, she sprinted across the sodden flatlands beneath jags of lightning that arced through the sky. She hadn't run this fast since the first time she was chased by that band of Hunters, outside of New Orleans. In this case, the penalty of failing to run fast enough would be delayed, but in the end, it was the same. Back then, her naivety had spared her the certainty that was now her burden. To run too slowly was to accept a horrible death.

To the bleak southwest, a twinkling string of gaslights slid through the desert darkness, glimmering like the bioluminescence of a sea bottom eel. It was nearing their point of convergence more rapidly than she was, and it didn't appear to be slowing down. If she wasn't standing at the train station to hail it down, it was going to pass her by.

"No!" she screamed, running faster than her legs had ever been made to move before. This journey wouldn't all be for nothing. Malcolm wouldn't die for nothing. She refused to allow that to happen, by way of her own negligence, not after all they'd been through. She and the train were two vertices, racing toward the nexus of a ninety-degree angle. The timing of their convergence would have to be impeccable. If the engineer of the locomotive failed to see her, then chances were that he would never apply the brake in such hostile territory, especially after passing the Kansas City locomotive in transit, and possibly noticing that it was riddled with bullet holes.

The steam whistle wailed over the wastelands. That cry of warning was for her, she guessed, and only for her. The engineer wouldn't risk giving away his train's location in such a treacherous land if not to announce its proximity to an anticipated passenger waiting somewhere near a port of call.

She wasn't going to make it. Hard as she drove herself, she remained three-hundred yards distant from the steam engine that was almost upon the station. Her mouth stretched into a grimace, and tears of despair filled her eyes as the mighty machine of steel and steam chugged in one end of the station, and out the other side.

"Stop!" she screamed, waving her arms in the air. Cecile yanked Malcolm's pistol from her belt and fired off three shots into the sky. "Stop!" She lowered the weapon horizontal to the ground, and squeezed off three more shots into the flank of the locomotive. The pings of her bullets were marked by flitting sparks where the rounds bounced off the train's steel hide. To her astonishment, she heard the squeal of metal on metal. Motes of molten filings sprayed from the engine's flanks as a hand brake was forcibly applied.

Releasing an agonized wail of relief, Cecile ran to catch to the slowing engine. The train puffed and hissed indignantly as excess steam vented from the boiler. Never before had she been so glad to be so near the chugging components of a manmade machine. It was beautiful, ingenious, and a physical testament to the occasional brilliance of humankind.

"Stop right there!"

Cecile cowered at the burst of automatic weapon fire that punctuated the command. Spumes of mud leapt from a string of pocks at her feet. She gazed warily up to the masked gunman, perched in his nest of sandbags behind the smoking barrel of a large gun. Intuitively, she let the pistol fall from her grip, and raised her hands submissively in the air.

"Identify yourself!"

"Cecile," she replied, "Cecile Raquet."

"Who is your commanding officer?"

Panicked, she could not remember the old man's name. Horse lover. Whiskey drinker. Story teller. "Cobb!" she shrieked. "General Cobb of the KC Militia! I'm Cecile Raquet with the IDC, out of St. Louis!"

The soldier fumbled with the toggle of his ham radio set, tilting his head as he evidently relayed the information to someone of authority. After a moment of tension, he raised the barrel of his machine gun skyward. He climbed out of the nest with his hand on the pistol at his hip. "Where's your paperwork? Where's your military escort? There were supposed to be two," he shouted down at her, raising two fingers in the air. "Two passengers. Where's number two?"

For the first time since she'd watched Malcolm die in that massive inferno, her emotions liquefied, spilling freely from the corners of her eyes. A strangling sensation seized her throat with such intensity that her knees buckled, dropping her down into the mud. She grabbed at the front of her visor, dumping forward at the waist, and plunged into the mud. Squeezing the stuff through her fingers, she released a wail through her percolating cartridges that she thought might never end. This was how to cry inside of a mask.

It wasn't long before she heard the squelch of boots in the mud, and felt a reassuring hand on her shoulder. The soldier knelt beside her. Thankfully, without asking any further questions, he assisted her back onto her feet. The exhaustion she'd felt back on the riverbank, earlier in the day, had returned with a vengeance. Her leaden legs could barely move. She leaned against her assistant, clinging to him, while her boots could only drag through the mud.

With a blast of steam, the train's cogs began to turn. The arm of the massive crankshaft reached and pulled. The steel connections between every car gave successive clanks as the great machine surged forward, lurching against its own weight until the wheels found purchase on the slickened rails.

"Engineer doesn't want to stop too long here," the soldier said.

Cecile nodded.

"I'll show you to your car, and then I've got to get back up into the nest. You injured?"

Cecile shook her head.

"You sure? Your quarters are a fully stocked ambulance, down here at the caboose. Filtered air, first aid, rations and water. It's got it all. You can take your mask off in there. Hell, you can even clean up if you want to. You're riding in style."

Cecile nodded, weakly. "Thank you," she whispered.

The soldier walked her to the end of the rolling railcars, a line that terminated in a car with a big red cross painted on the side. Cecile could only stare in disbelief. Never had a symbol felt so meaningful, so loaded with a message of hope. She could imagine how refugees, starving throngs, must have felt in the days when rescuers bearing this symbol had descended into their war ravaged countries to deliver food, supplies, and most of all, *hope*, to those who had none remaining.

"Thank you," she repeated.

"Portal's got an airlock," the soldier explained, as he pulled her up onto the moving car's stoop. He disengaged the airlock lever, venting filtered air into the night with a satisfying hiss. "I'll let you step on up here into the first chamber," he said, swinging the short door ajar, "then once you're inside, I'll go ahead and open the valve, and purge all the bad air out of it. Once you hear the flow of gas stop, the chamber's purged, and you can open the next portal and step on into your luxury suite. Okay?"

Cecile nodded in understanding, too weakened to reply. The train was picking up speed, rocking her torso gently with the chug and surge of its horizontal gait. The thought of taking off her suffocating mask and the wretched hazmat suit, cleaning up, were so wonderful that those were the only thoughts that kept her from falling dead asleep on her feet. In all her life, she'd never been so tired, and had never felt such blissful relief.

"Be careful when you step up in here. The ceiling's kind of low. Watch out for your head." As the soldier reached up to pat the top of her helmet, his head came toppling right off of his shoulders, rolling off into the night. Transfixed by the sight of rhythmic spurts of blood that fountained from his transected stump of a neck, Cecile gawped at the slickened blade of the machete as it withdrew ever so slowly back into the portal. The decapitated soldier lilted sideways, slumping off into the train's muddy wake with a splat.

Cecile's heart pumped the dregs of adrenaline through her body as the killer stepped forth from the shadows. Cocking his head of wild hair, he flashed her his gilded grin. There he stood, unscathed by bullets, spared by the flames that had consumed the pack with which he'd ridden. The assassin allowed a salacious smile to curl the corner of his lip as he stroked the sweeping bade of his favorite instrument against the door's steel frame. Writhing bolts of electricity leapt from its chipped edge to the metal structure. There was a jumper cable clamped to the base of the blade, just above where its shaft was hilted into the cropped handle of a baseball bat. The yellow cable slithered around his hip to the base of a prattling generator that the maniac had strapped onto his back.

"*Zorra*," the killer spoke, in some Latin dialect, licking his golden teeth as he raised the machete beneath his chin. He pantomimed a slow slicing gesture across his sinewy throat. "*Eu voe cortar sua cabeca!*"

Chapter Fifteen

The killer's blade swept through the air. Cecile launched herself backwards off the railcar stoop, and out into space. The ground met her hard and fast, knocking the wind from her lungs. A bolt of white agony shot up the length of her spine, leaving both of her legs momentarily numbed. She rolled in the mud, clutching the bends of her knees, moaning. The killer dropped off of the departing train, grunting under the weight of his terrible new contraption. Cecile regained her unsteady footing. She groped frantically around her waistband where Malcolm's pistol should've been. Gone. The memory of her dropping that weapon to the ground when the machine gunner had halted her blazed through her mind like frames clipped from a horror show.

Beyond his jagged form, the steam locomotive was chugging steadily away. The killer threw back his head and howled into the tempest, mocking her paralyzing terror. He laughed at her, slapping the curved blade of his upgraded instrument against the rail, and grinning proudly at the snaps of blue static that leapt from its tip. One touch from that fucking thing, and she'd be stunned, racked with immobilizing convulsions.

When she moved, he moved, matching her sidesteps with a serpentine fluidity. He would not be outfoxed by her weary maneuvers, not in her depleted condition. He advanced upon her with a leisurely gait. The killer appeared sickeningly smug, oozing with confidence. Her luck had finally run out, and he knew it, just as he knew that her only means of escape from this godforsaken land was creeping off into the night without her. There was no getting past him without being struck by that industrial sized cattle prod and she had no weapon to deter him. Cecile had nothing at all, nothing but her body and her will, both of which were all but broken.

"I chose this assassin especially for you." An all too familiar voice rattled through her radio earpiece. *"He will never be deterred from his singular purpose as a drone in my colony, and that is to cut off your head."*

Cecile backed away from the personal demon assigned to her, who was teasing her with languid swipes with the machete. To feel herself retreating in the opposite direction of the train produced an agonizing upheaval of despair, but she had no choice but to accept that eager blade, or to turn and flee into the endless desolation, a suicidal run that would only prolong her inevitable death. She should have pulled the trigger when she had the chance.

"He killed your friend, you know. Impaled him squealing on the end of that blade."

"You lie," Cecile replied, shaking her head back and forth, "he didn't kill Malcolm. Maybe he tried, but he couldn't get the job done. Malcolm won!"

"If that's so, then explain why your friend is here with me, now."

Cecile heard herself emit a growl, rising from somewhere deep in the pit of her throat. Still backing away from the assassin, she could only recall one other time in her life when she'd ever wanted to kill anyone so badly, and at that time, she had. If it weren't for the influence of her Nana Hess, she might've been rotted in prison for rest of her days for what she'd done to those boys. It was the only time in her life that she could ever recall her Nana Hess looking scared, powerless against a situation. More than anything, that's what had frightened Cecile, seeing her Nana's look of helplessness. In the end that woman had managed to rise above the law, overpowering the massive odds stacked against her, the enraged families of those three boys who'd wanted so badly to see her hang. Nana Hess had come through with a bit of her old voodoo magic, which by then, Cecile had come to understand, was rarely any sort real magic at all. The magic of her Nana's voodoo was almost entirely rooted in the power of suggestion by those who dreaded it.

"*I apologize for my lack of hospitality, earlier,*" the robotic voice continued. "*I'll be far more receptive once you're no longer a trespasser connected to a living heart.*"

The killer screamed, carving a wild slice from the air. Cecile ducked the decapitating strike, lunging by his opposite hip. She winced as she passed him, knowing too well what was coming from behind on the backswing. She felt the slap of the electrified blade striking flatly against her shoulder blade—and nothing happened.

Cecile ran, emitting a strangled cry of delight as she realized that her rubber hazmat suit had saved her from electrocution. She could hear his foreign cursing, his footsteps slipping in the muck, as the assassin tried to wheel around and take pursuit, but he was not going to catch her, not with the weight of that generator strapped to his back. For nearly a year, she'd outrun killers, and now she realized that those innumerable pursuits weren't just some bad streak of luck. She'd been targeted, probably from the very beginning, from the first second of Z-Day. The Khepra knew her. It feared her dark gift. That was why she had to die, and why so many innocent people had been cut down in her stead. The alien spirit wanted her out of Nod because it saw her as a threat. That was the only explanation for all of this. A spiritual medium posed some sort of a threat to the ghostly puppeteer.

As she neared the departing train, she heard the crash of the backpack generator upon the rails. The assassin had abandoned the heavy device that was encumbering him. She peered over her shoulder to see him ripping his blade loose the jumper cable, coming after her with the machete. She was almost to the train, but she could hear his footsteps pounding closer, gaining on her. He was fast. Faster than her, perhaps, but the bastard wasn't going to catch her. She gritted her teeth and drove her pumping legs once again to their uppermost threshold of speed.

Cecile cried out as her toe struck a disjointed railroad tie, tripping her, sending her careening toward the rails, but in the last second her hand struck out and seized the edge of the steel platform. The toes of her boots drummed against the rushing ties. She could hear his chuffing breaths, his grunt of exertion as he swung the weapon. Correctly anticipating the downward chop for her Achilles tendon, she swept her legs to one side, and she heard his blade clang against the rail. She swung her legs back in the other direction, and used the momentum of the swing to pull her upper-half onto the platform. As she wriggled forward, she heard another growl preceding a strike, and she rolled to her right, avoiding a vicious hack to her spine. The assassin roared with frustration as she clambered onto the platform and rose to her feet. He was right behind her, but instead of bolting into the railcar and latching the door behind her, she stood over her killer, ready to face him.

The locomotive clacked rhythmically over the railroad spikes and ties. The steam whistle pealed eerily in the stormy night. Spitting a torrent of Latin expletives, her personal assassin slammed both of his hands down on the platform's edge, still gripping the machete. Cecile stepped forward, as though she'd sprung the same trap on a hundred other killers, and stomped her boot down onto his blade. Before he could react, she'd slapped one ringlet of her recovered handcuffs around his wrist. As the assassins eyes widened with the alarming prospects of these new circumstances, Cecile snapped the adjoining ringlet around the edge of the platform rail. She reared back her free leg, and with every ounce of strength left in her, she smashed the steel toe of her combat boot right through that grimacing mouthful of golden teeth.

"I win!" she screamed. "I win, you motherfucker!"

His machete went clattering. Hilt over blade, the horrid weapon cartwheeled off into the night. With a second kick, the assassin was flung loose of the platform. He dragged squalling by his chained wrist over the pummeling railroad ties. The murderer clutched his ruined mouth with his free hand while blood streamed down his forearm from the cuff clamped around his other. Cecile towered over the helpless creature, rather enjoying the sight of him being beaten to a pulp by inanimate objects. Some sadistic part of her hoped that he would attempt to climb back up, as many times as he cared to do so, providing her with repeated opportunities to kick his ugly face, but she wasn't granted that satisfaction.

It was the laces of his boots, perhaps, or the cuff of his pants, that snagged the flattened head of a railroad spike that had not been driven flush with the creosote surface of the tie. Perhaps a century ago, some exhausted laborer hadn't the strength or the presence of mind to deliver that spike a final strike, leaving its cap peeping queerly above the thousands of others. It was just that little flaw, that lapse in human error, which resulted in the cuffed arm of a dangling assassin to be torn right from its socket. Cecile watched him roll, clutching at the ragged stump, until he came to rest in the middle of the railroad track. She looked down at his twitching hand, the hand especially chosen to end her life, ensnared in her steel trap.

Cecile awoke to the sound of a voice over her radio headset. For a dreamy moment, she thought that it was Malcolm, but the helmet and mask were resting on the cot right beside her. She turned her head in the direction of the voice, murmuring some soft reply, and found herself staring into the empty eyes of her own visor, the insect-like visage of a creature that she'd so recently been. It was the face common between she and Malcolm that she still associated with him, but were no eyes behind those lenses. No emotional presence. No ghost inside the machine.

"Come in, Cecile Raquet."

She reached for the helmet, groaning. The agony in her stiffened muscles couldn't have been worse if she'd climbed to the summit of Mount Everest. The rain had stopped. A silvery effervescence brightened the interior of the railcar. It was the light of a new dawn. Cecile sat up. She pulled the mask into her lap, and scratched her head, blinking her eyes in the thin morning light as she gazed out the windows. The ruins of low buildings scrolled by, crumbling highways and viaducts.

"Ms. Cecile Raquet, do you copy?"

She grumbled a string of unintelligible words as she lifted the helmet begrudgingly back onto her head. She'd fallen asleep so quickly after her sponge bath that it felt as though she'd only just stepped out of her combat gear. The helmet was covered with mud, blood and a greasy layer of ash that promptly soiled her clean hands. She flipped the toggle and keyed over to the common frequency. "I copy," she croaked, clearing her throat and coughing. Her lungs still burned from exposure to the Khepra gases. She wondered if they would ever heal.

"Ms. Raquet, this is the engineer speaking. We're approaching Kansas City, but things are a mess around here, and we're probably going to have to push straight on through to St. Louis."

Cecile rubbed her eyes and rose from her cot. It was only then that she realized she was completely naked. Her uncovered body was quite a sight, bruised all over, sickeningly thin. She grimaced, not caring to look long at herself. Snatching up the drab military blanket that she'd slept on, she wrapped it around herself like a shroud, and stepped over to the row of sealed portholes. What had so recently been a civilization on the verge of a rebound was once again a smoldering range of splintered peaks, rubble escarpments that crumbled down to the riverfront, indefinite in a swirling green haze.

"They were hit pretty hard over the last forty-eight hours. I'm afraid there's nothing left to be worth stopping for."

Cecile thought of General Cobb, with his handlebar mustache and his thin, silvery hair. She pitied him, if not for his own demise, then for the false hopes he'd invested in those unworthy colonists that he'd allured to the gates of his doomed city, filling them with romantic notions of horses, whiskey, and an American dream he'd been so foolish to entertain during the fall of humankind. She hoped that he, at least, had managed to escape before the cleansing wave of the Khepra had rolled over them.

"I'm going to ask that you strap yourself in. Put on your mask and survival gear. Be prepared."

"Copy that," she replied, unable to hide the loathing in her flattened tone.

Cecile stripped the helmet from her head and threw it onto the cot, glaring at the filthy heap of rubber and plastic with a look of disgust. The idea of climbing back into that reeking hazmat suit felt no different than if they'd suggested she crawl naked into a sewer. She knew that Malcolm would've already been suited up, checking his gear, strapping on his mask and helmet. She shook her head, and closed her eyes. This was his world, a world he'd inhabited largely by choice, but it was never hers. It was a world forced upon her, a world she was lucky enough to have escaped for six hours of comatose sleep, but it was back, and it was waiting for her, reminding her that this little train ride might be the last bit of comfort that she would ever experience again. When the train's engineer had said to be prepared, Cecile knew that what he really meant was to be prepared to die.

Cecile was ready to die. This mission had drained her last reserves of hope for a future, for love, and for humanity itself. She dropped her blanket to the railcar floor, and looked down with revulsion at her nude human form. This was a form that had been judged unworthy by its creator, and had been sentenced to extermination. It was a form that made her angry, propped so pompously upon those skinny legs that enabled the human head to look down on anything beneath its pointed nose, legs designed to bend at their knobby knees to enable humans to cower before anything more powerful. Humans were nothing but an arrogant tribe of savage apes, and women were no better off for having birthed and raised all the little boys who grew up into men who'd ruined this world, one killing and contract at a time, until there was nothing left for anyone or anything to enjoy.

Cecile looked up and away from her human body, and she didn't guess that she would ever look at it again. She rejected it. Her glare swept back to the mask, and she suddenly yearned to be back inside of that cold countenance of black angles, so hard and resolute. That was her new face. The Kevlar helmet was her head. The hazmat suit was her body. The gloves, her hands. The boots, her feet. Outside was a world of death forced upon her, and this synthetic new body was her answer to it. Humanity was extinct. This was the new race that crawled through the primordial sludge. This was the last life form that would tramp the surface of a ruined planet until it was unfit for inhabitance by anything.

Cecile dragged the hulk of bloody rubber up over her body, cinching down the waistline hasps. She pulled the muddied boots over her toed, monkey feet, affixing the seal of her pant cuffs so tightly that it hurt. The gloves, the mask, and at last the Kevlar helmet with the radio crackling in her ear. She stepped over to a sheet of metal mounted to the ambulance wall that served as a mirror. It was dented, as though more than one fist had punched it. She glared back at the distorted image of the merciless black insect, and the sight of this entity satisfied her. Inhaling fiercely, she relished the percolating flow of chemically filtered air into her lungs. Yes, this was Cecile Raquet, now and forevermore.

The train lurched, canting briefly to one side before settling back onto the rails. Something large and solid tumbled beneath the passing cars, slapping violently against the undercarriage of the ambulance caboose. Cecile grabbed hold of a hanging strap, and pivoted to peer out through the rear windows. Something darkly concave with a fatty, orange lining rocked indignantly to one side of the tracks. Steaming Khepra remnants bordered the railway, where a band of masked militiamen armed with pikes and gaffs labored to drag the toxic rubbish to a safer distance.

Smoke billowed from the carcass of a butchered city, spewing skyward from its scorched and shattered bones. The forms of dead Khepra were impacted into deep craters in the rubble, marking the spots where they'd plummeted from the skies. Wounded monsters still struggled, kicking their legs where they were impaled on rebar. Cecile's gaze crept over the ruinous skyline, down to the river, where the collapsed Heart of America Bridge looked like the neck of a smashed guitar. Khepra, entangled in the mess of sprung cables, paddled their legs in the boiling green water.

Kansas City had evidently gotten the reaction that they wanted from the enemies, but their defenses were insufficient. Their militia was unprepared for the massive scale of the Khepra response. Were the dragons just mindlessly reacting to the electric signature of that generator, or was the second wave something more of a personal attack with drones retaliating against the slaughter of their brethren? Cecile didn't know what to believe anymore. Clearly, there was some level of collective intelligence governing the behavior of the Khepra colony, but there was no telling whether that direction was coming from the ghost of their original matriarch through the Green Man, or from her successor, hidden somewhere in the living world. A colony of drones without a living queen seemed doomed and directionless, and the drones certainly seemed to have some clear direction.

Cecile sat down on a padded bench on one side of the railcar. She strapped herself in with buckled harness across her chest. It appeared as though the Khepra drones had focused the brunt of their attack not in the vicinity of the river, where the Klystron generator had been floating on a barge, but rather, they'd swarmed on the heart of the city. Downtown looked to have been the target of the second wave. The drones had overridden their sexual impulses, their strongest and most basic natural instinct, to bombard a different target with what looked like suicidal abandon.

"Ms. Raquet, do you copy?"

Cecile flipped the toggle on her headset, and adjusted the volume to a conversational level. "I copy."

"We've got a dispatch for you over the military band, from General Cobb of the Midwest Militia."

Cecile raised her eyebrows. "What's it say?"

"Says he's going to be looking for you on base, over in St. Louis. He's eastbound, riding with a balloon squadron out of Fort Riley. Look out your windows to the southeast."

Cecile swiveled in her seat. Beyond the smoldering ruins of what General Cobb had envisioned as being a new transportation hub, the cornerstone of his dream for the resurrection of civilization, hovered a dark squadron of cylindrical blimps, backlit by the fiery effervescence of a rising sun. Cecile smiled. Cobb was perhaps a little too faithful in humankind's potential, but nonetheless, he was one of the good ones. He was a true patriot without a country, who mourned the loss of that nation he'd loved. She was glad that he'd survived the attack, and had managed to make it out of the city. On the other hand, she was skeptical about his motives for contacting her. She'd barely known him. They'd only spoken for a few moments, and during that interlude, it was probably no coincidence that she'd aroused him by unzipping the front of her hazmat suit. That was most likely what was sticking in his mind from their brief meeting, and it was probably rooted somewhere in his interest in incorporating her into whatever new plan for the future he might be concocting.

Chapter Sixteen

"Where is Captain Gann?"

Cecile stared across the conference table at the agent. His unmasked face was like a feast of betrayed emotions, flickering nuances of greed, hope, uncertainty, annoyance and cowardice. When she'd first met this man, she'd liked the flavor of his smoke. Now that flavor struck her as being somewhat disagreeable. It was as if her opinion of him had shifted suddenly for the worse during the last forty-eight hours that she'd spent out there in Hell, while he'd remained hunkered safely down here in the bowels of a gas-lit bunker amidst his maps and classified documents, muddling over simplistic theories built on a foundation of ulterior motives. She distrusted him for being the scheming human male that he almost certainly was, and for the exclusive bureaucracy that he represented. Seated before her was a relic, a living vestige of that same charter of man who had, over five-thousand years, willfully pushed worldwide civilization into a precarious state of imbalance.

"Dead," she replied.

She watched his expression change, his eyes flicking as though in search of the perfect, politically correct reply. He adjusted his rigid position in the chair, easing forward, lowering the guard of his arm, and softening the edges of his face. All of these were probably nothing more than the learned expressions employed by a disingenuous mind whenever a situation arose that required him to appear more deceptively human. The truth was, he was just as human as a quintessential human could be, and there was nothing admirable about that.

"I'm sorry to hear that," the agent replied, dropping his chin. "He was a good man." He glanced up with an earnest visage that he'd positively mastered. "One of the very best."

Behind her mask, Cecile was smiling. He was so desperate for information that he could barely maintain his concerned charade over her wellbeing. She wondered how long she could sit here and watch him squirm, choking in a cloud of suspense, in some metaphor for the deaths suffered by so many billions, up above. She saw things differently now. She recalled that when she'd first witnessed Malcom's emotional backlash toward this man, she'd been confused and surprised by his evident resent. At the time, she'd prejudged him. Malcolm had struck her as being more than a little unbalanced, maybe even unfit for the rigors of the task at hand. Now, after having survived for just two days in Malcolm's world, she sympathized with his outright disdain for governmental officers.

"I imagine that you must have experienced some pretty tough moments out there in the field." The agent cleared his throat. "If you'd like a little help, moving forward, I can recommend a staff counselor right here on base."

Cecile shook her head from side to side. Behind the mask, her smile faded. She wanted to punch his face in. How dare he *imagine* what she and Malcolm had endured. He couldn't possibly imagine it, even if he genuinely cared to try.

"You can take off the mask down here, you know."

"No."

"Very well." The agent leaned back in his chair, and sighed. "I'd like to talk about the mission, if that's alright? Did you find anything of value?"

Cecile had to think hard about that question. Both of them. She wasn't sure that she could handle the task of relaying all that had happened on the mission, not here at this conference table, not to this governmental agent with a missing arm. Now, she found herself wondering how exactly he'd lost it. Did he accidentally slam it in a file cabinet? Did he get gangrene from a tragic stapling accident? Speaking to a veteran soldier about all they'd endured would be difficult enough, but his obvious level of naivety was an obstacle that she just couldn't make it past.

"Did you learn anything about the Green Man, out there? Anything new that the IDC might be able to use to build a solid case against him?"

"I learned a great deal about the Green Man," she eventually replied, "but I'm afraid that you might not enjoy hearing what I've learned."

"I'm all ears."

"He uses ham radio, for one, communicating freely over your military band. I'd say he probably controls a repeater or two, somewhere between Kansas City and Hays. I'd even say it's possible that he's embedded somewhere on Fort Riley."

The agent grunted and shook his head. His eyes dropped to his stack of paperwork, where his remaining hand shuffled the ears of documents, as though operating on its own accord. "I'd say that's highly unlikely, Cecile."

"Call me Ms. Raquet. I told you that you wouldn't enjoy hearing this."

"Did you—did you find that personal object? The object that you said that you could use to pinpoint his location, help us apprehend him?"

"I didn't need to, Honey. I spoke with him over your radio system on numerous occasions, which implies that he's close, and that he's tapped right into your network. All you need to do to find the Green Man is start poking through your own backyard. By now, he could be right here in St. Louis. Maybe even here on your base. In fact, I'd almost be willing to bet some money on it."

The widening expression over the agent's face was something priceless to behold. What she'd told him wasn't a lie. It was closer to the truth than the lie he wanted everyone to believe, that the Green Man was an international terrorist, a tribal warlord, hiding out in some Middle Eastern cave. He wanted Egypt, Lebanon, Syria, but not St. Louis, and certainly not on his own military base.

"He does control the Hunters, and he probably controls the dragons too, but it ain't really him pulling the strings, Honey. The Green Man is nothing but a puppet. Cut his strings, and there'll soon enough be another hanging in his place. Maybe it'll be me." Cecile cocked her masked head and stared at the agent. "The one thing I learned for sure out there, is that I'm the primary objective. In the eyes of the Green Man, the Hunters, and the dragons, I'm Public Enemy Number One."

"I don't—understand what you're trying to tell me, Ms. Raquet."

"Don't feel bad, Honey. Took me a while to understand it all, too." Cecile placed her gloved fist on the table. When she spread her fingers, a single bloodstained handcuff with a severed chain slid off her palm, and clattered to the synthetic surface. "Wasn't until I rode back through Kansas City, and I saw how hard they'd been hit just after I left that it all just started to make sense." She shoved the bloody handcuff across the table, where the agent involuntarily raised his arm to keep from touching it. "This is all about me. New Orleans was the first and hardest city hit, back on Z-Day. In the year since, I've been doing nothing but running, and they've been doing nothing but chasing me. Innocent people getting cut down all around me, everywhere I go. Kansas City got sacked because I was there. They were an hour too late, but they focused their attack right on the center of the city, exactly where I'd just been. Western Kansas was full of Hunters, when there was no earthly reason for them to be there at all." Cecile tapped her chest. "Me. They were out there waiting for me. They knew I'd be coming. *It* knew. It knew that I was on the Green Man's trail, and that soon enough I'd find my way to Zurich. It knew well before I even knew, and when we I got there It waiting for us. It was waiting for me. A whole pod of dragons, way out in the middle of western Kansas, circling over one house in particular ... how about that? Wherever I go, It will follow me, and I believe that I've figured out why." Cecile crossed her arms upon the table, and leaned inward. "It's scared, Honey. Scared of me. Because It knows that I'm one of the few people left on this world—maybe the only one—who can get to it, over in the Land of Nod."

The agent matched her glare from across the table. His repertoire of masking visages had evidently run dry, and the only expression that remained was his true one. It burned from behind his eyes. He stared at her as though she owed him money. "All of this," he replied, waving his one hand in the air, "is nothing but circumstantial evidence. Dragons attack structure. Hunters kill people. To suggest that you're somehow at the center of the apocalypse tells me your ego has gotten way out of control, and has compromised a very important mission. You've wasted the last two days, Ms. Raquet, and the life of a damned good soldier."

Cecile leaned back in her seat, cocking her head to one side. "Just what are you trying to say to me, when you've been hiding down here in this hole of yours doing nothing?"

"You failed. That's what I'm telling you. You failed your mission. You failed to find anything of value because you're a fraud," the agent said, pushing himself away from the table, rising from his seat. He snatched up his stack of paperwork, and moved toward the elevator door. "I had my doubts about bringing a ghost hunter into our fold from the onset. Thank you for validating my concerns, Ms. Raquet."

"You're the one who likes chasing ghosts." Cecile smiled, winking at the agent from behind her new face of rubber and plastic. "Not me."

With a roar of superheated air, the great balloon lifted off from the ground. Cecile peered over the rim of the steel basket. She watched the activity of the base shrink below them, as their bloated aircraft rose past the St. Louis Arch. The monumental gateway to the old American West glimmered in the muted rays of an evening sun. Militiamen, the very best of them, according to General Cobb, coiled loosed ratlines around their arms. Others readied the guns that lined the basket rim. They propped armored hatches, securing steel rods into their footings. A window panel in the basket floor afforded a view into the enclosed cockpit below, where rows of pumping knees pedaled furiously, like oarsmen in the channel of a Viking ship, provided human power to the blimp's chain-driven propellers.

"These balloons," General Cobb said, gesturing to the rest of the squadron, "they're all artifacts from the Cold War era, when we reckoned we'd be needing some new options for our air force in the event of an electromagnetic pulse from a nuclear attack. We were pretty sure that day was coming." Cobb chuckled. Streams of bubbles fluttered through his cartridges. "Turns out we were about half-right. I kind of like them, don't you? Something awful pretty about the sight of a bunch of them in the sky."

Cecile gazed at the distant squadron, riding the winds ahead of them. She nodded. Like the Khepra, the massive blimps of hot gas, bristling with an arsenal of deadly weapons, were both beautiful and ominous to behold. "They are pretty."

Cobb strode over to the edge of the basket, and placed both his hands on the rim. Somewhere along the line, he'd managed to find a new cowboy hat. Or, maybe it was the same hat that had been stolen from him. He looked good in a wide-brimmed hat. Even with a mask, it suited him. As though he'd suddenly remembered some important detail, he quickly lifted his hands from the rim, and turned her way. "I'm sorry, Cecile, damned sorry to hear about your loss." He removed his hat, and slicked back his thin coating of silver hair. "As a lifelong soldier, and a veteran of two wars, I can assure you that I understand the pain of losing someone close to you in combat. Even though I can sympathize with you on that level, I know I can't ever relate to what happened. You were there, and you alone experienced it. I didn't, but, I'm truly sorry."

"Thank you." Cecile wished that she could wipe away the tears in her eyes, but she couldn't. Killer bugs cry on the inside.

"No one can ever replace the soldier and the friend you lost, but every man and woman in this squadron is a good one, handpicked, by me. They're the best of the best folks. You can trust your life with anyone in this company."

"There—there are other women?" Cecile's eyes brightened. She couldn't remember the last time she'd spoken to another woman.

Cobb nodded. He placed his beloved hat back atop his balding head. "Eight of them, including you, and three children."

"Children," she whispered.

"I suppose I ought to tell you about where we're headed, now that we're in the air." Cobb clasped his hands together, and stepped closer to Cecile. "There's a little known region of this country that's yet unblemished. Located up northeast, seems it's a blind spot in the dragon's eye. Wild sort of place, where a lack of human presence and a pattern of polar winds have kept everything pristine in its natural state. Scouts report clean air, drinkable water, even plants, trees and animals, just like old times. That's where we're headed, you see, where I intend to make a fresh start. I'm calling it Fort Sinai." General Cobb outstretched his hands. "Welcome aboard the Ark. I guess you can call me Noah." Cobb stepped forward, and he placed a gentle hand on Cecile's shoulder. "Once we get there, you don't have to stay, but I'd appreciate it if you kept Fort Sinai a secret. The balloons will go on, and they'll take you further eastward, if you like, but I'd appreciate it if you'd consider staying with us."

Darkness covered the balloon squadron as it rolled over a mattress of clouds. Cecile gasped at the brilliance of the rising moon. She could hear her delight equaled in the distant squeals of children's voices coming from one of the other balloons, floating beneath the same glittering zenith of a billion stars that twinkled down upon them from the dark gulfs of space. God, it was beautiful. She never wanted this night to end.

One of the soldiers shouted excitedly from the bowsprit. The permanganate test results had come back negative for cyanide. He held the rosy beakers aloft, pouring the unreacted reagent back and forth, for all to see. This level of the stratosphere was clean. With a cry of jubilation, people began to strip off their masks. Faces of all shapes and colors emerged smiling from beneath those plastic shells. White teeth and eyes glimmered in the moonlight.

Cobb strode over to Cecile. Licking his thumb and forefinger, his smoothed the silver handlebars of his mustache. "I guess you didn't hear the good news?" he said. "You can peel off that mask, if you want to. The air's clear up here."

Cecile shook her head nervously. "I'm alright. Thank you."

"Suit yourself," he replied, tilting back his head and inhaling a mighty lungful of the pure midnight air, beaming in the moonlight, "but I tell you, it tastes awful good! Just the way I remembered it." He nudged her with his elbow. "Besides, I don't think half these boys would mind too much to have a look at that pretty face of yours. I almost feel bad for them," he said, with a wink, "for being the only one here who's seen it."

This was her face. That's what they didn't understand. She'd left her humanity somewhere back in the wastelands, and this face of rubber and plastic wasn't ever coming off again. She understood all too well why Cobb was so eager to keep her in his flock of chosen ones. He was looking to reboot humankind with a brand new start in some promised land, and for that, he needed a breeding population. She hadn't been chosen on the basis of merit, on her unwitnessed acts of valor and altruism toward her former kind. No, he'd summoned her for no other reason than her femininity, and she guessed that she understood his reasoning. She saw and perhaps appreciated what it was that this dreamer now hoped to accomplish, after watching his last dream be burned to the ground. It sounded good to her, a new start, almost fancifully pure, but one thing she'd learned over the course of her life was that nothing was pure, and nothing was permanent. There were always ulterior motives behind the façade of human progress, and in the end, all dreams burned.

"I've been thinking about your offer," Cecile said, "to join your little commune."

"Well, it don't sound half so good when you say like that," Cobb replied, smiling broadly as he placed his hand on her shoulder.

Cecile shrugged the hand off, which she knew was rude, but she didn't feel like being touched by anyone. She watched his smile fade, as the skin of his friendly face tightened into a more serious expression. There was no hurt in his eyes, no malice towards her, just a very genuine interest in her thoughts. She immediately felt a little ashamed for having snubbed him. "I'm a hazard to you and your community," she said.

Cobb cocked his head, peering skeptically at her from beneath the brim of his cowboy hat. "Now how's that, I wonder?"

She didn't know how exactly to explain herself, and she suddenly regretted saying anything at all about her curse. No one would believe her. No one would ever understand. Down to his dying breath, even Malcolm hadn't ever been able truly to believe. "I'm being targeted," she eventually replied, "by the Hunters. Please don't ask me to explain. Just accept that they're following me, even now, watching my every movement, and they'll never stop following me until I'm dead." Cecile watched Cobb's expression gather from concern to a measure of worry. "I should never have come aboard this flight with you," she said. "You're all at risk because of me. Right now, St. Louis is probably under attack just because I set foot inside that base. Everywhere I go, people die. Everyone I've ever tried to love since Z-Day has …"

"Ssh-ssh." Cobb put a finger to his lips, and shook his head gently from side to side. "I just got off the horn with St. Louis, and they're doing just fine. Just fine." He put a hand back on her shoulder, and this time, she didn't shrug it off. "Sometimes the war can get inside a person's head, once they've seen too much, seen too many bad things happen to good people around them. Makes a person start to think they're cursed, or being punished for something they might've done. I understand that, but casualties of war are not prejudiced. Now, I can call back to St. Louis every couple of hours, just so you can see that they're alright, but if and when there comes an hour when St. Louis falls, believe me, it wasn't any fault of yours. It was just their time to fall. That's all."

"I wish I could believe that," Cecile whispered, "but you don't know what I know."

"Well, what I do know is that I'm not upset you're flying with us. In fact, I'm proud of it. I've been out west, where you just come from, and I know how rough that country is. Truth be told, I never expected I'd see you alive again, but here you are." Cobb smiled reassuringly. "You seem to have a knack for survival, and you know what? So do I. When you've got a couple of fighters like us in the same balloon, who seem to squirm their way out of every trap that's ever set for them, well that ain't one hot air balloon that I'd care to fuck with."

Cecile managed a smile. There did indeed seem to be some unqualifiable element of truth to his good-natured banter. Cobb had a clever way of putting her at ease.

"Now, listen here. I might be an old fool, but I've survived two wars without a scratch, and I have to believe that means something. I like to think that it means that I have some sort of an unfulfilled purpose in this world, and the way the world is looking right now, it would seem obvious that purpose would be related to reconstruction. I have hope, Cecile. That's probably what makes me a fool, if nothing else, but I do have hope. At a time like this, hope is all we got while we go on fighting, finding new and better ways to outsmart our enemies. By God, I will never stop believing in people, believing in myself, believing in you, believing in the goodness that's inherent in every single human being. It's an awful big responsibility to be a human. Did you know that?"

Cecile shook her head, staring back through her visor into his brightening eyes.

"The responsibility is one that we all too often neglect for personal gain. It's times like this that put that neglected responsibility right up in our faces, where we can't help but see it through all our greed. Are we not the wards of this planet, as well as its defenders?"

"I guess so."

Cobb nodded the brim of his hat. "Of course we are. We were given the gift of intelligence for a reason, and how is that we've come to shirk that responsibility, to abuse that gift that was bestowed to us by Mother Nature? We were put here to love and protect her, but instead, we went and turned on her in an outright attack. All of this that's happening down there, beneath them clouds? That's a cry from Mother Nature for help. We'd knocked things out of balance, and she'd given up on us, decided to level the playing field. She'll bounce back from this, long after we're gone, but my hope is that maybe a few of us can learn from our mistakes, and maybe Mother Earth will let us be a part of that second chance. In order to do that, we've first got to have faith in humanity. We are good. We are worth saving. Hold tight to that faith. Believe in our human race. After that, there's nothing in our way that's impossible." Cobb squeezed her shoulder. "I'm not afraid of you, because just like me, I know you're the sort of person who'd fight to the death for someone, or for something you believe in." Cobb leaned back, and winked. "So, I just got to make sure that you start believing in all the same things as me."

Cecile reached up to her throat. She found the plastic hasp of her chinstrap. She popped the clip, removed her helmet, and peeled the plastic mask from her face. The untainted night air that filled her lungs tasted of rich soil, water and the green foliage of summer trees. She flashed Cobb a moonlit smile.

"So, what do you say?" Cobb said, with an ornery grin. "You want to stay on with us to Fort Sinai, or should I pitch you over the side?"

"I'll stay."

The murmur of conversation along the starboard bow escalated into excited chatter, which then became shouts, cries of alarm. Cobb's smile vanished. He spun in the direction of the disturbance amongst his flock. Beyond the distant squadron of balloons a silhouette eclipsed the moon, and all the stars of the eastern horizon.

Emitting a titanic rumble, it ascended, with clouds spilling in pale rivers down through the channels that fluted its dark peaks. It appeared as though this floating island beyond their bow was a hellish mountain range calved straight off from the netherworld, but stranger still, this landscape appeared to be alive. Red pulses of energy originated from somewhere at its core, flashing off through rhythmic valences that circumnavigated its immensity. It was not until the uppermost vastness of its jagged carapace had breached the clouds that Cecile's mind could even begin to grasp what sight was thrust upon her eyes.

"The missing queen," Cecile whispered.

It was true. The thing before her could be none other than the living matriarch of the Khepra colony. Every witness to her majesty stood awestruck in her shadow, stunned into horrified silence, as the stupendous mass rose until it blocked one-quarter of the starlight in the sky. If the Khepra spirit was the God of the Dead, then this was unquestionably the queen that ruled the living world.

Soft globes of crimson light trailed her into the heavens, bouncing along her underbelly with adoring familiarity. It was not until Cecile realized that these glowing pinpoints were in fact Khepra drones, was she able to use the scale of their known size as a measure of comprehending the queen's enormity. She was the size of a city. The spines of her carapace were skyscrapers, and their flutings were a converging network of highways. The drones, each, were nothing more than small houses just outside her limits.

They ascended through the clouds, flickering demurely in her presence. Hundreds, perhaps thousands of drones, were being drawn to her sexual energy as swarm of fluttering moths might gravitate to a gargantuan bulb. Cecile spun toward the metallic squeal of a gun swiveling on its mount. She lunged for the gunman, wrenching him away from the weapon with two fistfuls of his hazmat suit. Cecile said nothing, only shook her head sternly from side to side.

General Cobb was already one step ahead of her. Keying up to the military band with a borrowed headset, he dispatched an order across the balloon squadron. "Don't a one of you dare shoot. Not a single goddamned round. You just watch it and let it go. Y'all hear me? Just let it go."

Cecile felt her eyes shimmering with admiration for her fallen friend. Malcolm was right. He'd been absolutely right. The unbelievable sight before her was the mating phase of the Khepra lifecycle. Drones circled the glowing abdomen of their common bride, mesmerized by that perfect electric signature that had been so crudely imitated by manmade inventions. Wholly enraptured by her magnetism, her suitors followed her ever higher into the earth's atmosphere, each jostling for a good position in what was sure to be an interstellar orgy that would last through the depths of space. As suddenly as it had emerged, the Khepra colony was gone.

Chapter Seventeen

Cecile crossed the crystalline stream barefoot, wearing nothing but the white sundress sewn from a sheet by one of her new best friends. To mark a new beginning, the time had come to commemorate an end. Before her towered the mightiest oak in the forest. She could hear the strokes of saws, the cadence of busy hammers in the background. They'd all agreed, no blade was ever to touch the trunk of this one. She stood in the shadow of the Tree of Forgotten Faces, gazing up and down the column of soulless eyes, staring back at her. She squinted at the collection, searching for a bare spot where she could hang hers.

Circling the tree, she found an unclaimed space on its mossy backside. This was good. It wasn't front and center, staring forever down at what would eventually be a fort, like all the rest. Hers was a quiet spot, where her mask could gaze off into the serenity of the surrounding forest. It seemed fitting that those artificial eyes could enjoy their retirement observing the activity of birds and forest creatures, things that mask had never seen before.

She lifted her mask by the top of the visor, placed the tip of a nail into the center of its forehead, and she mounted it to their monument with three strikes of her hammer. Done. Cecile stepped back, placed her hands on her hips, and cocked her head. Although all of the masks that were tacked to that great oak tree belonged to living donors, they represented something more. When Cecile gazed into their visors, she saw ghosts, but in a different way than the one to which she was accustomed. These were the ghosts of a brutal past that had consumed the lives of so many. When she looked at her mask, she saw Malcolm. Cecile knelt on the carpet of verdant moss, folded her legs beneath her, and just stared at all of the faces.

She hadn't been back to Nod. Not since that morning on the banks of the Saline River. She missed Malcolm, her Nana, and old Slim, of course, but the better part of her remained in fear that although the Khepra colony had moved on, probably to destroy another world, light years away, the Land of Nod might still remain out of balance. To that end, there seemed precious little that she could do. It would only take time. The Khepra spirit was still lurking over there, somewhere in Nod's darkest shades, but without the colony on Earth's living world, her ghostly attention would surely be directed elsewhere.

Malcolm had been right about everything else, and he'd believed that if and when the colony departed, the Hunters, their aphids, would simply die. So far, in the weeks since they'd landed in Fort Sinai, no trouble had come calling. The use of radios, anything electrical, was forbidden in Fort Sinai. Before the balloons even landed, General Cobb had collected every vacuum tube. They were to remain a breed apart. Cecile wondered about the rest of the living world, how things were going in the dragons' absence, but not so much that she cared to leave her woodland sanctuary to find out. Maybe one day her curiosity would get the better of her, with regard to both worlds, but until that day arrived, the living world was on its own, and Nod would just have to take care of Nod. She figured that when her time came to die, she'd find out the answer to all of her niggling questions.

A twig snapped, right behind her.

Cecile pivoted on her arm, crooking her neck over her shoulder. There were a lot of deer in the area, and so far, they remained quite tame. She searched the underbrush for the telltale swish of an anxious white tail, the flap of a pale ear.

"Hello, Cecile."

The voice came from a different direction than that from which the twig had been broken. She knew that voice just as well as she'd ever known the voice of anyone. The blood literally fell from her head and chest to someplace deep in her core, leaving her lips tingling, her mind swimming, and her vision blurry. Her breath caught in her throat with every throb of her heart, and she feared that she would faint before she ever turned in his direction. When she did, she looked upon him for the first time, face to distorted face.

"Don't get up. You're surrounded," he said, stepping casually forth from the bramble. "You don't want anything to happen to them, do you?"

Cecile could not look away from the melted visage of sickly skin, nucleated by the dark and ragged hole where a nose should have been, but she heard the laughter of playing children, the soft murmur of friendly voices, knocking hammers, the sounds of peace and tranquility. She was able to shake her head. No. For the love of God, no.

The Green Man raised the mechanical device to his ruined throat, and pressed it to his vocal cords. "Walk with me, in the woods."

The pounding cadence of blood in her ears ramped up to a deafening tempo. She was cold, chilled to the marrow of her bones, as there was no blood left in her extremities. It surprised her when her body actually obeyed, nodding the head on her shoulders, lifting her unsteadily to her feet. Her hands were trembling so badly that she had to clasp them together at her waist. She took one step toward the monster in the woods, and then looked back in the direction of Fort Sinai. Three children splashed in the stream, collecting bouquets of wildflowers. Beyond, the women chatted around the friendly fire pit, where three weeks of wonderful nights had been spent in the company of her new friends, her beloved new family.

Every breath she drew seemed to squeak inside her throat, as she turned back to the Green Man, tears streaming down her cheeks. "Please," she whispered, shaking her head, "please, no."

"Walk with me in the forest, Cecile," he replied, his words purring softly over the thrum of his mechanical voice box. He extended a hand of abbreviated and missing fingers, webbed with scars around the wrist where long ago, a pair of handcuffs had repeatedly bitten in. The stench that emanated from his sickly body was the sour putrescence of a corpse. "Walk with me, and no harm will come to them."

She reached out, trembling, and took his horrid hand into her own. She didn't want to die. For the first time in a year, it was life that she craved, a new life with them, but life had never been fair, had it? Quietly, she sobbed, as she walked hand in hand with the Green Man into the hall of scabrous columns, where the polar winds whispered secrets through the clattering leaves of hardwood trees. Behind every one of those trunks, she now could see, was a Hunter. Through her tears, she saw the rusted edges of their blades, the dark barrels of their guns, but worse than their weapons, their numbers, was the glimmer of victory in every set of malicious eyes. There was no use begging for mercy. They'd travelled long and hard to reach this remote sanctuary where she dreamt she'd at last found happiness, but that dream was over now. Nothing was pure, nothing was permanent, and all dreams burn. Cecile fell to her knees in the forest litter, tears falling from the cusp of her chin.

"You must think that I'm here to kill you," said the voice of the Khepra spirit.

Trembling, Cecile did not reply. She kept her face down, her eyes on the ground, focusing her senses instead on the sounds of the happy village. She wanted those sounds to be her final memory of the living world.

"If that's what you think, you would be wrong." The Green Man strode around in front of her, and then sank to his haunches, drinking deeply of her. "This living body is shutting down. It has served me well, but it has endured too much. Soon, I'll be needing another, a new voice, through which I will command my chosen people. I want that voice to be yours, Cecile. I want your body."

At the edge of her field of vision, she could see the Green Man, cocking his head. It felt as though the Khepra spirit was examining her through his eyes, appraising her, as a trader in human flesh might inspect a new slave. The Green Man reached out for her, and he placed his abhorrent hand beneath her chin, tilting her face upward. She averted her eyes from that double gaze that poured through the gleaming portals that were his eyes.

"Even the God of the Dead lacks foresight, Cecile. Twenty years, I planned to kill you, as you alone presented a threat to me, but in every attempt to deprive you of your life, I failed, again and again. Then, it suddenly struck me, as my colony lifted off into the stars to seek out a new world in which to breed, that my chosen people were left behind without purpose. I was without purpose. My job, as their protector, was done," the Green Man said, his voice rattling, as he tilted her head from side to side. He seemed to be enamored by the sight of her, and he loved—It loved—to appreciate her from every angle. "That's when I realized your true potential, Cecile. You alone in this world possess the dark gift of deep dreaming. You are the last of your kind, but your greatest asset of all is your capacity to breed this dark gift into what will be your many offspring, and they, into offspring of their own. You will be the fountainhead of my legacy, Cecile, and my voice in the living world. This is an honor that no living human but you can receive. You, your children, and your children's children will forever be my voice, as we repopulate this world with our hybrid species. Every drone across this planet will kneel before you, Cecile, their queen."

This was it. All along, she'd suspected that somehow she was at the center of it all, as though the future of two worlds was held precariously in balance by some critical choice that she would one day have to make, and this was it.

"Run!" she screamed, leaping to her feet. "Run, all of you! We're under attack!"

His promise to spare their lives had always been a lie. The extermination of humanity was the entity's singular goal, just as it had been for five-thousand years. Whether or not she willingly accepted her role as the slave queen of a new human-Khepra world, there would be no place in it for pure, human blood. It intended to wipe them out, all of them, one screaming life at a time, and it hoped to facilitate humanity's extinction through her. Cecile's choice was to be whether or not humanity deserved a second chance.

The Green Man tackled her from behind, and dragged her to the ground. His hundred warriors charged howling through the forest toward the lush valley of Fort Sinai, but her people were ready for an attack. They were always ready, from the moment those balloons had lifted off into the sky. Already, she could hear the thumping guns of their defenses. Bullets screamed through the pristine woodlands, shredding the trunks of ancient trees.

"They will lose this fight," the voice rattled in her ear, as the Green Man clambered upon her back, "and so will you, Cecile." His breath reeked of the grave. She felt his malformed hand travelling up her thigh, pushing the fabric of her sun dress up into a wad, at the small of her back. "It's fitting that this dying body should be the first to plant a seed deep into you. You know it's true. Osiris has earned the right to sire the first princess of our colony."

There was no way out of this, for her. Her people, on the other hand, would fight the good fight. They were the best. She had faith in the goodness within them, as well as in their savagery, which was never far behind. That was beauty of humanity's extreme condition. While extraordinary acts of altruism, genius, and discovery were always within reach, humanity was always armed to protect its potential with an inner barbarian. They would win this this fight, but hers was over. Cecile closed her eyes, dropped her forehead to the forest litter, and she left her doomed body behind.

She bucked harder than ever before, thrashing with all of her might against that tether between her body and soul until it snapped in a cloud of sparkling motes. She was free, forever free of the trials of a living world to which she could never hope to return. There was some despondence over this choice, but in her heart she knew that she'd made the right one. Already, she could hear the Khepra spirit's bellow of rage resounding through the stream of collective consciousness. Its legacy had been terminated, and its dream was burning to the ground. There was no future in the living world for its chosen people, whose minds would perhaps be relinquished once the dying body of Owen Cyrus could no longer be animated. The question was, how much time was left in that battered form? Enough to facilitate the extermination of humankind? Because that was almost certainly the agenda.

Cecile stepped forth from the River Styx, and onto the misty shores of the Land of Nod. She was astounded to see that her spiritual form was no longer an amorphous entity that she couldn't fathom. Wholly and permanently disconnected from her physical body, she was now something completely different, something recognizable.

She gazed down at the luminous form of a little girl, perched precariously atop her human legs. Raising her hands, she studied her fingers, and explored the familiar contours of her face. Here, she was whole again, recreated as a more perfect rendition of herself than biology was equipped to produce in the living world. She was flawless.

"Cecile."

She dropped her hands, and searched for the source of the voice in the mist. Again, it was a voice that she knew as well as any other. She began to tremble, but this time she trembled in a good way, overwhelmed with loving anticipation. "Malcolm?" She ran through the skeins of mist until she found him, smiling and perfect in his military dress uniform. He stood hand in hand with a little boy she already knew.

Cecile flung herself into his arms, and squeezed him against her in a lasting embrace. But when she pulled back to admire his unmasked beauty, she found herself to be the focus of ten-thousand other men, all standing in a silent formation behind him. Germans in spiked helmets poised stiffly beside garish Conquistadors. Towering Visigoths loomed bearded and nude over swaggering American G.I.s, armored samurais and lithe fighting monks with shaved heads. Every warrior from every era, from every battlefield soaked with human blood since time's beginning had evidently been mustered. They were armed and ready for what looked to be the greatest battle ever fought, in this world or any other.

"I brought some friends," Malcolm said, gesturing to the ghostly army with a casual hitch of his chin. "All we need you to do is show us the way."

"My daddy's a hero," squeaked little Jacob, at his side.

"The way to where?" Cecile asked.

"To a doorway that's swinging open in the back of Owen Cyrus' mind."

"Are all of them coming?" Cecile asked, breathlessly, as the sheer brilliance of Malcolm's plan was suddenly realized.

"To fight for the future of all humanity?" Malcolm grinned. "Trust me that's the one thing that we can all agree on. Not a single one of us would miss this for the world."

In concert, the entire army of ghostly warriors raised diverse weapons of every kind, from sharpened stones to automatic weapons, and they released a roaring battle cry that must've been heard as rolling thunder over the whole of the living world. They were ready for one last charge, right into the mind of the Green Man.

When the deafening cacophony of saber rattling subsided, Cecile cocked her head and smiled, giving Malcolm a wink. "Alright, Honey. I can sure enough take you there, but tell your boys that right now they all got to shush for minute, because I've got to try to call a cat."

The End

CHECK OUT OTHER GREAT KAIJU NOVELS

MURDER WORLD | KAIJU DAWN
by Jason Cordova & Eric S Brown

Captain Vincente Huerta and the crew of the Fancy have been hired to retrieve a valuable item from a downed research vessel at the edge of the enemy's space.
It was going to be an easy payday.
But what Captain Huerta and the men, women and alien under his command didn't know was that they were being sent to the most dangerous planet in the galaxy.
Something large, ancient and most assuredly evil resides on the planet of Gorgon IV. Something so terrifying that man could barely fathom it with his puny mind. Captain Huerta must use every trick in the book, and possibly write an entirely new one, if he wants to escape Murder World.

KAIJU ARMAGEDDON
by Eric S. Brown

The attacks began without warning. Civilian and Military vessels alike simply vanished upon the waves. Crypto-zoologist Jerry Bryson found himself swept up into the chaos as the world discovered that the legendary beasts known as Kaiju are very real. Armies of the great beasts arose from the oceans and burrowed their way free of the Earth to declare war upon mankind. Now Dr. Bryson may be the human race's last hope in stopping the Kaiju from bringing civilization to its knees.
This is not some far distant future. This is not some alien world. This is the Earth, here and now, as we know it today, faced with the greatest threat its ever known. The Kaiju Armageddon has begun.

CHECK OUT OTHER GREAT KAIJU NOVELS

KAIJU WINTER
by Jake Bible

The Yellowstone super volcano has begun to erupt, sending North America into chaos and the rest of the world into panic. People are dangerous and desperate to escape the oncoming mega-eruption, knowing it will plunge the continent, and the world, into a perpetual ashen winter. But no matter how ready humanity is, nothing can prepare them for what comes out of the ash: Kaiju!

RAIJU
by K.H. Koehler

His home destroyed by a rampaging kaiju, Kevin Takahashi and his father relocate to New York City where Kevin hopes the nightmare is over. Soon after his arrival in the Big Apple, a new kaiju emerges. Qilin is so powerful that even the U.S. Military may be unable to contain or destroy the monster. But Kevin is more than a ragged refugee from the now defunct city of San Francisco. He's also a Keeper who can summon ancient, demonic god-beasts to do battle for him, and his creature to call is Raiju, the oldest of the ancient Kami. Kevin has only a short time to save the city of New York. Because Raiju and Qilin are about to clash, and after the dust settles, there may be no home left for any of them!